THE QUEEN
OF LIMNOS

TONY WHITEFIELD

Published by Karpasi Press,
Printed by Tender Print Australia

First published in Australia 2020
This edition published 2020

Cover design, typesetting: WorkingType (www.workingtype.com.au)

The right of Tony Whitefield to be identified as the Author of the Work has been asserted in accordance with the Copyright, Designs and Patents Act 1988.

ISBN: 978-0-6487976-0-9
pp284

To Despina

CONTENTS

Glossary of terms   vii

Chapter 1   An old man and a temple   1

Chapter 2   If it is to be it is up to me   10

Chapter 3   A certain chain of events   13

Chapter 4   Samothraki   24

Chapter 5   Polyxo's plan   30

Chapter 6   Murder most foul   34

Chapter 7   The new Queen of Limnos   59

Chapter 8   Thomas and Sikinos   63

Chapter 9   A boat is coming   69

Chapter 10   Twins   103

Chapter 11   A witless man   112

Chapter 12   Some bad news   118

Chapter 13   Nemea   128

Chapter 14   Orpheus   135

Chapter 15   It's a boy!   150

Chapter 16   Kratiras   155

Chapter 17   *The Dionysus Wine Festival — part 1*   167

Chapter 18   *The Dionysus Wine Festival — part 2*   180

Chapter 19   *Captain Korelli*   188

Chapter 20   *The King of Athens*   192

Chapter 21   *A short life*   196

Chapter 22   *Visitors*   204

Chapter 23   *The Golden Vine*   214

Chapter 24   *Athens*   220

Chapter 25   *Oinoe*   231

Chapter 26   *Samos to Myrina*   242

Chapter 27   *The Trojan blockade*   252

Chapter 28   *Dionysus Wine festival revisited*   255

Chapter 29   *Hypsipyle's last days*   260

Cast of Characters   267

Authors note: 271

Suggested Reading: 275

GLOSSARY OF TERMS

Amphora	Ceramic jug for food and liquid storage, usually with two handles
Chiton	A common form of loose-fitting linen worn by both sexes
Chryse	A small island east of Limnos, but today sits below the water's surface. In ancient times, it was visible and accessible from Limnos by foot.
Colchis	Now modern Georgia, Colchis was the Argonauts destination to locate the fleece. Also, considered to be the possible homeland of the Amazons.
Dionysus	Greek god of wine and winemaking, vegetation, grape cultivation, festivals and having a great time.
Kithara	Musical instrument — related to the lyre, and an early incarnation of a modern guitar. Made from wood with gut or sinew strings.
Krater	Ceramic mixing vessel for watering down wine.
Larnax	A small type of closed ceramic coffin, but could be made of wood
Limnos	An island in the north-eastern Aegean Sea.
Mandra	Small stone building for animals
Oinoe	Ancient name of the modern-day island of Sikinos in the Cyclades.
Piraeus	Port of Athens

Plateia	A village square were people sit at tables to eat, drink and talk.
Samothraki	A mountainous island to the north of Limnos.
Stadia	Plural of 'stadion', which is roughly measured between 185 to 192 metres.
Thera	Ancient name of the island now called Santorini.

CHAPTER 1

An old man and a temple

I have always loved island sunsets. That magical moment as the deep blue sky slowly melts into the sea and a single beam of light reaches out from the fading sun to dance on the gentle waters lapping at my feet.

As I grow older, sunsets have taken on a whole new meaning. When I was young, I took the end of each day's sun disappearing for granted, and did not pay any attention to them. Now, each one is a wondrous gift, to be treasured every night for the remainder of my fading life.

How rude of me not to introduce myself. Here I am, babbling on about sunsets, and I have not told you who I am. My name is Peter, but there is a good chance that you have never heard of me. My life is not a story worthy of telling. I suppose you may think that odd, given that I am a story teller, but my life really is not that interesting. Others have had far more interesting lives than mine.

Before I say any more, I must tell you a bit about my name. While I go by the name of Peter, the name I was born with was Petros. But a chance visit to Limnos by a boat one day selling all kinds of wares was captained by a sailor called Peter. I was a young boy of about two at the time, and apparently, I could not pronounce my name of Petros. If truth be told, I could not pronounce anyone's

1

name correctly, but for some reason when Peter came to the port, I could say his name perfectly, so I also became known as Peter. My mother often told me a story that I would run after Peter and yell out 'Peter, Peter, Peter!' I cannot remember any of this, but who can argue with a mother's recollection of their child's first words?

These days, I live a remote and solitary life on Chryse, the small, flat but fertile island due east of Limnos. Most people from the known world do not even know Chryse exists, but believe me, it is a beautiful place to be. I have a simple stone mandra where I am fortunate to share the warmth in winter with my beloved sheep and goats. In summer, we live day and night outdoors in the open fields. The animals spend their time grazing on green pasture all over the island. They know of no stone fences to keep them in, but being on Chryse means that there is a natural barrier surrounding us all. By day they are free to wander, and by nightfall, they dutifully return home.

These days, I am the only human inhabitant on Chryse. Many people were scared off the island some years back after an earthquake destroyed the one and only village. The whole island shook for minutes, devastating houses, fences and temples, returning them all to piles of wood, stone and rubble. I do not blame the villagers for leaving. Most just simply headed on foot in waist deep water, carrying their meagre belongings to neighbouring Limnos. The larger island seemed to escape the effects of the catastrophe, so my fellow islanders walked to their new homeland on a very windy day and rebuilt their lives. They named their new village Keros, because according to local legends, that word meant windy, and they arrived on a day when the winds were quite strong.

Even though my little island paradise has noticeably sunk into the sea, I do not think it will sink further any time soon. For now, my animals and I will continue to coexist.

Limnos is the better-known island in that part of the world, but for me, Chryse is home. I have a special attachment to this island, which I find difficult to put into simple language. This again may seem strange considering my occupation, travelling around the Aegean from island to island and village to village telling stories that could and often did last for days. You might say that I have a way with words, but ask me to describe why I love Chryse, and I am as incoherent as a newly born baby.

I entertained all kinds of people with poetry, monologues and a multitude of mythical tales, but later in my itinerant life, one particular story was by far the most popular. No matter where I went, my reputation preceded me and I was asked for one story above all others. Even though it now takes four full days to reveal from start to finish, audiences never grow tired of it. I was once accused of making it all up, but that is just not true. All of it happened. When I first began telling this story, it would last about half a day. With the passage of time, life experience, audience participation and chance meetings with people who claimed to be eyewitnesses, or who knew of others who claimed to be eyewitnesses to certain events, gave me much more to work with and in the end….well, I will just have to let you decide.

This will be the last time I tell this story as I am now old, and my memory will only fade with the years. I am therefore passing this tale on to you now, so listen well. It is considerably annoying growing old! Believe me. I still see the world in the same way as I did all those years ago, but when I see my reflection in the water, I think to myself — who is the old man and what have you done with Peter? But my mind has not departed just yet!

Why is this story so special I hear you ask? Did I not also tell stories about the siege of Troy, of Jason and his team of rowers looking for a special sheep's coat, the seven generals marching against the city of Thebes to rightfully restore a King, about the heroes of Greece, and mighty warriors? Yes, I did, but I will let you in on a small secret. This series of events I am about to entertain you with combines those famous tales and then some. It is a tale of romance, betrayal, smelly murderous women, music, slavery, mighty female warriors, man eating serpents, all interwoven with a little humour and a lot of love. The mention of smelly, murderous women always seems to captivate an audience's attention.

Before I start, let me explain how I came to know this account and how certain events in my life led me to where I am today.

When I was young boy, my father and I would spend all day with our flock of sheep from early in the morning until late at night on Limnos in a small village located in the centre of the island. Arising before the sun awoke from its nightly slumber underneath its great velvet blanket, we would pack a small cloth bag containing some bread, cheese and dried figs. There was no need to take water, because Limnos has many dry-stone wells all over the island. I had heard stories as a boy that these wells were built by the Argonauts, during their stopover in Limnos before travelling on to search for a particular golden sheep's coat. I did not even know that sheep had golden wool, but that was what people said they were after. Later in life, I learned the truth about the Argonauts, their time on Limnos, and how their influence on people's lives will last for generations to come.

On this one particular day my father and I were resting near the temple dedicated to the mighty Hercules. He was one of the Argonauts you know, and this temple was erected near where he stayed on Limnos with a beautiful young woman by the name of Komi. In the time they spent together, Hercules and a small number of Argonauts helped build some wells, cleared land and set up a farm for Komi to manage. The land was extremely harsh, and had quite a few large rocks that needed to be moved. This proved no problem to the strongest man alive in all the world, and his deeds resulted in Komi and other women dedicating a temple to him after he left. Komi and Hercules were quite the couple, albeit for a very short time. He may have been a strong man, but in her arms, he was as meek as a new born lamb.

Most people have heard of the twelve labours of Hercules, but are extremely surprised to learn of his direct connection to Limnos. I fear that this small and seemingly insignificant part of his extraordinary life seems destined to be forgotten, but I hope my story will allay that fear and keep his vibrant flame alive.

During the summer months, our sheep needed to rest from time to time in shade, and we needed to sit and eat lunch. Watching sheep at this time of day still amuses me. Some just put their head under the belly of the nearest animal while still standing, some actually find shade from a tree or stone wall and stand with their heads touching the stone and some just lie down. This particular day, while we were resting at the temple to escape the midday heat, we soon discovered we were not alone. An old man was also there, but instead of resting, he was picking up any fallen stones and placing them back in perfect order along the walls and specifically around the altar stone. He had a straw broom and was sweeping the dusty, earthen floor, giving the old temple a much-needed face-lift. I had never seen it looking so clean. I had never seen him before.

Apart from an old chiton, the temple sweeper had horse hair belt around his waist, a pair of well-worn leather sandals tied just above his ankles, and every now and then he wiped his brow with a cloth attached to the broom handle to keep sweat out of his tired old eyes.

His mind appeared to be lost in thoughts from a time long since passed. Either by accident or on purpose, he did not seem to know that we were watching. Now I think about it, he knew exactly what he was doing, and that we were carefully watching his every move.

We offered him some water, bread and cheese, and asked him to sit with us. He sat and ate his food, drank his water and did not say much apart from thank you. All this time he was resting on his broom like it was a faithful walking stick.

After a final mouthful of cheese, he slowly and carefully stood up to start cleaning again, offering no new words, but he did

5

mumble something to himself as he cautiously approached the mighty stone altar. We let him go about his business, glad to have some company. Without uttering another word, he finished his cleaning and simply walked away. He left as silently as he came.

Many weeks went by without seeing him again, until one day late in the summer, when we were about to bring our sheep closer to home, my father and I visited the green pastures near the temple for the last time for that season. The old man was sitting there with his bread, cheese, and this time, some wine. He looked like he was expecting us. To my surprise, it was he who asked us to sit for a while, and share food and drink with him.

I was very fond of wine at that time in my young life. The quality of wine coming from Limnos was what the island had been best known for. It was quite possibly, the finest wine in the whole of Greece. Many people came to our island and purchased wine by the ship load to take back to wherever they came from.

But I digress. The old man had appeared on our last day at the temple for that summer, and as I said, it was he who asked us to join him. Little did I know, but he was about to tell us a story that was to become my life's work and indeed, my life's obsession from that moment onwards. He asked my father and I to sit with him, and when we sat down, he produced the most wonderful goats' cheese, dried figs, fresh bread, and pointed to a large amphora of wine sitting next to the recently cleaned altar. The amphora was the largest and most beautifully decorated drinking vessel I had ever seen.

It was made from the finest red clay and decorated with pictures of a boat with many oars, a sheep with a golden hue, men in various fighting poses, and two women, one who had twin boys at her feet. The woman with the twins looked sad, yet beautiful, and other women appeared beautiful, but had a wicked look about her. I had no idea what these stories were about, but listening to the old man soon made these images come to life.

We sat there looking at this magnificent object of art, and he saw that we were in awe of its size and beauty. When the old man poured some wine into a small cup, he offered it first to my father and then to me.

He told us little of his own life, but he did say that his name was Timotheus. I thought at the time that his name was familiar, but I could not quite remember why I knew that piece of information. Maybe it was his kind face and gentle manner, but it was as though we had known him for many years.

For the remainder of the daylight hours, and then long into the night, my father and I sat and listened to his most wonderful tale. All I can remember of that day, and night, was listening, eating, drinking wine, and remaining speechless the whole time. My father was a good talker, but he too could not speak. Timotheus had us captivated. In fact, we were there for so long, we all watched the sun rise the next morning.

As the sun rose, and we had eaten all our food, Timotheus quietly stood up, and thanked us very much for hearing his tale. He said that we could keep the amphora and its contents. As he left, he turned to me and spoke.

"Peter. This story is now your responsibility to share with the world. Do it justice. But remember, you are a Limnian first and foremost, and Hypsipyle was our first Queen. If she were alive today, I am sure she would approve".

At that time, I had heard stories about Queen Hypsipyle, but nothing like those tales Timotheus had told us. He had made her seem human, and gave her substance that you can only gain from meeting a person with first-hand knowledge and understanding.

"The amphora is a gift from me to you both. I know it is in good hands now. Goodbye, and thank you for listening".

This time he departed without saying another word. My father thanked him for sharing his story, but already, my mind was spinning. Not from the wine, but from what he had told us. Well, maybe a little of both!

7

After Timotheus left, we took the very tired sheep back home, and went to our own beds. My mother was hysterical. You know how mothers can be.

"Where were you? I was worried sick all night? What do you mean by keeping the boy away for that long?"

I am sure she raged for quite a while longer, but we were too tired to really listen or care. All I could say to her was that we were alright, and would explain everything tomorrow, but for now, we just needed some sleep. From what I remember, we slept for the rest of the day, and all night. Strangely enough, the sheep did the same, which is very odd for sheep.

For the next few months, life returned to normal, except that we were now the proud owners of the best wine amphora in our village. We became the envy of all our neighbours. For many years after, my father would use this specific amphora to store his best wine in. Everyone who drank with us commented on how well it tasted and what a splendid looking vessel it was. Now that I think further on this, my father most likely put any old wine in it, and because of the art work people automatically thought that the wine was special. This idea of adding artwork to clay amphorae holding wine was something Limnians became particularly good at, and it was not too long before the idea took off all over the Aegean. People made a lot of money selling their worst wine in colourfully decorated amphorae. Why are people so gullible?

The days of autumn were spent doing the same things as we had done for generations, but for me, all I could think about was what Timotheus had told us, and his words. What did he mean by saying that it was now my responsibility? I was still young, and by definition, I should not have had any particular responsibility, apart from looking after our animals and helping my parents. I felt different after meeting him. I felt grown up.

Before this chance meeting had occurred, I was a shy, but inquisitive boy. I spent my days listening to people talk and observing them at work. On the farm, at the port, and in the temples, my favourite time passing obsession was to listen and to observe all people around me. When elders asked me questions, I gave one-word responses, sometimes extending to a phrase, but never replying with a question of my own. Now, it was different. I wanted to ask questions. Both my parents noticed this change in me, and soon told me to stop asking so many questions. I could not help it. I had to know everything. But most importantly, I wanted to learn about Hypsipyle. After all, she was a Limnian, and so was I. For the rest of my days, this was to be my life. After all, who could not be fascinated by stories of murderous smelly women, heroes, war, disastrous events and love?

Chapter 2

If it is to be it is up to me

Before I begin — don't worry, I will tell you when it is about to start, there are a few more things I need to clear up. After Timotheus left, I wanted to find out from others in the village, all they knew about this strange old man. That simple task didn't take very long as no one seemed to know anything about him. They did not know where he came from, even though he had been living a quiet existence on his own for a number of years just outside our village.

You may or may not be aware of the terrible event in history that is known around the world, as the "Limnian deed". I can see by your nodding that you are aware of this event. I will talk about this later, but there is one important fact that was kept secret for a long time. It had always been assumed that after the deed, there were no males left living on Limnos. No males at all! Well, that is not quite true. There was one man and his son who escaped with their lives and lived alone and as it turned out, quite successfully for many years.

The wife of this man knew her husband and son were missing because they did not come back to Myrina with the other men after one of the Samothrakian fishing visits. After some time, she firmly believed that they must have died in Samothraki. Let me tell you what really happened: The father and son stayed behind on

Samothraki for two extra days — telling the other men that they had some business to attend to. After two days, they secretly left for Limnos, but instead of going to Myrina, they travelled to the far north-east of the island and lived alone and out of site. Everyone thought they had died on Samothraki, and nothing more was ever said. The reason these two did this is that the father inadvertently heard some women discussing what they would do when the men came back home. With the future of his young son in mind, they hatched a plan. That son was Timotheus.

What became of his father I hear you ask? I will get to that soon enough. The two lived a life of solitude, oblivious to what was happening in Myrina, which at that time, was the main village on Limnos. Timotheus and his father caught fish, raised some goats, and lived a sparse yet comfortable existence in an area abundant in naturally growing food. The father died one day while coming back from Chryse collecting shell fish. He slipped on a rock hidden from view under the surface of the water, hit his head on another rock and drowned. As simple as that. Timotheus found him later and buried him near where he died, just behind the high-water line.

Timotheus explained to me that many years after the island once again became populated with males, he returned to Myrina, told people he was from another island, and now wanted to live on Limnos because he had heard so much about the place. Strangely enough, no one questioned him on where exactly he came from and he was fully accepted into the community. Little did they know.....

Timotheus did contact his grandmother Antonia. She was extremely happy to see him alive but kept his true identity safe from prying ears and inquisitive neighbours. They secretly met just outside Myrina every day to talk. No one ever suspected Timotheus was her grandson because by then, he was considerably older than any one remembered and totally unrecognisable. Timotheus was unable to contact his mother, because she died of a broken heart a year after her husband and son went missing.

11

However, his years of solitude had meant that he preferred to live alone, even though he was living just outside the village. There was one other woman who did know his identity. Can you guess who? Remember I told you about Komi and Hercules?

Hercules left Limnos with the rest of the Argonauts and never set foot on the island again. That means, he never saw his daughter — Atsiki. She lived with her mother Komi for many years, and after Komi died, Atsiki devoted her life to looking after the temple both she and her mother had built in remembrance to her father Hercules.

Atsiki and Timotheus met and one thing lead to another...well you can probably guess the rest. With the temple being so far away from Myrina, many village people never visited that part of the island, and Atsiki and Timotheus could live in relative obscurity and peace.

It was only a few short years after Atsiki died, that Timotheus went back to the north of the island to once again be alone. I met him when I was only about 10 years old, that wonderful day I told you about. He must have been nearly 80 years old, but had the heart and soul of a man much younger.

OK, now I think you are ready for the story.

CHAPTER 3

A certain chain of events

King Minos of Crete wanted to protect the important sea trade routes from the Black Sea to Crete and every island in between. Due to its strategic position at the entrance to the Black Sea, Limnos was the ideal place for King Minos to send an important member of his family, so one of his grandsons Thoas was chosen for this important task. Like his brother Oenopion, who Minos dispatched to Chios, Thoas was an ambitious young man and keen to help the family in any way he could.

King Minos knew that Thoas could not achieve all this as a single man so he searched for a suitable woman for him to wed. Minos was informed of a potential young woman from Iolchus, who was the daughter of King Cretheus, and by all accounts, a beautiful woman and a suitable match for his grandson.

To help Thoas achieve this significant trade objective, Minos approached King Cretheus of the newly created city of Iolchus, to see if Thoas could wed Cretheus' daughter, Myrina. Such arrangements do not seem to work most of the time, but when Thoas and Myrina met for the first time, they fell in love immediately.

Thoas took his new bride to Limnos, and quickly renamed the main village on the island in honour of its new queen. Before Thoas and Myrina arrived, the village had been called Anemoessa, which meant 'a windy place'. The new name was greatly appreciated by the local residents because it was named after a lovely woman, and not a meteorological event. While Limnos never had a King and Queen before this, local people took them to heart and loved them as if they had been born there. It had been only a year since the arrival of the royal couple to Limnos, but Thoas and Myrina proudly welcomed a new little person into their lives — their beautiful daughter, Hypsipyle.

In a very short period of time, Limnos had gained a King and Queen, and was now a major contributor to the conduct of trade all throughout the Aegean. The island had access to imported goods and was relishing the chance to export its own produce. The lives of people rapidly changed due to this sudden expansion of trade, and the arrival of a baby to the royal couple was certainly a cause for celebration.

A new kind of prosperity emerged. No longer a backward island growing only enough food to feed itself, Limnos now grew more food and introduced many more varieties of fruit and vegetables which seemed to thrive in its soil and climate. Prior to Thoas' arrival, Limnian inhabitants rarely fished beyond their shores, not venturing far and certainly not sailing out of sight of the island. King Thoas encouraged a type of daring in the fisherman, and taught them many skills of navigation his father and grandfather taught him.

Thoas introduced many new ideas and changes to the islanders. New products were grown locally and traded for items not available on Limnos. With an increase in trade, people began to change their lives for the better. Trade also allowed Limnians to become healthier due to their improved diet. King Thoas also commenced a major construction undertaking on the rocky promontory overlooking Myrina's main port. He realised that the village needed to guard itself against any attacks from neighbouring islands and pirates, so a proper fortification of the area was deemed necessary.

Hypsipyle grew up in the newly constructed palace and seemed to enjoy her childhood. She had many friends, and local children were constant visitors to the royal household. The palace was more of a community centre than the official residence of a King and Queen. Soon after Hypsipyle was born, Thoas asked one of the local women, Polyxo, to be the child's nanny. She graciously accepted the role and became more of a part of the family than a palace employee. Polyxo was permitted to marry and have her own children, but only she and her daughter were permitted to live in the palace. She did have a husband and four sons, but they lived on a farm outside of Myrina.

The relationship between Polyxo and her own family was not seen as anything other than normal. Her husband Evangelos and the boys lived and worked on their farm, but each week, Polyxo and all her family dined together in the palace with the royal family. Evangelos didn't seem to mind this arrangement with Polyxo because he understood she had a primary responsibility to young Hypsipyle.

The first 10 summers of Hypsipyle's life were quite uneventful. Polyxo's daughter Katerina and Hypsipyle became best friends and could be seen in each other's company every day. Like other young girls in the village, they played by the beach, took walks up to the new castle on the nearby hill overlooking the main port area, spend time playing around water fountains, and helped their mothers whenever possible.

Hypsipyle was a natural leader amongst the young village girls. Not because she was the daughter of a king and queen, but because she could speak well, was confident, knowledgeable, and was a good listener. She was treated normally by the people in Myrina, which was how her parents wanted it to be. Thoas and Myrina were more like the guardians of the village cultural and economic life, rather than a royal family instructing village people on how to behave.

Hypsipyle didn't want to be considered a member of a royal

family. Not thinking of herself as a potential Queen, she did her best to fit in with people from the village as an equal. She desperately wanted to be '*just one of the girls*'. When new families came to live in Myrina from the mainland and from other islands, any new girl immediately joined the gang. Many of these girls said later in life that initially, they had no idea that Hypsipyle was the King and Queen's daughter. That news came as a surprise to both the new girls and their families. The differences in birthright soon became irrelevant as they treated Hypsipyle in the same way they treated each other.

The population of Limnos grew as a result of increased trade. People were actively encouraged by Thoas and Myrina to plant and grow new agricultural produce, such as more grapevines, olive trees, wheat and fig trees throughout the island. With this increase in agricultural produce for local consumption and trade, the need for new skills arose, such as boat building, flour milling, house building, cheese making, dry stone wall construction and farming. People were further encouraged to build farms outside the village, and to explore the rest of the island for new and prosperous sites.

Even though the island is quite large with an abundance of lush and fertile farming land, in those early days many of the newly constructed farms were close to Myrina, where farming land was quite harsh. It was not until much later that farmers extended their farming to other parts of the island to make better use of the land quality. The Trojan siege had a lot to do with this, but there will be more on that later.

Many more donkeys were introduced to Limnos, and farmers saw benefits immediately. Not only in the active work necessary for heavy farming, but as a form of transport to and from their farms. Donkeys seemed to thrive on the grasses of Limnos and had no trouble with the climate. One enterprising family saw the necessity of building a donkey park in Myrina, where all farm donkeys could stay during the night time before their owners took them to work in the fields each morning. This park was beneficial to famers as previously, they housed their donkeys in barns next to the family home each night.

These years in Myrina were carefree for the young Hypsipyle, but all this changed in the year of her 11th summer. Queen Myrina became very ill, and died quite suddenly. There was nothing the King or any of the apothecaries could do to help her. Nothing worked. King Thoas and Hypsipyle were deeply upset and affected by the sudden death of Queen Myrina. She was loved by all Limnians, and her death came as a complete surprise.

Hypsipyle's nurse Polyxo became a kind of defacto mother to her immediately. In Polyxo's personal life, her husband died a year before, and Thoas and Myrina had comforted and supported both her and her children. Polyxo's sons were old enough to live alone on the farm, but the King still felt a responsibility to them as he did for Polyxo. Life after the Queen's death was difficult, but Hypsipyle found the necessary comfort and affection from her father, Polyxo and especially Katerina.

Life returned to normal for the people of Limnos following the death of Queen Myrina. They continued to thrive with the existing trade deals, and some families started to expand their farming needs much further away from Myrina, but still only a day or two away from the village. During summer months, men and their sons spent considerable time away from home working with their animals and growing crops. To cope with this separation, men built small mandres on their farms closer to where their crops and animals were.

This was a time in the not too distant past, when all people on Limnos were living in harmony with each other. Women looked after all things to do with the household and raised their children. Children played, grew up and assumed the traditional roles assigned to them at birth once they reached a certain age, which was very young!

Change was coming, and no one knew what it was nor when it would come. The newly found wealth created in part by King Thoas and the increase in Aegean trade meant that the newer crops and farming methods required attention. Families became wealthier, but it was the men who seemed to want more. When men came home from their farms, they thought that their wives would be happy to see them, and glad to have them back home. The men became more demanding in their sexual favours, and by and large, the women dutifully obliged for the greater part of the year.

However, one thing was changing. While men were away from home tending to the family farms, women also became slightly more demanding. The one thing they demanded was the right to be left alone for 10 days in early summer so they could perform women only rituals at the Temple of Aphrodite. Previously, women did perform these rituals, but only for one day, because they believed that a single day was not enough. Women thought that in a whole year, ten days was not much to ask for. Men flatly refused this and continued as normal — demanding sex with their wives whenever they wanted.

Polyxo did not have a husband, and was free to decide for herself. She could devote time to their important rituals, but for married women, this was not possible due to the insistence of men for women to be completely subservient. So, she devised a plan to help married women participate in a ten-day retreat. Her plan was a brilliantly simple one.

The idea came to her some time ago after talking to a man who had just finished unloading his boat in port one day, and was enjoying a quiet refreshing drink of unadulterated wine, possibly in Ambrosia's wine bar. He was telling her how his wife and some of her friends had begun to eat raw onions and garlic on a regular basis. Although this was not an uncommon food item to consume, what he said next stayed with her for a long time.

"When she does it, her breath stinks. My donkey doesn't even go near her. The kids stay away too, preferring to spend time with our animals. She says it is for 'medical reasons', but I just think she wants to be left alone. Fortunately, it doesn't last for long, and she stops eating them after a few days."

Talking to some women one day, Polyxo outlined her thinking.

"I know how we can keep our men away from us so that we may pay our respect to Aphrodite and celebrate together without carnal interruptions. What we are seeking is not unreasonable. My plan is simple. We make ourselves as unattractive as possible. We do not wash. If we do wash, it will be in salt water. We will not change our clothes. We will eat garlic and onions daily. We will also rub onion over our skin."

Some women thought that this was a great idea, so the next approaching summer, they experimented with Polyxo's plan. It worked exceptionally well, and at the end of 10 days, they washed in fresh water and rubbed essential oils into their skin. As you can imagine, men were grateful and after a 10-day absence due to the stench of their women, men came back for their usual relations.

Seeing how successful the trial was, women who did not follow Polyxo's plan in that first summer vowed to do so the following year. Many men told their wives that they did not approve of this idea, and forbade their wives from participating.

Polyxo thought that the plan worked so well after one season that she and the women decided to try it again, but this time, and for the proper rituals to be undertaken in Aphrodite's name, all contact with any male — husband, son or father was not permitted for the 10 days.

When the men heard about this, they were furious. A delegation of men was despatched to King Thoas for his advice on what to do. The King could not advise them immediately, and suggested that they should let one more year go by before deciding on a plan of action. Secretly, Thoas agreed with the women and thought they had a good argument to conduct their own rituals without male interference, but he did not let the men know his true feelings.

The farmer most aggrieved by his wife's refusal to have sex with him for those 10 days was a man called Stelios. So outraged that his wife had turned away from him, Stelios sought the opinions of other like-minded farmers who it appeared shared similar thoughts. Each of these other men were equally shocked their wives could abandon them for 10 days.

Stelios and the others demanded to speak to the king. Thoas agreed to see them and invited them into the palace. Stelios took upon himself to be the spokesman.

"King Thoas. You have done a wonderful job bringing trade to this island. We have all benefited so much from this, and our lives are so much richer for it. Our children are happy, and our granaries and stores are full and we are truly appreciative. But we may have a problem soon with our wives. To keep up the supply of goods to trade, we need to spend much more time at our farms outside of Myrina, sometimes requiring us to be there for days at a time without coming back to the village."

"Our wives are demanding that for 10 days at the start of the summer season, they be left alone to prepare their offerings and other things at the temple of Aphrodite. As you know, in the past this event has gone on for 1 day, where we were happy to let it occur."

"But for 10 days? This is not acceptable. They do not need 10 days to pay their respects to Aphrodite. What could they possibly be doing? The women have now taken to not washing, eating garlic and onion and smearing onion all over their bodies. The stench is unbearable to us. Even our sons are turning away from their mothers, grandmothers and sisters. The old women whose families have grown are also participating. We cannot get anywhere near them. They refuse to have sex with us."

At this stage, Stelios was frothing at the mouth, with his fellow sufferers agreeing and nodding furiously with every word spoken. The King simply sat on a cushion and listened quietly. Stelios continued to speak.

"We demand that you do something."

King Thoas sat for a while, with his right elbow cupped in his left hand while he rubbed his chin with the thumb and forefinger of his right hand. Stelios was sure Thoas would agree that something needed to be done, but he did not expect the words from King Thoas that came next.

"As all of you know, I have been without my dear wife now for three summers. You knew her — she was a wonderful woman, a gracious Queen, and caring mother to Hypsipyle. People said that I would soon get over it, but believe me, you never do. I hear what you are saying Stelios, but if our women feel the need to take 10 days in a year where they are to be left alone to pay respects to Aphrodite, which is not a new thing to them, I do not think that this is a problem. I have been without my wife for a lot more than 10 days."

The King probably said more, but Stelios and the men did not hear any of it as they were shouting at him in disagreement. Not surprisingly, they stormed out of the palace because they didn't obtain the answer they were looking for. A meeting was called at Stelios' mandra outside Myrina for the next night. Word quickly passed around to all men that the meeting was to be held, and their attendance was essential.

The meeting began at sunset, and Stelios stood on a large rock at the entrance to his farm and quietly beckoned them to come closer so that he did not have to speak loudly. This particular night, there was no wind, so agitated men's voices could travel a long distance. Stelios' farm was above Myrina, and if he spoke loudly, he thought he may have been heard in the village below. He began calmly.

"I have heard rumours from fishermen on Samothraki that their women are being starved of male company. A great number of men

21

from Samothraki have joined a strange cult where they must go without sex for 6 summers to prove worthy of the High Priests."

"I have heard that too", said one of the gathered men. "They just leave their families and go to the temple. Women and children are left behind."

"I hear that young unmarried women are most concerned because the men who enter this cult are young", said Stelios. "Do you want to know what I am thinking?"

Stelios outlined his plan. It was breathtakingly simple. Men would go to Samothraki, find these young unmarried women, and bring them back to Limnos to help with farm work.

"The first thing we must do is to bring these young women to Limnos, under the guise of a ploy based on a fake pirate attack."

"How will we explain this to our women?" asked one of the gathering men.

"Easy. We don't say anything to them. We go to Samothraki as usual for trade purposes, but in this instance, our return cargo will be young women!"

The Limnian men were still confused.

"We travel to Samothraki for trade all the time, weather permitting. We will do so again, taking over some of our produce, which is nothing out of the ordinary, so that our wives do not suspect anything."

"We return with young women, who we will explain are here for their own protection."

"How will we do that?"

"Again, this is easily explained. When we return with a cargo load of women, we say to our wives that Samothraki was under a pirate attack, and we managed to save these women while their men battled with pirates. Remember to add that we only just managed to escape with our lives."

"But how do we explain the women on our boats to the women in our beds?"

"We tell our wives that we offered to keep these young women safe until it was time to return. We can house them at our mandres, and while they are here, they can help with our agricultural endeavours."

"This must be the story you tell your wives. In addition, you must maintain give the impression that you remain totally upset with their 10-day Aphrodite devotion idea. If you can do this successfully, our wives will not suspect anything is wrong."

Stelios knew that most of the men would have no problems with this story line. Everyone came back from the gathering on his farm in a jovial mood. They were convinced that their wives would not mind, and be quite amenable to having these women working on their farms.

What could possibly go wrong with this simple plan?

CHAPTER 4

Samothraki

When Limnian produce was ever sent to Samothraki, a maximum of two, but mostly only one boat would have made the journey. Trade between the neighbouring islands had been irregular for many years, whereas trade with Imbros and Samos had grown significantly. Stelios knew that he desired at least a dozen boats to make the Samothrakian journey, so he required an amendment to his plan.

Because trade with Samothraki was still relatively sporadic, and Stelios believed he could convince Thoas to allow travel to the island with many men and boats on the ruse of an educational trip to explore new trade possibilities. After explaining to the King his plan for a trade expedition to Samothraki, Thoas was very excited and agreed to Stelios' view of sending many men to learn, discuss and swap ideas with farmers on their nearest northern island neighbour.

On the nominated day, 12 boats gathered in port and steadily filled with produce for sale. King Thoas himself farewelled the flotilla and wished Stelios a safe journey. The weather was favourable and over fifty men set sail for Samothraki and arrived before nightfall.

Prior to the arrival of Stelios and his group on Samothraki, the young women were told that they would be travelling to Limnos to spend time learning new farming techniques and would be returning shortly. They were also told that the reason for this excursion was to strengthen relationships with their closest neighbouring island, and that they were specially chosen for this most important role. Apparently, they all believed the deception.

Early in the morning of the next day after arriving on Samothraki, Stelios and the men loaded the girls on to the boats and prepared to leave for Limnos. Farewells between the girls and their families were made at the port, and the cargo of human produce prepared for the short journey to Myrina. Once safely away from land, each boat captain had been instructed to explain to each young girl the true purpose of their visit to Limnos, and if they breathed a word of it to anyone, or sought help from anyone on Limnos, they would be killed immediately. The girls were told that they would be spending all their time working on farms and during the 10-day Aphrodite rituals, would be expected to offer their bodies to each man as required, and when required. As we can imagine, these girls were terrified, and most likely never expected to be returned to their families ever again.

On arrival in Myrina, Stelios marched directly to the palace and asked to speak to Thoas. He told the King of a pirate attack on Samothraki, and he and his Limnian men just happened to be in port and could safely evacuate the innocent young women to Limnos so as to escape potential slavery. Thoas said that bringing back these poor innocent young girls was the right thing to do and suggested to Stelios that he and the others should house the girls on their farms. King Thoas further suggested that the girls might contribute to each family by working on the farms. Stelios enthusiastically agreed with these suggestions and promised the King that as soon as it was safe for them to return, the men would dutifully take the girls back. King Thoas believed him without question, and asked Polyxo to let the women know of the situation with the Samothrakian women, and that to keep them safe, they would be put to work on farms, away from the village.

Polyxo was furious. She knew what Stelios had intended, but could not really say anything as she had no direct proof. Polyxo did manage to speak to one of the young women, and was told about a pirate attack, and that they were thankful of being saved from a life of slavery. Because her story was not at all convincing, Polyxo assumed she and her Samothrakian friends were on Limnos against their will.

A meeting of women took place at the Temple of Aphrodite the next day, where Polyxo attempted to explain her thoughts, and how she believed the new farm workers were nothing more than sex slaves, and for each married woman to be very aware of their husband's actions. Surprisingly, almost all woman disagreed with Polyxo. They said that they believed their husbands, and would go out of their way to help these young girls feel at home — even though they were to live and work on the farms.

I have heard stories from many sources that in the first few days, women from Myrina took food and clothing to the newest arrivals out on their family farms.

By the time the sun had disappeared behind the horizon twice, all Samothrakian girls were safely housed on a farm. Where a farm did not have an adequate house for the new arrivals, new buildings were constructed. It has been said in the years since this event that the houses on each farm were in better condition than the homes in Myrina itself. All men approached this task of housing construction with a vigour never before seen on the island.

Women in Myrina were not suspicious of their husbands' motives at all because they had no reason to be. They were proud that their men were helping these young women enjoy a good life until they could be returned safely to their own island. Men argued that by building proper houses on their farms, they were improving them by having somewhere comfortable to live in when they could not get home to the village. The Limnian women trusted their husbands.

Polyxo did not trust one word of this make-believe story about farm improvements. She said to other women on many occasions, this is wrong, this is not right, and all the men are doing is keeping a sex slave out on their farms. No women believed her, and were getting annoyed at her constantly speaking about this. At that stage, they all completely trusted their men. Even King Thoas was saying that it was wonderful what the men were doing for these poor young girls from Samothraki.

It was not long before some cracks began to show in the thin veneer of the feeble excuse built by Stelios. One by one, men were making up excuses to stay overnight on their farms for longer times than they had ever done. Excuses such as — I need to stay tonight to keep a watch on the new lambs/foals/kids/chicks...I was so tired after spending all day planting new trees/vegetables/vines....I had to stay as I was so tired after ploughing new fields/digging a new well/clearing land/rebuilding the stone fences...you get the picture. Men were spending more nights on their farms.

At first, women in Myrina did not think it was at all suspicious that men spent more time on their farms, as long as they brought home enough food to feed the whole family and additional produce to be exported. The continual excuses by men to remain on farms for extended periods were believable. But that time of the year was fast approaching where women wanted to be alone, so they immediately started the new ritual of not washing and making themselves ugly, smelly, unsightly and unbearable to men. Women were expecting a fight on their hands, but surprisingly there were few arguments. Instead, men were saying things like, "you have your 10 days — you deserve it. We will stay out of your way and go to the farms, so you can be alone".

For the first time since the Samothrakian girls arriving on Limnos and the Limnian women wanting their 10 days of celebration and devotion to Aphrodite, there was no argument with men. Women thought that it was their smelling bodies and appearance that was having the desired effect, and men played up to that by saying they would leave them alone. Without wanting to appear too eager, men would continue to show false anger at their smelly wives, and appear to give in to their demands for a 10-day celebration period. Women thought they were winning the argument for the first time and were convinced that it was their smell and ugly appearance that was putting men off.

To any outsider who visited Limnos, relationships between men and women appeared to be normal. The reality was much like watching a duck on a pond, where what can be seen is the serenity of a duck wading effortlessly about the pond, but below the water line, the duck's little webbed feet were furiously paddling to stay on course.

Men were playing their part too. Stelios had spent considerable time schooling men on what to say and how to say it to their wives. On the surface, women were extremely pleased they could finally have their 10 uninterrupted days of devotion to Aphrodite, and men were more than happy to go to their farms. Women honestly thought that eating garlic and onion, not washing and rubbing onion on their skin was a ploy that worked to keep men away and give them time to be alone.

I also need to enlighten you about another grand idea by Polyxo, with the full blessing of King Thoas. Polyxo could see that her utterances were not making any favour with the women. No one agreed with her thoughts on why Samothrakian girls were on Limnos. Polyxo may have had ideas that there were to be no men on Limnos soon, but she certainly did not let anyone know of those innermost personal feelings.

Instead, she asked the King if women could begin to take a more active role in the loading and unloading of boats entering and leaving the port of Myrina. King Thoas thought this was a marvellous idea, and before too long, it was quite normal to see women and a handful of men performing these tasks. When vessels came to Limnos to offload goods, they did not care *how* it was done — only that it *was* done. It was the same for loading boats with goods for export. Many of the bars and food stalls in the port area were operated and run by women. When asked by sailors on these boats why more men were not around, the answer was simply this; they are on the farms growing the produce we are now selling. Also, when sailors from these visiting boats were taken to the nearest bar to consume wine, they certainly did not seem to care who served them.

Without anyone noticing, Polyxo was orchestrating a vision of life on Limnos with no reliance on men for help and assistance. While she may not have said so at the time, it certainly appeared that way. Boats came to Limnos full of imported goods and departed with exported goods, and sailors drank far too much in port side bars. Nothing seemed to be out of the ordinary.

Women who gained work at the port were grateful they had some other responsibilities apart from housekeeping, food preparation and child raising. They learned new skills, and a number of new port side businesses soon blossomed. Of course, bars and food stalls at the port did a good trade, but so too did brothels. To draw attention away from the lack of men working on the docks, Polyxo cleverly set the scene of things to come.

Before too long, the second year of women only rituals conducted over a 10-day period ended, and a steadily increasing number of men did not rush back to their families in Myrina after devotions were concluded.

CHAPTER 5

Polyxo's plan

I think I need a wine. Aah, thank you. What a beautiful drink this is.
It was now two moons since the rituals had concluded for the second year. Polyxo quietly convened a meeting of women at the temple of Aphrodite and this time, attendance had significantly increased since the last gathering. When she spoke, all ears were listening and hearts pounding. To add to the gravitas of the situation, a cool breeze blew unusually early for that time of year, and clouds moved in to cover a falling sun.

"Women of Limnos. I told you before, but no one was listening, or you did not want to listen. Either way, please hear me now."

She went directly to the point. No small talk, just a passionate plea from her heart.

"Our men have deserted us. This charade of having Samothrakian girls working on farms is nothing more than a sex slave operation. There were no pirates on Samothraki. Our men were annoyed at us wanting *more* time to devote to Aphrodite. Remember the first time we asked our men for more time? We pleaded with them. We tried to use reason. Remember what they said? No! Why do you want *more* time? You cannot have it. We won't allow you to have *any* more time."

"What did we do? We made ourselves unattractive. We made

ourselves smell. What did they do this first time? They stayed away, but they were definitely not happy. You all thought that the ploy worked. On one level, it did, but it caused an unexpected outcome."

"Our men were so disgusted at us wanting 10 days to ourselves, to conduct all the appropriate rituals necessary to please Aphrodite, they hatched a disgusting plan with the men from Samothraki."

"There were no pirates. It is true that many men on Samothraki leave for a number of years to join a strange new cult, where women are not permitted, and men go without sex for the entire time they are cult members, but the young girls on Samothraki are not in any danger or starved of male company. Not all men enter the cult, and there are many men who choose not to. There is no problem."

"How do I know this? A number of you have benefited greatly in learning new skills concerned with trade between islands. I know that you do your work diligently, not talking to any men that appear on our shores from other lands. I am different. I talk to them. I ask them about where they are from, and what problems they might be having back home with crops, families, pirates and a host of other topics. I have shared many stories with these men as they begin to loosen up after a few kraters of wine and after a visit to our brothels. Men are such lambs after they have had their needs and carnal desires met. They tell me anything. They also see me as no threat as I am without husband, and they are certainly not interested in bedding an old woman like me."

"A week ago, one particularly unremarkable boat arrived carrying dried figs and barrels of salted fish. It was unloaded without problems and then loaded up with our flour and olive oil for the return voyage."

"One of the questions I ask each boat captain is 'where are you from', and to my surprise, they said Samothraki. Immediately, the captain saw my surprised expression, as this was the first boat from that island in a long time. I immediately asked how the pirate situation was."

"What pirate situation, came the quick response."

"You know, the pirates who are threatening your land and taking young women as slaves?"

"Never heard of it. We do get pirates from time to time, but we have not had any pirate trouble now for as long as I can remember. Why do you ask?'

"I had to think fast. I did not want to alert the captain, and give away too much information. Then came a question from the captain that I did not expect".

"I hope our girls are doing well here. They can learn many more farming skills on Limnos than they could possibly learn on Samothraki due to our mountainous land. We thank you for giving them this opportunity. By the way, when are they coming home? Their families miss them?"

"Again, I had to think fast so as not to arouse any suspicion. Clearly, this captain was under the impression that their young women were here on some form of farming work experience, and would soon return with the knowledge necessary to add to their agricultural expertise.

"Soon, I believe." "What more could I say?"

"After some wine and a quick trip to the bars and brothels, followed by a good night's sleep to help clear their heads, the captain and his crew set off for Samothraki with Limnian produce, none the wiser as a result of my questioning."

Polyxo relayed this story to the gathered women, who were by now, shaking their heads in disbelief and starting to get a little annoyed at the situation. Sensing a growing unease with the attitude and serious actions of their men, Polyxo continued.

"We need a new beginning. We need a fresh start. Our men's minds have been corrupted with these sex slaves and they have totally forgotten us. Our sons' minds are also being corrupted. Our fathers and uncles are totally corrupted. We need to cleanse our island of this disease."

Prior to this meeting, women were wary of Polyxo and her rants against men, but this time it was different. They were not suspicious anymore of her words. They were beginning to come around to her way of thinking. Little did any of them have any idea of what she would propose. Polyxo was physically shaking with rage, but underneath, there was an inner calm.

"I have had a dream. The god Phoebus came to me and promised that we will have new marriages and life will begin again. Our men need to go. They must be killed. All of them, boys, old, young — all of them. We must have a fresh start where we are equally in control of our lives, and not dependent on men for anything. We cannot be treated in this way ever again. We will send a message to the world that Limnian women are not to be taken for granted. All we wanted was a time to ourselves, a time that was rightfully ours, without any interruptions, without any interference, and then life was to return to normal. All we ever wanted was to be left in peace for this time each year to be amongst our own kind and pay our due respects to Aphrodite. What did our men do? They lied to us. They claimed that they had to go to Samothraki to help fight pirates, and instead, came back with a bounty far more wicked than pirates. They ignored us. They corrupted our boys and our fathers went along with this."

Can you imagine the reactions to these words by Polyxo on the gathered women after hearing this? You would think they might have been totally opposed to the outrageous plan for cleansing the island of its male disease, but that was not the case. One by one, each woman started to nod her head and agree. The men had to go. Just like that. If any of the women had private doubts regarding Polyxo's plan, they did not publicly voice any objections. Polyxo was convinced all women were in complete harmony. Perhaps they were.

CHAPTER 6

Murder most foul

After the meeting, women casually drifted back to their homes and continued on with life as usual. Boats came and went, and no foreign captains thought it was anything but normal to be greeted at the port of Myrina by women working the docks and serving wine in bars. Limnian men spent most of their time at the farms, and also did not think it was anything but typical behaviour that women took to working at the port.

Polyxo did not spend much time at the palace looking after Hypsipyle, as the young royal was fast approaching womanhood. Hypsipyle also enjoyed meeting the boats and talking with ship captains and their crews. All of these workers on visiting ships knew that Hypsipyle was the daughter of King Thoas, so there was no trouble. If there was even the slightest hint of trouble, Polyxo stepped in to sort it out. She was gaining a fierce reputation as a peace maker and problem solver.

Limnian men could not believe their luck. They honestly thought their wives agreed with having the Samothrakian young women on farms was a good idea. In the mind of Stelios, he had done a great job convincing all Limnian women the new farm workers were just that — farm workers. He had no idea the women knew the real story, and were now secretly plotting their murderous revenge.

When men did come home to spend nights with their wives, they were not demanding sex, and nor were their wives.

At this stage, Polyxo did not have a specific plan of how to permanently rid the island of all males. It was a plausible concept supported by the women, but no details had yet been established.

One warm and calm night, when all males were not staying out on the farms but unusually back in town and celebrating at the temple of Dionysus, an idea came to Polyxo. The reason for the celebration was to give thanks to the goddess Demeter for an excellent wheat crop. She observed the men in a jovial and cordial mood at the temple, albeit after many wines, but it was a happy occasion. In those days, the Temple of Dionysus was high on the hill overlooking the secondary port of Myrina, where the wine bars and brothels were located. Here, men felt safe, and this particular night, they made appropriate libations to both Demeter and Dionysus, and conducted the normal sacrifices where families were invited afterwards to feast on sacrificial lambs.

Polyxo observed the happiness of men that night, and thought that it would be an ideal place for a murder to take place. She had the location planned, but now for the method. She also noticed the husbands and farmers invited all boys and older men who may or may not be farm workers to join in the celebration.

This particular night, the Samothrakian female farm workers were invited to attend the festivities. For the first time, these young women were all together in Myrina at the same time, enjoying the celebrations at the temple site high on the hill. As luck would have it, there was little or no wind that night, and the temperature was quite warm — unusually warm for that time of year.

In simple language, it was a perfect night for such a celebration. But the Limnian women were anything but in a celebratory mood. The invitation extended to each of the slave girls to be there made the women furious, and now more than ever, completely determined to carry out the planned murder.

King Thoas and Hypsipyle were asked to make the initial sacrifice, whereby Thoas dutifully slit the throat of a ram, and Hypsipyle poured the first wine into the earth to please Dionysus. Everyone appeared happy, but the women of Limnos disguised their thoughts of disgust under a thin facial veneer of perceived happiness. By now, they were becoming impatient, eager to extract revenge.

When the evening finally drew to its inevitable and predictable conclusion, with many men falling down suffering the effects of too much wine, it was the slave girls who stepped in to take them back to their farms on donkeys. A group of women could not contain their anger any further. They were shouting obscenities as the slave girls led each donkey carrying their inebriated cargo towards the farms. Polyxo rushed to the women urging them to hold their tongues. She was worried about her plan being exposed too early. But there was no way a drunken man slumped over a beast of burden was in any position to hear vague threats of imminent doom.

But what exactly was the plan? Next morning, Polyxo gathered a few of her closest friends and described her thoughts.

"Last night, the celebration and libations paid to the goddess Demeter was for the harvest of an excellent wheat crop. In Crete, Demeter is also considered the goddess of sleep and death, as well as for grains and fertility."

One old Cretan custom is to celebrate Demeter as the goddess of sleep through use of poppies, and it was widely known that poppies can be used in a special concoction to promote sleep.

While Polyxo explained the Cretan custom, she stopped, paused and sat on a rock, looking at some colourful flowers growing between two other rocks.

"I think I have it."

Polyxo thought some more and then spoke in a soft, careful and at times excited voice.

"Why don't we mix a concoction of herbs and flowers with wine, to make the men sleepy and drunk. For many years, women of Limnos have been adding to water, varying levels of opium juice gained from poppies growing wild about the island to help babies sleep, for aching teeth and to help older arthritic people with bodily aches sleep better."

The use of poppy juice was a remedy for all types of ailments and conditions that had been used since before anyone could remember. One of the benefits of using poppy juice was there was no odour once mixed with water or wine.

Suneva, one of the women present at the meeting and an old friend of Polyxo's from when they were children, said that she often ground some seeds from a plant growing near her family farm and added it in with water.

Suneva's mother had a wealth of knowledge about local plants and their herbal usages. While not remembering the actual name of the plant, Suneva remembered her mother giving this drink to her and her siblings if they were having trouble sleeping during unusually warm summer nights.

She said "Why not add this in as well, so that the men would be drunk, happy, and then fall asleep with vivid dreams? I have not used it for a while, but I remember that it also does not have an odour, so when mixed with wine, the new drink would smell of wine only. What do you think?"

The plan was gathering pace. Bring the men to the Temple of Dionysus, offer them a special party with ram sacrifices, and supply plenty of wine laced with opium juice and a herbal remedy for instant sleep. That should do it!

Before any more elements of the plan could be discussed, Suneva said. "I have another idea. Why don't we try this out on one of us first?"

"What do you mean Suneva?", asked Polyxo.

"I mean that we should test it first on one of us to see that it has the desired effect. That way we will be able to ascertain the right consistencies, and estimate how long it will be before men start to fall asleep."

After a short moment of quiet, where each woman thought about this, Polyxo broke the silence.

"I'll do it. Suneva, gather some of that herb, and I will harvest some poppies. Ambrosia, bring some of that sweet wine from your bar down at the port. Can we meet back here at sunset tomorrow, so that I can drink our newly flavoured wine?"

At sunset the following evening, Polyxo brought her poppy juice, Suneva gathered a handful of herbs from the unknown plant, and Ambrosia had a small amphora of sweet wine. No one knew what consistencies to mix, but they were too impatient to wait any longer.

Polyxo took the wine amphora, a beautiful looking drinking vessel used for special guests in Ambrosia's wine bar. Ambrosia used this amphora and others like it for captains, and men she particularly liked when they arrived for a drink after loading or unloading their boats.

Polyxo took only a small amount of her poppy juice, added some of the sleeping herb from Suneva, and mixed it together with a pestle. These two ingredients made a thin, clear paste that was luckily without any discernible odour. Ambrosia poured in some of her sweet wine, mixing it gently with the already thickening paste. Soon enough, the paste dissolved and what was left.... was wine!

Polyxo did not say anything at first. She drank slowly from the cup, and sat down.

Nodding her head, she said "Nice. Nice. Very nice".

"How do you feel?" asked Suneva.

"Nothing yet", said Polyxo. "Give it a bit more time".

"I think you should walk around a bit, like the men will do at the party", said Ambrosia. "Maybe dance a bit too".

Polyxo agreed, but had trouble standing up. Suneva and

Ambrosia helped her to her feet, taking one arm each and walked her about for a short time. They even danced together.

"My legs feel heavy, but I feel ….ha..ppyyy…". At this point, Polyxo collapsed, falling into the arms of Suneva and Ambrosia. She was asleep, and smiling.

Suneva and Ambrosia gently took Polyxo back to the palace trying not to arouse suspicion, but were met by Hypsipyle at the entrance.

"What has happened to Polyxo?"

"One minute she was talking, and the next she said she felt faint", lied Ambrosia.

"Quick, bring her inside. She needs to lie down. I will see to it that the other slaves will look after her."

Ambrosia and Suneva helped Hypsipyle take Polyxo into her room. Two of the palace female slaves came quickly once they heard the commotion outside, and offered their assistance to get Polyxo into bed. She must have been a strange sight. In a deep sleep, and smiling!

Polyxo woke the next morning to find a room full of people. The two slaves were standing at her bedside either side of her head, Hypsipyle standing behind them, Suneva and Ambrosia standing at the foot of the bed gawking at Polyxo.

Lying profusely, Polyxo asked what had happened. One of the slaves said "Hypsipyle, Ambrosia and Suneva brought you home after sunset unconscious, but smiling, and we all helped you get into bed".

"I can't remember anything", said Polyxo, but before she said another word, Ambrosia spoke.

"Don't you remember, you had a drink of water last night and started to feel faint. Suneva and I took you by the arms and brought you back to the palace. By the time we arrived here, you had passed out. How do you feel"?

"I feel fine. Honestly, I feel fine. Now can you all leave me alone while I go about my morning ablutions?"

Everyone left the room immediately, but Ambrosia doubled back at the last moment to return to Polyxo.

"Now, how do you feel, and tell me what you can remember from last night."

"It worked, didn't it? I remember mixing the wine, flowers and herbs, drinking it, and I think we even danced a bit. Is that true? I remember that I was flying over Myrina, looking down on all the people below. I swooped down lower to show people what I could do, but no one seemed the least bit interested that I could fly. All they thought I was doing was imitating a bird! It did not appear to be any big deal to them that I could fly. But after that, my next recollection was waking just now to see you all looking at me."

"Come to think of it, there was one other thing. In my dreams I visited a place that was very beautiful. It was somewhere I've never travelled, so I can't remember much more about it than that!"

Polyxo and Ambrosia embraced. No more planning was necessary. They knew what the required recipe was to make men feel happy and fall asleep. Ambrosia agreed to meet up with Suneva immediately, and then all three would meet at the temple that night.

Sunset came and all three conspirators stood in front of the temple altar. Polyxo explained that she could not remember anything after dancing. Ambrosia said the time between her dancing, and Polyxo declaring her legs felt heavy, was so short, they were all convinced the consistency of the special mixture to wine was good enough. No more testing was needed or necessary, but they did agree to make some slight variations in levels for young boys, young men, and older men.

The three women talked about these levels in some detail. They needed to know the volumes of wine and additives necessary to plan for the party. Once that was decided, Polyxo said it was time to gather all women, but before that, they had one more idea.

Next morning, Polyxo, Suneva and Ambrosia went to see King Thoas at the palace. It never dawned on them but in the palace, there was only one male, while all the rest were women. King Thoas did not have any male slaves, only Polyxo, who was Hypsipyle's nurse, her two daughters, and two female slaves.

Thoas agreed to see them. Hypsipyle was also there.

"How can I help you?" asked Thoas. Polyxo responded.

"We have an idea that could see normal life return to Limnos. The women understand that our desire to have 10-days to celebrate and pay our respects to Aphrodite have had unfortunate consequences on the lives of all males on the island. We can see that we have been extremely selfish in these desires. We thought that we were right, and our men would understand our needs and wants, but now, we see the error of our ways, and the heartache that this has caused."

Slightly confused and surprised, Thoas said "Go on".

"The men were right in shunning us, as we made ourselves ugly, smelly and revolting. They went to Samothraki for trade purposes, inadvertently helped defeat pirates, and in doing so saved a lot of innocent young women from certain slavery, or even death. They were right in bringing these unfortunate and blameless young women here to work on our farms until it was safe to return home. They should be thanked, not scorned."

"But we women were obstinate, and could not appreciate the good things our men were doing, and how we shunned them in their time of need, just to have 10 days to ourselves. Our revolting appearances and selfish manner made our men shy away and live apart from us on farms outside the village. Our sons and fathers too were shunned by us, as we ignored their needs."

"Here is what we propose. We all sincerely apologise to you and our men for ignoring them, to you our beloved King for our selfishness, and to our sons and fathers for shunning them. We think it is time to take the young farm workers back to Samothraki, as we will return to normal relations with our men for evermore. After these young women are reunited with their families, we will have a big feast and make libations and sacrifices to Dionysus at the temple, and give ourselves to our menfolk once more."

"Ambrosia and Suneva have been helping me see the error of our ways, and have helped prepare the feast. Ten rams will be sacrificed, one for each day we spent in our own selfish endeavours, and a special blend of wine and herbs will be served to all males, both young and old, by all females."

Thoas was so happy. He suspected there were tensions between men and women, but he could not find a solution as all people appeared to be living in harmony.

"What a wonderful idea. We will set the feast for seven days from now. I decree that all citizens of Limnos be in attendance for this great feast at the temple of Dionysus, and the farm workers must be taken back to their families on Samothraki immediately."

Thoas went straight to see Stelios and told him of the feast. At first, Stelios thought the King was joking, but soon became apparent that he was serious.

"Stelios, gather all the sailing vessels you need and return all farm workers to Samothraki. Our women have seen the error of their ways, and will forgo their demands to spend time away from males at the temple of Aphrodite. They have started to wash and will from now on, refrain from eating so much garlic and onion, and will be immediately rubbing their bodies with essential oils once more. Stelios, your wish has come true."

On hearing these words, Stelios was deeply suspicious, but as he thought about it further, he felt justified in his now changed position. He was happy that the women had backed down and agreed to return to life as normal. Stelios felt vindicated.

He organised a quick meeting of all men at his farm, and at the same time Polyxo arranged for women to meet at the temple to Aphrodite to explain the plans for a new beginning.

"Our women have backed down. We won! They are even

preparing a special feast for us, so we can return to our normal homes and our normal lives."

"The King has asked if we can take the girls back to Samothraki without fail. Our women have given up their ridiculous notion of needing time alone from us to celebrate at the temple of Aphrodite. We won!"

"Now for the good part. Our women are so contrite, they are planning a feast in our honour. We will have 10 rams to sacrifice, one for each of the days they wanted alone, and a special wine from Ambrosia's bar. You know how good her wine is? I am told it is a special brew just for us. They promise that we will remember this for the rest of our lives. Men, we have won."

Just as Stelios was speaking to all men, Polyxo was addressing the women.

"The King has asked us to prepare for a feast in seven days' time at the temple of Dionysus. At this feast, we will be serving a special wine, coming from Ambrosia's wine bar, and containing special additives. This special wine will be served to our husbands, sons and fathers. We will also be sacrificing 10 rams, one for each of the days to dedicate and pay our appropriate respects to Aphrodite. It is time for a new beginning."

"The special additives will make the men happy and fall asleep". They will appear to be drunk. Once they have fallen asleep, we will commence our new beginning. It is time to shed blood and start again. We must rid ourselves of this disease on this special event, that has spread to all males, not only men, but sons and fathers too."

"All slave girls will be spared, and returned to Samothraki in a few days' time. This will of course depend on favourable winds. I trust the gods will be on our side. On the night of the feast, we must not drink the special wine. Ambrosia will have our untainted wine in a separate amphora."

Hypsipyle did not know of any of this. She had no part in Polyxo's planning and was not aware of the level of anger built up in the women towards all males. Her life with Thoas in the palace meant that she was kept sheltered from the tribulations of everyday life. Even Katerina, her best friend from childhood was keeping this secret from her. That was until Katerina decided to let Hypsipyle know what was going to happen at the feast and immediately afterwards.

Katerina was still living in the palace with her mother Polyxo. She was becoming extraordinarily active in the management of portside operations and possessed some form of official authority from the King. Thoas trusted her with these roles and actively encouraged her to become much more involved.

With six days until the feast, it was time for Katerina to let Hypsipyle know of the new beginning. Early on this particular day, Hypsipyle and Katerina were sitting at the port, watching one of the early morning ships leave for Lesvos loaded with Limnian produce. Katerina asked Hypsipyle to remain totally silent and not to interrupt, as she had something very important to say.

After the plan was outlined, and the reasons for it, Hypsipyle gasped and held her hand over her mouth so that she would not cry out load or scream. Katerina took her hands and held them tight. The murder of all men included killing the King!

Katerina held Hypsipyle close and whispered into her ear.

"But I have my own plan. I know my mother wants all males to be killed, but I know that we cannot do this. You and I can save the King, but we must keep it a secret. We have to save Thoas, but no one can ever know. If our scheme is discovered, I fear for our lives."

Hypsipyle was crying. Not because of a promise to save her father, but the notion of killing all males. Katerina did her best to explain it, but it still did not make any sense to Hypsipyle. Katerina was adamant that if Hypsipyle did not go along with the plan, or warn any male of it, she too would be killed.

The two best friends took a walk along the beach towards the temple of Dionysus. Passing the temple, they climbed to the top of the cape and gazed out towards a distant Mt Athos rising majestically out of the sea.

"My idea is to inform your father just prior to the feast. He won't have time to escape before this without drawing attention to himself. If he does escape, it will be obvious to everyone that he has been warned, and you and I will be in mortal peril."

"We need to prepare a small boat and hide it away from the village, in a bay a few stadia away from the main port. Next to the bay is a cave. Remember that cave? We used to play there when we were young."

Hypsipyle remembered it and said to Katerina that a small boat could easily be hidden there.

"With so much activity happening this next few days in preparation for the feast, men taking the Samothrakian girls back home, with the young boys and fathers working on farms, no one will think to go to this place. As you know, there are no farms nearby because of the rocky cliffs above. It is the perfect place to hide a boat."

Katerina and Hypsipyle concocted an elaborate plan in an attempt to fool everyone on the night. After making the appropriate libations as befitting a King at a feast such as this, Thoas will appear to drink the same wine as other men, but instead, drink a different wine, weaker in strength than anything else so as to not get him drunk. He will then act as if he was drunk and pass out, like other men should do. Hopefully, this ruse would not arouse any suspicion from other men, and certainly not from the women. Hypsipyle will make an excuse at the time to take Thoas back to the palace where he will be killed and put to sea in a larnax, as custom dictates.

Once at the palace, King Thoas will quickly gather some clothing, food and water and go immediately to the cave to make his escape. Katerina and Hypsipyle will then return from the palace after pushing a fake larnax into the sea, carrying the Kings authentically bloodied sword so that other women would believe that she had killed her father. This authentic blood will come from a pig already sacrificed at the palace earlier in the day.

Two very different boat trips had been planned to leave Limnos within a few days of each other. One single boat carrying the current King away from Limnos to a destination unknown, and the other boats to return each of the young women to Samothraki.

At the beginning of the celebratory week, all available boats were moored in the port in readiness for the return voyage of human freight. Some of the men who had had the benefit of a young farm worker were complaining to Stelios about the sudden change of plan, but Stelios was a very convincing man. He must have been extremely persuasive as no man openly challenged him to stop the boats. In his mind, he truly believed he had won the battle and their wives would once again perform any task demanded, and at any time.

Weather permitting, it was decided to leave for Samothraki on the following morning. Preparations were made hastily for each young girl to travel from the farms directly to the boats, and to be guarded in case they thought of trying to escape back to the farm.

At the same time, Hypsipyle and Katerina had managed to find a small boat for the King's journey, and carefully hid it in the cave.

Morning arrived with winds not favourable for travel to Samothraki, so no Limnian boats took to the sea. Polyxo was starting to feel as if the gods may have been against her. But within one day, winds shifted sufficiently for the flotilla of young human cargo to be returned. The port area was alive with many people packing provisions on the boats in readiness for the hopefully calm journey to Samothraki.

In a boat travelling with the main group was Damianus and his young son Timotheus. Damianus had never taken a slave girl for himself, because he was still in mourning for his dear wife who had died when Timotheus was a young child. Damianus and

Timotheus lived on the edge of the village and had a farm next to their house. They had some vegetables and grape vines growing, but spent much of their time fishing in a small boat.

When they were children, Damianus, Stelios and his younger sister Erika were best friends. They would go everywhere together, playing along the water's edge, around the temples and on the hill overlooking the port area. As they all grew older, Damianus and Erika were developing their friendship in a way which excluded Stelios. He could see his younger sister falling in love with his best friend, and was more than likely jealous of the blossoming relationship.

Stelios was so outraged at losing his best friend, he jealously and openly forbade him from marrying Erika. Both Erika and Damianus ignored Stelios and married each other. The petty jealousy culminated in Stelios never talking to each of the newlyweds ever again.

Damianus and Erika had a son who they named Timotheus, and together lived a happy existence until Erika developed a debilitating illness when Timotheus was only two years old. Stelios was convinced Damianus caused his sisters illness, and was even more angry. The bitterness between former best friends was never healed.

Enough of the past — now back to the story.

Damianus was very good friends with Ambrosia and often visited her tavern for a wine and some freshly baked bread. He had his preferred seat by the front of the tavern facing the port area, where he could enjoy a drink of wine and gaze out over the water. One afternoon in her tavern, when she thought Damianus could not hear her, Ambrosia was overheard talking to some other women about a special concoction to add to wine for the upcoming feast. He thought he heard the words 'new beginning', and Damianus left immediately. He had always thought the women had every right to take as much time as they wanted to in order for proper sacrifices and libations to be made to Aphrodite. He could see how angry they had become, and was acutely aware that men were spending most of their time on farms with their slave girls.

After he left, Damianus walked along the beach towards the port to focus his thoughts and to think about what he was going to do next. With pieces of strange conversations overheard in Ambrosia's bar playing on his mind, seeing women who only a few days ago were very angry with men, to seeing now a complete change around in female behaviour and attitude to these same men, he knew something was not right and made his mind up to escape.

His plan was simple. As a fisherman, he was used to visiting all parts of the island accessible only by boat. If he was unable to make it back to Myrina by nightfall, he would simply pull his boat up onto the sand and spend the evening.

He remembered one such place on the north-eastern coast of Limnos, where fish were plentiful, and food could be grown easily without anyone suspecting who was living there. In this particular part of the island, he had always thought that it would be an ideal location for a village, and frequently wondered if one day he could build a house and live there on a more permanent basis. Damianus had visited this part of the island on many occasions and had even planted a variety of fruit and fig trees, and even had some water melons growing for when he visited during the warmer months.

Damianus was now planning for his departure along with the fleet moored in port. Once back home, he told Timotheus to quickly pack some clothes for a fishing trip leaving immediately. Minutes later, both Damianus and Timotheus were in their boat ready to leave.

After all the boats carrying slave girls had left port, Damianus and Timotheus made a number of purposefully clumsy attempts to leave. No one seemed to mind, and they left well after the main fleet departed. On the way, they started to row slowly, as the lack of wind prevented them from hoisting a sail. None of the boats ahead took any notice of them lagging well behind. Once the main fleet rounded the north-western tip of Limnos, Damianus was completely out of sight. He stayed hidden until he was certain they were both safe.

When positively convinced of their safety, he and Timotheus headed due east, hugging the coast line while the main fleet made their way north into the open sea. Soon after he turned east, a strong wind picked up and was immediately favourable for the fleet heading to Samothraki. Now, Damianus felt safe. He and Timotheus quietly rowed to the place he knew they could hide. And hide they did. For the next 10 years, these two lived a peaceful existence in a bay surrounded by prime agricultural land and plentiful fishing stocks.

After Damianus and Timotheus had not returned to Myrina with the main fleet, they were thought to have been lost at sea, and that was that!

Three days after leaving for Samothraki, the men returned to Myrina, eager to take their rightful place as the head of each family. Amongst the men, expectations and excitement about the upcoming feast now only one day away were high. It was seen as a sign from the god Dionysus himself that events were unfolding in a way acceptable to all men. For them, it was not a new beginning, but a return to traditional values. Wine, feasting, sex on demand and family!

For the women, they were seeing it totally differently. They believed that Aphrodite was assisting them and therefore they were justified in ridding the island of its curse. They did not see anything wrong in killing all males, as they believed the goddess Aphrodite was in agreeance with them on this matter.

One day to go, men are back home, and preparations for a memorable feast were well underway. Men were seen singing, dancing and laughing. Women were also singing, dancing and laughing. If any outsider sailed into Myrina on the afternoon before the feast, they would probably have thought that these people were the happiest they had ever seen. But looks were deceiving.

Feast arrangements were almost completed. Ambrosia and Suneva mixed the special ingredients in readiness to be added to wine later. Ten rams were led into a pen behind the temple, oblivious to their imminent destiny. Meals were prepared and completed and all fires extinguished before retiring for the night. Men, boys and older men slept soundly, while women slept nervously.

Morning came with the usual cacophony of cocks crowing, birds chirping and sheep bleating. The water surface of the beach seemed like oil, with hardly a breath of wind to cause a ripple. The day's chores started as normal with eggs collected from chickens, water collected from town wells and embers stoked in each home to prepare for cooking and especially for warmth. It was the start of the summer period, but nights were still cool and each day took some time to warm up.

Men went to their farms to collect vegetables and do whatever needed doing at that time of the year. Some pruned trees, some weeded garden beds, some repaired stone fences while some milked their sheep. All in all, it appeared to be quite a normal day. Every conversation in every corner of the village for that day centred around the upcoming nights feast.

Hypsipyle spent the day with her father. Wherever he went, she would follow. They spoke very little, simply appreciating the everyday things in life, like cleaning the palace and preparing for that night's feast. King Thoas had no inkling of the drama about to unfold, and Hypsipyle who was still harbouring many mixed emotions, just wanted to be in his company for as long as possible.

Polyxo quickly performed her normal morning tasks at the palace and then walked the short distance to see Ambrosia and Suneva, who were both at Ambrosia's bar in the port. All variations of the special additives had been mixed the night before, and now each was carefully poured into the purposefully marked

wine amphorae for boys, young men, older men, but most importantly was the untainted wine for themselves. For the rest of the
day, Polyxo, Suneva and Ambrosia made a point of visiting all the
women in Myrina to reinforce the new beginning and to make sure
none were wavering in their resolve. Many of them commented
that although they had not had much sleep, they were prepared
and ready to accept the consequences of their actions.

By early afternoon, Polyxo realised one important part of the
new beginning plan had been overlooked. That was — how do you
dispose of nearly 500 bodies after a mass murder? Originally, she
thought the solution was to carry each body up to the cliff and push
them over the side onto the rocks and water below, hoping the sea
would carry them away. But her knowledge of currents and wind
suggested to her that some bodies may eventually wash up along
the western coast of Limnos for days to come. Any boats coming
into port would no doubt see this and begin to wonder what had
happened. This was potentially going to be a huge problem.

However, the solution to the issue came rather quickly. Last
time the men had a feast at the Temple of Dionysus, she remembered they built a large fire, to cook the sacrificed animals and also
to keep warm in the cool night air.

Polyxo thought that they could quickly construct a larger fire
to cook the sacrificed rams, but built to such a size that could be
used as a funeral pyre. Her excuse if asked by any men was that
it is to be a large fire because everyone from Limnos will be there
and they need a fire of that size to keep warm after the feast.

Pleased with her logical thinking prowess, Polyxo went directly
to Stelios' farm, explained her large fire idea and asked him for
help to build it. Stelios said it was a wonderful idea and asked ten
men from nearby farms to carry firewood to the temple site. Once
others saw what was happening, they too joined in, and before long,
over 30 men were constructing a huge mound of wood and kin-
dling. By late afternoon, just before sunset, the biggest sacrificial

fire anyone had ever seen on Limnos had been built next to the temple.

Problem solved.

At sunset and everyone made their way to the temple site for a special feast. For half the population, it was a feast to recognise a return to the values so long held on the island. For the other half, a feast to close a chapter and start a new beginning.

King Thoas commenced the feast by ritually cutting the neck of the first ram. After him, Stelios took care of the second and then eight other senior men completed the task. Each ram was bled in the correct fashion and at the conclusion of the tenth sacrifice, they were slaughtered and prepared for cooking. Everyone was happy. Each animal was led to its death quietly and within the bounds of normal sacrificial animal rituals.

For the first round of drinks, Ambrosia served wine only, without any additives, apart from water. King Thoas made the first libation and poured a cup of wine on the ground in front of the alter.

The first course of the feast consisted of bread, olive oil, honey, dried figs and cheese. Once the meat was cooked, women took it on themselves to welcome men back to the family by serving all males ahead of any female. The second course was now ready. Men were particularly in a good mood, and helping their sons to enjoy their watered-down wine. Older men joined in by talking about how much they could out-drink each other and were starting to play drinking games.

Ambrosia and Suneva announced they had prepared a special wine for the second course, to accompany the meat. A special amphora was set up on each table, and a new set of drinking vessels were presented to each male, young and old alike. The men were ecstatic. Hypsipyle helped Polyxo, Ambrosia and several other women pour wine for each male into the special new cups.

Hypsipyle, who had hidden a slightly adulterated wine mixture under the table for the King, gave her beloved father his drink. All other males were also given their new cup with the fully tainted wine and asked to wait until Polyxo made a small welcome back speech.

"King Thoas — we women deeply apologise for all the pain we have caused you and to the male population of Limnos by our petty complaints that we were not permitted to spend 10 days in devotion to our goddess Aphrodite. It is clear that we were wrong, selfish and inappropriate in making ourselves smell in order to achieve our goals. We apologise once again, and hope that you enjoy this special wine prepared by Ambrosia for this feast dedicated to the god Dionysus. From tomorrow, there will be a new beginning. Drink this wine in celebration of this new start to life on Limnos."

King Thoas took a small mouthful, poured the remaining drops onto the dry ground and raised his empty cup in the air. His speech was short and to the point. "To a new life".

All the men of Limnos did the same soon after.

The wine clearly tasted good, as most men came back to Ambrosia and her wine helpers for a refill as soon as they could.

Young boys were delighted at being able to join in the celebration, and they also came back for more. Older men continued to play drinking games with each other, still bragging about how much they were going to drink that night.

Polyxo was overjoyed. Her plan was succeeding. Men were drinking, dancing around the big fire and singing songs. Women could not keep up the demand for wine pouring into cups, and Ambrosia thought that she might run out of the special brew.

King Thoas, who had consumed a watered-down special brew was feeling light headed and told Polyxo he had to go back to the palace to lie down. Polyxo did not think anything of it, and asked Hypsipyle to accompany him back to the palace to make sure he arrived. To avert people's eyes away from the King and his daughter leaving, Katerina started to dance around the fire and coaxed the young boys to join them. Young boys did what young boys do. They ran, not danced around the fire. Young girls were staying with their mothers helping serve wine and food.

Once safely inside the Palace, King Thoas was given a concoction to counter the effects of slightly tainted wine. He took it gladly, and said that he now felt much better.

Hypsipyle was standing next to him and asked her father to sit and listen. She had rehearsed this next speech many times, but was still unable to articulate exactly what was on her mind.

She explained what was happening to the men at the feast, why the women were upset, Polyxo's plan, how she and Katerina had hidden a boat, and told him that they would not see each other for a very long time but that he had to leave immediately from a cave on the other side of the village to where the feast was being held.

Thoas was completely stunned, but the effects of the wine followed by the sobering up potion rendered his thoughts a little vague. On one hand he wanted to march directly back to the fire and put a stop to the carnage about to happen, but Hypsipyle said one thing to convince him not to follow that course of action.

"Father, if you are discovered alive, my life will be in mortal danger, and there will be nothing you can do about it."

"You must leave now. Katerina and I have packed some clothes, food and water for your journey. Please go to the cave."

Hypsipyle lovingly embraced her father and with a heavy heart, said to him that she hoped to see him again one day soon. Without any more talking, a teary Thoas turned away from his only daughter and carefully negotiated the path down towards the cave.

Alone in the palace, and before returning to the feast, Hypsipyle took her father's ceremonial sword, smeared it in the blood of a previously killed pig, and sat on the floor next to her fathers' throne. With the thought of having lost her mother as a young child, and now potentially seeing her father for the last time, Hypsipyle burst into tears. Wiping away eyes with a cloth, she lovingly placed the smeared sword down on the floor and joined Katerina at the feast.

Back at the fire, the young boys started to tire noticeably, but were still laughing as they sat on the dry ground. Men also stopped dancing and they too sat down feeling tired, but very happy. Some were laughing as much as the boys. Old man drinking games were slowing down considerably.

At the table where wine was being dispensed, women were looking in amazement at the unfolding events. They could not believe what they were seeing. The fire was burning brightly and all around it, young boys, some men and one or two of the older men were now lying down sleeping. The strange sight was that all of them were smiling.

Stelios was the last male standing, and managed to stagger closer to Ambrosia. He said "I don't know what that wine is, but I doubt I'll ever taste another like it for the rest of my life."

"Thank you, Stelios. I'm glad you like it,", said Ambrosia, at which point he promptly dropped to the ground laughing. He too passed out from the effects of the special brew and with a huge smile.

With all boys and men asleep on the ground, the women rounded up the young girls and quietly ushered them back to their homes to shield them from the sight of what was about to happen next.

Together with the mothers, Hypsipyle and Katerina walked back into the village with the girls and made sure they arrived home safely. Soon after putting their daughters to bed, mothers came back to the temple.

Ambrosia, Suneva and a small group of other women packed up the wine cups which were scattered all around after they had fallen from the hands of sleeping males.

Hypsipyle and Katerina returned to the palace to find the larnax, and carried it to the beach. Inside, they placed a small pig, which had been killed earlier that afternoon by Thoas. Together with the pig, they added in some of Thoas' clothes and trinkets from the palace. Before casting it off into the sea, Hypsipyle took her father's ceremonial sword and smeared it with more pig's blood. She doused the larnax with lamp oil and with the help of Katerina, dragged it into the shallow waters. As if by magic, there was a mild off-shore wind and after the vessel was set alight, it drifted gently off into the deep water and out of sight.

I have never told the harrowing story of what transpired next in detail. Normally, I leave out the particulars of what actually happened, because I do not really know. The events must have been so frightening, many of the women involved simply forgot, or refused to tell anyone later what occurred. Possibly the latter!

Polyxo started the slaughter by finding each of her four sons. Without any hint of regret or fear, she quietly killed each of them with a quick slit across their throats.

Methodically and carefully as if in some form of trance, women took knives used for the purposes of slitting the throats of animals and went to find their male family members. One by one, each woman found who they were looking for, and slit their throats where the bodies lay. I am sure many of the women that night had second thoughts prior to killing their sons, husbands and fathers, but after Polyxo had dispensed of her family first, they put away those thoughts and joined in the slaughter. Still, some must have been reluctant, and I am sure many had tears, but they honestly believed that the gods approved of this drastic action.

No one was talking. The off shore wind started to blow harder. That was the only sound. Once each woman had completed her deeds with a knife, she wiped it clean and passed it to the next woman.

Hypsipyle saw her opportunity and walked slowly up the hill carrying her father's sword, dripping in pig's blood. In her left hand, she was holding the bloodied chiton Thoas wore only a short time before at the feast. Polyxo stopped what she was doing and looked at Hypsipyle in amazement. Without hesitation, Hypsipyle threw the chiton and sword into the fire.

Polyxo asked "Where is the King?"

Turning her head, Hypsipyle looked out to sea where the burning larnax could just be seen, drifting further away, out of sight and perhaps, out of consciousness. When any hesitant woman saw the burning larnax, and believing that young Hypsipyle had murdered her own father, they gained much needed strength.

Polyxo nodded in appreciation. Women who did not have a male family member, helped those who did, carry lifeless bodies to the edge of the fire pit, and heaved them on to the flames and embers below.

To cover the stench of burning flesh, essential oils were also added to the flames. This had the effect of masking the atrocious smell, and acted as an accelerant. Luckily, the wind was kind, blowing the smoke out to sea, in the same direction the fake funeral box of Thoas was moving.

Additional logs of wood were added in order for the fire to burn more deeply. This was no ordinary funeral pyre. This was a mass murder. Unlike an army burning its dead after battle, where the names of deceased soldiers are called out and carried on the wind, there was complete silence from all those present. Apart from the intermittent sound of crackling flames, no words were spoken.

One last piece of Polyxo's plan needed to be done. To help with a story line, all boats moored at the port were set alight, slightly adrift so as not to set fire to the wharf. The purpose of this was twofold. First, in the morning, young girls will wake up and notice no males around, so a story will need to be concocted. The story was told to those who asked that once the men awoke in the early morning, they went to their boats, and sailed for Samothraki. Any remnants of burning boats will be explained by saying the men burned them so they could not be followed. If asked why all males sailed for Samothraki, women will be able to say "We just don't know". Second, burning all the boats meant that any women would not be able to leave Limnos if they so desired.

Hypsipyle could not sleep at all that night once back in the palace. All she could think about was whether her father had made it safely to a better place. The next morning, she went down to the cave to make sure her father had indeed left. When no boat was found, she smiled and silently wished him a safe journey.

Polyxo, Suneva, Ambrosia and several other women remained awake all night feeding the fire with more wood, to make sure there was no evidence of burnt bodies visible in the ashes. Winds had remained favourable all night, blowing any smells and smoke out to sea, but in the morning, all wind had stopped.

At the port, some of the other women too had stayed up most of the night, to make sure no charcoal remains of boats could be seen. Once satisfied that nothing was visible above the water line, they returned to their homes and fell into a deep sleep.

Apart from those who remained at the temple site all through the night, Myrina was strangely silent for most of the morning. Sheep, birds, roosters and donkeys could not be heard. The usual noises of the morning were replaced by sounds of water gently lapping the shore line. Young girls were not woken by the normal morning symphony of animals waking to greet the day and slept longer than usual.

When children finally woke, they went about their everyday business of playing and helping with house chores. Apart from sleeping in, to them it appeared to be a regular start to a day, probably because they had become used to not having males around in the village.

A new beginning had commenced.

CHAPTER 7

The new Queen of Limnos

With the sun reaching its highest point for the day, Hypsipyle cleaned out her father's room and stacked his clothing, footwear and other personal effects in the fireplace. She took an ember from the great fire of the night before to the palace to burn all his belongings, not wanting anything to remain that would remind her of the past. Katerina watched from a distance but did not say anything. Like Hypsipyle, she was still numb with the memory of what had taken place the night before.

On Limnos, it is possible for a storm to be raging in the north of the island, yet not a drop of water will fall in Myrina. On the morning after the murderous feast, young girls were asking where all their brothers and fathers were. They were told the males took all boats on a major fishing trip to the north of the island and potentially all the way to Samothraki. They were also told a large storm could be seen brewing in the north, and perhaps the fishing fleet could be sheltering in a harbour somewhere.

A later addition to the fabricated story at the time was the men had heard of a potential pirate attack on Samothraki, and they may have attempted to see if they could assist in fighting the pirates.

The young girls were happy with these answers, and as there

were no boats in the port, and large dark clouds were visible in the distance. Before too long, they stopped asking when boats would return. They simply got on with being young girls, helping their mothers with daily chores, and playing together. Many mothers were now saying that the storm must have been very bad, and started to explain to their daughters that the men might not be coming home.

It is possible that some mothers, if not most of them, were now attempting to convince themselves of this story, and putting the real reason for the lack of males on the island out of mind, as it was so shocking to contemplate their actions. Their visible grief towards the young girls was probably genuine enough, but the truth was now well and truly beginning to be buried in a myth. A myth that was to remain for many years.

Two days after the deed, Polyxo asked all women to meet at the palace. She told them of important matters that required immediate attention. Sunset was the appointed time of the meeting, and the palace was full. Polyxo did not seek Hypsipyle's permission to use the palace. Once most of the women were seated, Polyxo rose to speak.

"What is done, is done. We cannot go back. We cannot change the past, only influence the future. Our daughters seem to have settled into a routine now, but there is one important thing we need to do."

"You saw Hypsipyle carry King Thoas' bloodied sword and chiton to the temple, and throw them into the fire. The King is dead! We have no King, nor any need for a King, but tradition dictates that we do need a monarch."

There were muffled cheers, but they were somewhat subdued and low key. Polyxo continued.

"We need a new leader. Hypsipyle has shown by her actions that she is worthy of this role."

"Hypsipyle, will you be our Queen?"

Hypsipyle had an inkling that she would be called to be the new Queen. Katerina had whispered something to her earlier in the day, so Hypsipyle was ready and prepared, although she secretly hoped the true King could still be alive.

"I accept, and will try to be fair and honest like my mother and father before me."

Women rejoiced and assured each other of good times ahead, and promised a new beginning with the island's new Queen.

With that brief ceremony out of the way, women returned to their homes and to their new lives. They began to share time equally between the family farm and the village residence. Together with their daughters, women had to learn the intricacies of farming. It was a challenge no women shirked. They took to farm work with as much vigour as those who previously learned about loading and unloading boats in the port.

So, just like that, all males of Limnos had been murdered, a story about a big storm and a possible pirate attack concocted to explain their disappearance, and now plans were underway to move on as if nothing of any consequence had ever happened. What Polyxo did not know, was that not all Limnian males had died.

For the next year, life on Limnos did move on. Boats came into port every week, questions were asked as to the whereabouts of any men or boys, and the answers varied, depending on who asked. If they were captains who had visited before, they did not ask, assuming men were out working on their farms. For new captains and inquisitive crew, answers ranged from 'they are on the farms', 'they have gone fishing at the top of the island', or even 'they must have gone to Samothraki to help fight off pirates. Obviously, portside workers had to know not to give that response to any boats from Samothraki.

Captains of visiting boats accepted the answers given, and never challenged Ambrosia or the new Queen. All they wanted was a good cup of wine and a visit to the fine Limnian brothels.

The new Queen relished her role as monarch. But in the back of her mind, she never stopped thinking about what may have happened to her father.

CHAPTER 8

Thomas and Sikinos

Whatever became of King Thoas? While most ordinary people at this time would have been terrified on their own in a small boat, this was not the case for Thoas. He was no ordinary man.

When Thoas was a young boy in Crete, he was fascinated with sailing, fishing and anything to do with water. His mother Ariadne taught Thoas and his brothers to swim at a young age, and was often seen either on the beach, at the port, or in the water.

As Thoas grew older, he developed excellent navigational skills, and his grandfather, King Minos encouraged him to explore the large island in his boat. Sometimes travelling with one or two of his brothers, Thoas would often stay away from home for days at a time, venturing not far offshore at first, but as his experience grew, further out to sea. His brothers did not share the same passion or skill necessary to sail boats away from Crete, so Thoas would go alone, which he preferred. He loved to visit islands immediately north of Crete, and sometimes as far north as Thera.

This navigational skill proved helpful in Thoas' life shortly before being sent to Limnos. He had sailed many boats to all the islands north of Crete as far as Skiros, and although never having been to Limnos, he certainly knew where it was.

To be placed alone in a small boat at night by Hypsipyle was not frightening to Thoas. He knew what he needed to do, and after he was sure that the boat was far enough away from Limnos, he set sail south for Skiros and landed his boat on the northern tip of the island, spending a few days resting out of sight of any people. Once he had replenished his water supply and picked any fruit he could find, the next leg of his journey took him to Andros island. Travelling at night, navigating by stars was his preferred time, and it was not too long before he landed again in a place he had been to many years before.

Following a similar pattern of keeping out of sight and away from people, Thoas managed to find some slightly out of season figs and other food growing in an orchard. He rested for two days and set off again. Not originally having a plan of where to finish, Thoas remembered an island not far from Thera, that he believed was relatively uninhabited, and had a natural water supply. The island was Oinoe, and he thought that he could stay there for long enough until deciding where to live on a more permanent basis.

Thoas grounded his boat in shallow water inside a safe but small bay on the island of Oinoe, rolled out exhausted into the water and crawled up to dry land. Thoas fell asleep immediately on the sand.

Not far away from where he beached the boat, fishermen had witnessed Thoas come ashore, and collapse on the beach. They went to his aid and helped him drink some water, before Thoas fell back into a deep sleep once again.

They nursed him until he could stand and walk around unaided by others. Curious to know something about this lone sailor, Thoas told them he was a grape grower from the village of Mythimna, Lesvos, and had to escape with his life after pirates came to raid his village. Stories like this were common throughout the Aegean, and the fishermen had no reason to doubt Thoas' claims. For a start, they had never heard of Lesvos, but then again, they had not heard of many islands. Fishermen from this island rarely travelled far from their home, only sporadically venturing to islands close by. Thoas told his new friends that he was married once, but his wife and daughter had been murdered. They accepted Thoas, who by this stage had told them his name was Thomas. Also, luckily for him, none of the fishermen had ever visited Crete, but they knew it existed.

Even though Crete was relatively close geographically, it was not uncommon for people on the islands around Oinoe to never visit their much larger neighbour. Unless a fisherman was a skilful sailor, he would have no reason to travel to Crete, so Thoas thought his true identity was safe for the time being amongst these people. From now on, he would become Thomas and assume a new identity.

Thomas regained his strength with the fishermen's help, and started to explore the island. It had been many years since he had visited Oinoe, but in those days, his knowledge was limited to the coastline, never really exploring inland. He was instantly struck by the bountiful water supply and soil quality. It appeared to him to be far more fertile than Limnos. He thought the rich soil would be ideal to grape growing, and asked the fishermen if anyone had thought of growing and making wine. They said that none had ever really contemplated that, and that all their wine was imported from other islands.

Thomas had seen enough on Oinoe to believe he had some sort of a future there, and made the decision to stay. He envisaged the grape growing potential this small island had and immediately began a search for a place to once again, lay down his roots.

Oinoe had one village, much like Limnos, but Oinoe was a much smaller island. He quickly became known in the village, and it was not long before he had built a temporary house and taken a parcel of land to plant grapevines. His new fishermen friends agreed to bring him some small vines from islands they visited. Thomas planted all these vines on his land and they began to grow almost immediately.

Thomas met Daphne, a much younger woman from the village, possibly 20 years younger, and soon fell in love. Together, they built a simple solid stone house and cleared land around the property for planting and growing food. They were married and Daphne with her new husband soon announced that she was pregnant. For the next eight months, Thomas and Daphne were blissfully happy planting vegetables and fruit trees and cultivating grapevines. Although he wanted to be truthful with his new wife, Thomas could not tell Daphne he was really a King from Limnos, and a grandson of King Minos of Crete. It was difficult keeping this secret but he knew that if he told her, there was a chance his daughter's life could be in danger. For now, he had a new life, a new wife, and they were expecting a child.

At that time, the population of Oinoe numbered approximately 300 people, and until Thomas came along, fishing and limited farming were the principal source of income and sustenance for the islanders. After Thomas arrived and started clearing land for grapevines, a small group of neighbours started to do the same.

Thomas wept tears of joy the day Daphne gave birth to a son, who they named Sikinos. Sadly, Daphne died soon after the birth due to complications during delivery. Convinced that his existence was somehow cursed, Thomas buried his wife and commenced life as a sole parent yet again. To take his mind off his problems, Thomas totally devoted his life to Sikinos, and could be seen taking him everywhere on the island. Having a son was something he always wanted, but he never forgot about Hypsipyle, and often wondered how her life was turning out. From time to time, Thomas remembered Myrina and Hypsipyle, and life on Limnos, but reality had a way of reminding him that there was another human totally dependent on its father.

For the next few years, the wine made from Thomas and Daphne's vineyard became better with each passing season. Sikinos loved working with his father in the grapevine orchard more than with vegetables or fruit trees. By the time Sikinos was ten years old, he knew as much about grape growing and wine making as anyone on the island.

In fact, for those ten years, Thomas had all but forgotten his past life on Crete and Limnos, his two wives, and his only daughter. Sikinos was such a joy to him, the two became inseparable.

Young Sikinos also had started convincing more people from Oinoe to think about growing vines of all varieties and tastes. With such enthusiasm for his work, Sikinos spent as much time helping others in their vineyards as he did with his own father. Thomas did not mind at all. In the short space of ten years, Oinoe was becoming known for the quality of wine produced, not necessarily for its volume. The island was too small to produce quantity, but the quality of wine due to its climate, water and soil content soon became known throughout the Cyclades.

Thomas and Sikinos began experimenting, taking existing vines and grafting them with others. Sikinos was learning this technique from visits to other islands with his father, and listening to people who have tried, failed and tried again. After every trip away from the island he was eager to get home to try something new. Oftentimes, the trial planting would fail, but from time to time, new plants would grow, and new varieties of grape emerged.

Sikinos' experimenting helped him and his father achieve greater yields, not only for themselves, but for all other wine makers on Oinoe. Thomas' first island friends, the fishermen, became part time wine exporters, in addition to their fishing trips to other islands. Instead of importing wine, Oinoe was now exporting far more than it consumed locally. These fishermen were forever grateful to Thomas for introducing them to an alternative way of life and existence, and income. It seemed to encourage them to want to stay on the island and grow larger families.

News quickly reached Athenian wine merchants about new wine varieties from Oinoe, and some of them visited the island soon after to see what all the fuss was about. They were impressed with the quality of wine, and convinced Thomas and Sikinos to sell some of their produce to them so they could see if anyone in Athens liked it. With the permission and blessing of Thomas, one of the wine merchants encouraged young Sikinos to visit Athens to learn more about growing, grafting and wine making. By this stage, he was only 16, but his knowledge and level of maturity was that of someone much older. He was also growing into a man. Thomas was proud of his son, and encouraged him to visit Athens to learn as much as he could.

At that time, Athens was not the bustling metropolis that we know it to be now, but an ever-expanding village owing to its proximity to the recently constructed port of Piraeus. This port helped the village develop quickly, and soon Athens became a vital commercial and trading centre.

On the next visit from the Athenian wine merchants to buy wine from Oinoe, Sikinos booked a trip back with them. He was so happy. He was off to the largest wine festival in all of Greece, and he was going to be learning from the best. His father Thomas could not have been prouder of his son.

CHAPTER 9

A boat is coming

One particularly uneventful day started out as any other, with Katerina walking along the beach to the hill overlooking the port and climbing to her favourite vantage point to sit, stare blankly at the water and contemplate life. She was still deeply troubled by the shocking events of a year ago.

After sitting for most of the morning, she thought she could see a strange looking dot on the horizon, due west of Limnos. The only thing visible in that direction on any given day was Mt Athos, but this was slightly to the south. The dot appeared to grow in size, and it was rising and falling with the water. Could it be a boat?

This boat was different. Not the usual transport boat brimming with supplies, but a magnificent vessel with what appeared to be dozens of oars on each side. It was by far, the strangest looking boat she had ever seen. Katerina came running down, careful not to fall on the treacherous rocks and meandering goat tracks. She went directly to the palace to call for her mother.

"There is a boat coming, there is a boat coming", she yelled.

"Boats come and go all the time. What is the problem?"

"Mother, this does not look like a trading boat. It is much slimmer, and appears to have dozens of oars on each side. I think I can hear a drum too."

Polyxo immediately suspected pirates, so she hastily arranged for women to put on their armour and for archers to take up position on the hills either side of the beach where the boat was likely to land.

In the past year, Polyxo and Hypsipyle had taken it upon themselves to learn how to use bows and arrows. They feared they would eventually have to defend their island — so they prepared an army of women warriors.

Myrina could only be defended on the port and beach side, but not on the land side. If any pirates did ever come to the village, they would have been stupid to arrive via the port. Pirates could at any stage in the past year, if they knew the land around Myrina, easily have landed anywhere else on the island and simply walked into Myrina through the back door!

The boat was getting closer, and most women were standing along the beach, or strategically positioned in various locations on the southern end of the port, on castle hill. These turned out to be a completely useless positions, as the boat veered left and headed for the smaller hill north of the port. When they saw the boat change direction, the archers ran down from the castle, along the beach and onto the smaller hill. In that time, those on the approaching boat could see clearly the reception they were about to receive, so they remained stationary off shore, strategically out of arrow range.

Wearing armour and surrounded by at least 60 women with bows and arrows, Hypsipyle and Katerina stood together in the shallow water, intrigued by the now motionless boat.

From the boat, one person dived into the water and cautiously swam towards shore. Hypsipyle did not know if it was a male or female, but she stood still and waited.

It was a man. Hypsipyle took two steps forward, raised her right hand with her palm facing him and spoke.

"Stop right there. Who are you and what do you want?"

Before the man could walk up onto the beach, he stopped in

waist deep water and replied "I am Orpheus and we wish you no harm. Please take me to your King."

"What are you selling? Your boat does not look like it has anything we need."

Orpheus tried to take a step, and the archers either side of Hypsipyle raised their bows and aimed directly at him.

"That is rather difficult to explain."

Being a musician and not a warrior, Orpheus had not noticed the archers and bystanders on the beach were all women. His eyes were directly locked on Hypsipyle's, as his feet sank slowly into the wet sand.

Shifting his stance ever so cautiously, Orpheus spoke again. "If you take me to your King, I can explain. My friends in the boat will remain there until I return."

"Come, but I warn you. My archers are a little out of practice, and nothing would give them greater pleasure than to shoot some arrows at your friends if they move any further forward."

After leaving the soft wet sand, Orpheus looked around and was amazed to see only women. He thought it may have been a trick, wary of men suddenly appearing out from behind trees and buildings if he showed any signs of evil intent.

Turning around to the boat, Orpheus gave a wave indicating they should wait for further communication. Excited mutterings could be heard amongst the bystanders. Even though they had seen men in the last year, unloading and loading boats, they had never seen one walk up out of the water, and not such a good looking one as Orpheus.

Orpheus was 21 years old, and the most attractive man anyone had seen for a long time. He was deeply tanned with toned muscles, piercing blue eyes, soft hands and long blonde hair tied back in the nape of his neck. He looked like a god emerging from the water!

Hypsipyle, Katerina and Polyxo lead Orpheus towards the palace, entered the main gate, walked through the courtyard and into the throne room. Orpheus looked around to see where the

King was, and was surprised when Hypsipyle sat on the ornate wooden chair.

"We have no King. My name is Queen Hypsipyle, and this is Katerina and Polyxo, my senior advisers."

"As I said, I am Orpheus, and I speak on behalf of Jason, our leader. We are 49 men and one woman, and we are on a journey of discovery to find a special woollen fleece from a ram that we are led to believe is in Colchis."

"What is so special about the fleece of a ram that is only found in Colchis? We have plenty of rams here. Take one, and go home. Consider it our gift."

Just then Hypsipyle remembered that he said 49 men and 1 woman.

"Just go back one step Orpheus. Why do you have 49 men and one woman? That makes no sense to me. Why one woman?"

"Her name is Atalanta, and is the best archer in the whole of Greece. She is better than any of the men on our boat at what she does and we may require her particular set of skills on our journey."

"An archer you say?"

"No. Only joking. She is our cook. But we will still require her skills if we are to survive."

"Why 49 men then? What skills do they possess?"

"Where do I start? Jason is our leader and patron of the expedition. When we return successful, he will be the King of Iolchus. Some are excellent fighters, some mighty warriors, some are athletes, farmers, one is a boat builder, one is the strongest man in the world, one can navigate by the stars, some are cooks, some are the sons of Kings from all over Greece, one is a physician and one is the best musician in the whole world."

"We mean you no harm, Queen Hypsipyle. But may I ask you a question?"

Hypsipyle looked at Katerina and Polyxo. They both nodded in agreement.

"Just one? What is it?"

"I don't see any men. Where are they?"

"Our men, my father the King included, left us some time ago to fight pirates in Samothraki."

"When are they coming back?"

"You only asked for one question. That was it", said Katerina, thinking she had won a small battle.

"You are right. May I ask some more questions?"

"We have been rowing for two days now, and we are tired, hungry and thirsty. May we rest here for a day or two and then we'll be on our way?"

While this conversation was taking place, several women arrived at the palace and stood quietly at the back of the throne room to listen to what was being said.

One of these women, Komi requested and was given permission from Queen Hypsipyle to speak.

"I need some work done at my house, and it seems like this boat has plenty of men who could help me. Some of us wouldn't mind if these men could help us before they leave."

"Let me go and ask the rest of the women."

Hypsipyle asked Orpheus to return with her to the beach. Following behind them were Katerina smiling, Polyxo scowling, and Komi smiling.

Hypsipyle looked at the women standing on the beach, and noticed something interesting. They were not scowling like Polyxo, but smiling like Komi and Katerina.

It was at this point Queen Hypsipyle made a decision without consulting Polyxo, who clearly would have disagreed.

"Swim back to your boat and let them all know that they are permitted to come ashore, but to leave any weapons on the sand here. If any do not, my archers will start practicing on live targets. Is that clear?"

"Yes, that is perfectly clear. We mean you no harm."

73

Orpheus swam back to the boat and spoke to Jason, who by this stage was beginning to worry they might not be able to rest. He told Jason that they could all come ashore, but to leave all weapons on the beach. He also told the crew that there were no males on the island. All on board were very sexually aroused at this news, all except Hercules and Atalanta.

Slowly, the boat made its way as far as it could before running aground on sand. Thirty of the front rowers jumped out into the shallow water to heave the boat onto the beach while the back rowers pulled on each oar. Once all rowers were on dry land, their weapons were placed in a neat pile a short distance above the water line

I am going to stop right here, because I want you to try to imagine the scene. There were hundreds of women on the beach staring at this boat. On the boat were 49 young, fit, healthy looking men wearing very little, muscles bulging after rowing for two days, jumping into the water, soaking wet, and walking in slow motion through thick, wet sand. Can you picture that scene?

Ok, back to the story.

The Argo was hauled up onto the beach, so that it would not float away. All the exhausted rowers sat on dry land for the first time in two days. Orpheus spoke to one of the men, who did not sit with the others. Instead he walked up to Queen Hypsipyle and knelt down on one knee, hands out in front of him, carrying a red coat with purple trimmings and what looked like different action scenes woven into the fabric. Hypsipyle thought this must be the captain, or leader, or someone very important as this garment was simply the most outstanding coat she had ever seen, better than anything her father wore.

"Queen Hypsipyle. My name is Jason, and I am the leader of this group which consists of the finest, athletic and talented people in the whole of Greece. Please accept this garment as a token of our appreciation. My crew and I wish you no harm. We come in friendship. All we ask of you is that you let us stay for some time to allow us to quench our thirst, fill our stomachs, and rest so that we may continue our journey to Colchis."

"Stay as long as you deem necessary Jason. Rest now, and tell your friends that you are all welcome to join us in a special feast tonight at the palace."

"Thank you, kind and gracious Queen. We accept your invitation and will be pleased to join with you in celebration of our welcome and for our future travels."

It had been over a year since these Limnian women had laid eyes on so many men at the one time. Not all of them worked in Myrina, so they would not have seen any men on boats visiting the port with cargo to sell and to take away. Already they were silently looking at these rowers and thinking what work they could get them to do back on their farms, in their houses, in their beds or anywhere they wanted.

Quite a few of the women rushed towards the new arrivals and offered water, bread, olives, figs and to wash their clothes. Some men disrobed immediately and thanked the women for their generosity and kindness.

You should have seen where the women's eyes were looking! It had been nearly two years since their husbands were murdered, but regardless of the past set of tragic circumstances, these women still missed male company.

Tired and exhausted, the crew of the mighty Argo sat on the beach and rested. Some fell asleep immediately.

Jason and Hypsipyle walked up to the palace to continue their discussions.

"Tell me about the rams' fleece. Why is it so special and why does it take all of you to find it? Are you expecting trouble?"

"The main purpose of our journey is to find this particular fleece. We have heard stories of a special breed of sheep in Colchis whereby the fleece attracts flecks of gold when laid down on the bottom of running streams. If there is any gold in a stream, and the fleece is stretched out on the bottom, flecks of gold will attach themselves to the fleece as the water gently passes over it. If this is true, it means we can mine the precious metal without too much work on our part. The time and effort saved would be a major benefit to us. That is, if this rumour is true."

Jason was not concerned he was sharing any confidential information, as he knew these women would not be competition and try to beat him in finding the fleece. He had the best crew and best boat for the journey.

"There is also another reason for our journey, and it is equally important. This boat is the first of its kind, purposefully built for such a voyage. It has been designed for many circumstances, and this trip will hopefully allow us to improve our boat building skills to allow these kinds of vessels to go anywhere, in any condition."

"The reason we are taking so many with us is that we do not know what trouble lies ahead, and we need to be prepared for anything."

Hypsipyle could see some sense in that.

"How long will you spend on this quest for a golden fleece Jason?"

"As long as it takes. We need to prove once and for all if such a fleece exists. If it does, we will buy it, or take it, whichever happens, but we will be prepared for it."

"Queen Hypsipyle. May I ask you some questions."

"Of course."

"Where are your men? Are there any men here on your island?"

"One year ago, our men and young boys left for a fishing trip to the northern coast of the island and were headed for Samothraki, taking all our boats. The next morning, a terrible storm appeared, and we believe that all males perished. We do not know if this is exactly what happened, but none of them, young boys and old men included, have ever returned to explain what took place. No bodies were ever found. We still live in the faint hope that one day they will return, but as it has been well over a year now, and that hope has all but evaporated."

"Why did all the males leave? Surely some would have remained to protect you?"

Hypsipyle was always prepared with an answer for this question, as it had been asked by many before Jason.

"You can see by our reception today Jason, we are not incapable of looking after ourselves. Why all the males left together is still an intriguing question that I am afraid we may never find out, but the fact remains that they did and we are still here."

"Was there ever a King?"

"My father, Thoas. He led the fleet, which is why I think something happened to them. He would not leave his people voluntarily."

Hypsipyle was partially truthful. The men did go to Samothraki for fishing, and it is an island to the north of Limnos! She was not about to tell Jason that all males were killed and her father may be alive somewhere. She certainly was not about to tell him the truth.

Before he returned to the crew, Hypsipyle gave Jason some water, bread and cheese. He thanked her, and said he needed to have a rest, and was looking forward to the evening where he and the Argonauts would be formally welcomed.

Jason walked out of the palace and took the road back down to the beach to eat the food provided by Hypsipyle, drink and fall asleep on the sand. Many of his men were sleeping, and glad to be on dry ground.

All afternoon, women were making excuses to wander down to the beach. There were dozens of partially naked men asleep on the sand. Some were completely undressed, waiting for their clothes to be washed and dried. All over Myrina, women were making excuses to visit the new arrivals, to see if they needed anything extra.

"I'm just going to see if they need some figs."

"I want to let them know that their clothes are nearly dry. I'll just go down there now and tell them."

"I have to take some extra kraters of water. Would anyone like to help me?"

"I'll come with you."

Hercules was keeping a watchful eye on the men to see that no harm came to them, and was also keeping an eye on the boat, to see that no harm came to it. But specifically, he was carefully guarding the stockpile of weapons to see that none of them were taken away. Their journey had only just begun, and he did not want it to end after their first stop.

In the meantime, amidst all the comings and goings of Limnian women to the beach, an exhausted Jason lay down on the sand and drifted off into a restful and much needed sleep.

One of the crew members however did not sleep. Atalanta wanted to talk to the women that had been pointing their arrows at her since they first beached the Argo.

The archers were still keeping an eye on the sleeping men while Atalanta approached.

"Do you mind if I talk to you? I am not in need of any sleep at the moment, and I would like to see your weapons."

"You can talk to us", said one of the Limnian archers, "but you cannot touch our weapons."

Noticing the way they held their bows, Atalanta could see immediately that the archers were quite inexperienced. She assumed, and rightly so, that none of them had ever fired an arrow in anger at a person, or even an animal for hunting. She wanted to gain their favour, and thought of an idea without revealing her true identity and more importantly, her ability and expertise with weapons.

She approached the woman who acted like the leader of the group and started a polite conversation.

"I have an idea," said Atalanta. "See that tree down at the end of the beach. See the knot in the branch about half way up the tree, on the right-hand side. It is about the size of a lemon. Would you agree?"

"Yes, we can see it. So what?"

"I doubt if your best archer could fire an arrow and hit that knot in the tree from here."

"No one could hit a target like that from here. It's impossible."

"Are you sure? It's not that far. I think I could hit it easily."

Atalanta did not let on to these women what her specific skill was, and why she was a member of Jason's crew.

The best archer walked over to Atalanta. "My name is Aspasia, and I am the best archer here, and that target is too small, and too far away. I might be able to hit it once in every 5 shots, but it is very difficult."

"How about you fire 10 arrows at the target. I predict you will miss with all of them. Then, give me one shot, and I promise you I won't miss."

All the archers laughed the kind of laugh when someone else stubs their big toe on a rock, but Atalanta and Aspasia were not laughing.

"Ten arrows you say," quizzed Aspasia.

"Yes, ten. Start whenever you want."

Aspasia took her bow and fired the first shot. It missed. Not even close. She fired another eight and they all missed, but she was getting closer. At least some of the shots struck the tree. Her hands were trembling. She was the best archer on Limnos and she had just missed nine shots. One to go. She waited for her hands to settle, wiped her brow free of stinging sweat somehow finding a way into her right eye, raised the bow, loaded the arrow, aimed, released and missed everything yet again.

A collective groan went around the group of eager onlookers.

"Are you happy? I am the best here and I missed all 10 shots. The target is too difficult to hit from this spot. No women or man could strike it. It's impossible."

Aspasia sulked her way back to the rest of the group, gently placed her bow on the sand, folded her arms defiantly and stood staring at Atalanta.

Seeking reassurance from the rest of the group, and speaking to no one in particular, Aspasia said "no one can hit that target — right?"

"Now that I think of it, it is a long way from here. You may be right. It might be impossible, but may I now take one shot at it anyway?"

Aspasia, feeling quite proud of herself for getting close to this impossible target, was convinced that this woman from the Argo would have no chance.

"Go ahead. One shot."

"Before I take my one shot, may I please use my own bow that was taken from our boat? It is in the pile of weapons over there."

Not for one moment thinking that any bow belonged to Atalanta, Aspasia said "Sure, but I'll get it. Wait here."

Atalanta described the bow to Aspasia, who then strode to the weapons, found the bow, and brought it back, admiring its characteristics and feel. It felt strong. Now she was completely convinced that it must belong to one of the men aboard.

"Here it is. You have one shot", she said as the weapon was handed to Atalanta. "Here is one arrow."

Atalanta gently held the arrow, found its centre of balance and liked its feel and craftmanship.

Watching from the beach amongst the sleeping crew was Philoktetes. He knew Atalanta's ability, and apart from himself and Hercules, she was the next best archer on the Argo. He knew she could hit this target 10 times out of 10, but he was not about to spoil her demonstration.

Aspasia and the other archers were chuckling.

"No one can hit that."

"Impossible."

"Not even a man could strike that target."

Imagining what was about to transpire, Philoktetes casually strolled over to the archers and joined in the chuckling.

"Forgive me for this interruption, but you are right. No one could strike that target. I might be able to get close in 10 arrows, but Atalanta is our cook. She does not know the first thing about archery. There is no chance that she will come close to that target."

Philoktetes was rather pleased with his story about Atalanta being the cook, as she hated cooking. Atalanta joined in the ruse by saying that she was a cook, but also loved a challenge. She knew what Philoktetes was doing and added to the charade.

"Let me introduce to you, the best archer in all of Greece, Philoktetes. If he says he would have trouble making this target, maybe you should listen to him. But I still think I can do it with but one of your arrows."

"Go ahead Atalanta. There is no way you can strike that target from here. Not even if you were 20 paces closer. Not even if you were 10 paces from the target" said Philoktetes.

Feeling superior, Aspasia said "yes, go ahead. One arrow. Impossible."

Before Atalanta could even pick up her weapon, Philoktetes snatched her bow, selected an arrow, and asked "May I go first?"

"Why not? If you are who she says you are, maybe you could get close to it? But I still think it is impossible."

Philoktetes nodded, and then carefully studied the target. He looked around to gauge the wind direction and strength and esti-mated the distance to the tree. Placing the arrow in its correct position, he took stance, aimed and released.

The bowstring fizzed and the arrow flew in a graceful arc towards the target, missing the knot just to the left by the width of a little finger.

"That was close" said Aspasia, who had never seen such a dis-play of archery before. Not even her late husband, who had been Limnos' best archer, could have got so close.

Philoktetes had intentionally aimed at this very spot but did not dare admit it to the admiring band of part-time archers. Atalanta silently chuckled, as she knew Philoktetes had aimed to miss. She was quietly impressed with how close he could actually be without striking the intended target.

Disappointed with his shot, Philoktetes walked back a few steps and gave the bow to Atalanta.

While this was taking place, Aspasia said under her breath to the other women that she had never seen such accuracy. They all nodded. None of them had ever seen it either.

Now it was Atalanta's turn to display her skills. In one fluid motion, she took the arrow, placed it in its correct position, gently pulled back the bow string, and released.

Bullseye!

All eyes were on the target. Atalanta was suppressing a smile. She said "That must have been a lucky shot. May I have one more to show you that it was pure luck?"

Without taking her eyes from the arrow quivering in the knot of the tree, Aspasia handed over another arrow.

Same result. Bullseye.

"All right. How about I go further away, say 20 paces."

Aspasia handed over another arrow, reluctantly. By this time, she was rubbing her eyes in amazement. Collectively, all the archers were standing with mouths wide open and eyes even wider.

Same result, now the target had three arrows firmly wedged together.

Philoktetes could see the Limnian archers were now completely confused. He asked if he could go back 30 paces more and have another shot.

Atalanta handed him the bow, and Aspasia gave him an arrow.

Bullseye! Now there was no room on the target for any more arrows, but not to be outdone, Atalanta asked for one final shot. She retreated further along the beach to double the original distance.

Everyone was shaking their heads. Not Atalanta.

"Let me try one final time."

At twice the distance from when they commenced, Atalanta fired her last shot, splitting the arrow Philoktetes just fired, and striking the target.

Aspasia asked "Who are you?"

Philoktetes stepped in to respond. "We are very sorry to have deceived you. We mean no harm. Atalanta is not our cook. She and I are the best archers in the whole of Greece. That is why we are on this voyage with Jason. If you like, we are his personal bodyguards."

Aspasia knew that she and the other women were in the presence of archery royalty. She was not upset or annoyed at being deceived but thrilled at the possibilities of what could be learned from these two experts. Without asking the other women, she spoke quickly.

"While you are here, can you please help us? As you can see, we need help. Just a few lessons. Please."

"I am sure we can do that tomorrow at first light", said Atalanta. "But first, I believe a feast is in order."

Aspasia and the other archers had never imagined there could be such accuracy over such a long distance. When Philoktetes and Atalanta finally returned to their crew, Aspasia and the archers could not believe their luck. They were about to learn from the best. In a high level of nervous excitement and anticipation, they could not wait until the morning.

Some of the Argonauts were waking up after a brief rest and were sitting on the beach talking to each other. Orpheus climbed onto the Argo to retrieve one of his kithara's. On the voyage from Iolchus, he did not row, causing many of the others to wonder why he was on the voyage at all. Jason responded by saying each of the crew members had been chosen for their specific and different skills. Orpheus was a musician, which elicited great consternation amongst the rowers, straining with their muscles on the oars.

Typhys the helmsman was most annoyed at first, because

Orpheus sat directly beneath him, and he thought that having a musician at his feet was not conducive to a well-run ship. He was heard to ask early on in their voyage "Why do we need a musician?"

About half way between Iolchus and Limnos, Orpheus picked up his kithara and started strumming, making up songs as he went along. Playing in rhythm with the rowing, each rower began to forget the pain in their arms and backs, and became mesmerised by his music. It seemed to act as a soothing balm for aching muscles.

Jason was also heard to have said rather abruptly to Typhys "Now you know why he is here."

Sitting on the beach at Myrina, Orpheus again picked up the kithara and played once more, creating yet more new songs as he went. This time, it wasn't the Argonauts who were listening, but Limnian women and children coming to the beach to offer succour.

I am not going to try to sing any of his songs because they were improvised at the time, and quickly forgotten, but in doing so, Orpheus established his credentials as a talented musician, capable of taking everyday events, people and situations, and turning them into lyrical poetry with music.

In his repertoire, Orpheus sang on his own, encouraged his audience to join in, sang sad, happy and romantic songs, but most of all, accurately reflected the mood of the occasion as he deemed necessary with his music.

Hypsipyle heard the music on the beach from the palace, and quickly came to hear its source. She too was enthralled at how someone could simply make music so effortlessly, as if it had been sung hundreds of times before.

"Orpheus, please bring your instruments tonight to the feast. That was beautiful. We have never heard such melodic and interesting music before."

"It would be an honour Queen Hypsipyle. I look forward to it."

"As do all of us."

Watching from the bow of the Argo was Hercules. Keeping a close eye on the weapons, and making sure the boat did not drift back into the sea, he sensed that his fellow crew were not in any danger, and finally allowed himself a short rest. Like the other Argonauts, it was the first real respite he had had since leaving Iolchus.

Constantly trying to live up to his image as a strong man all the time must have been tiring in itself, and Hercules soon fell into a deep sleep. His pulsating rhythmic snoring could be heard all over the beach, and it wasn't long before Orpheus picked up on it and started to sing songs about the noise emanating from Hercules' throat. For a gifted and talented musician like Orpheus, he had no trouble using the rhythm of Hercules' snoring to make an instant tune. His method of song writing was to first hear a rhythm, then hum and strum the kithara. When he was satisfied with the sound and melody, he experimented with key words and phrases. To the untrained ear, it seemed like he was a musical genius, but to Orpheus, it was little more than a well-rehearsed method of song writing and performance.

Enough of how to write songs. Bring me another wine.
Myrina was buzzing with activity in preparation for the welcome feast. Ambrosia had to draw on additional supplies of wine from her vineyard, but this time, there were no special additives. Women were busily preparing food all afternoon. Each and every farm had something to offer, and a number of sheep had already been slaughtered and prepared as soon as the feast was announced.

Polyxo sat alone outside the palace on a marble step, scrutinising and carefully observing the activities unfold before her. During the day, many women went to her and not Hypsipyle to seek her permission if one or more of the men could help with some work on their farms. Aspasia and the archers asked Polyxo for her blessing so that Atalanta and Philoktetes could train, or at least, give some guidance in the finer points of archery. Polyxo agreed with these requests, and sensed that her idea of a new beginning had already started.

Not knowing how long these men would stay, Polyxo told Hypsipyle that this was the kind of new beginning that she had envisaged. Hypsipyle was happy, and began to prepare for the feast.

"Hypsipyle, may I speak with you?"

"Of course, Polyxo."

"My Queen. I have been thinking a lot since the arrival of these strangers. I agree with you that we should be offering gifts such as this feast tonight, instead of being robbed by them at a later time. But this alone will not ensure our survival into the future. We could be attacked by pirates at any time, and it is only through good fortune that this has not occurred. But what if we had been? How easy was it that this boat came to our shores today? These men appear to be friendly, but the next visit might not be."

"Many of us are getting old, and won't be alive for much longer. Time will eventually catch up with us. But we face a greater problem. If we do not produce sons, who will lead us into the future, who will yoke our oxen and look after our farms when there is no one here save for a few old women? This visit by these strangers is our new beginning. The solution is right at our feet. Offer these strangers our homes, our animals and our marvellous city. Spread the word to all women here in Myrina."

Hypsipyle thanked Polyxo for being so forthright.

"Polyxo, I agree with everything you have said. This is our chance to be re-born. I will spread the news to each woman here. I am certain our very survival will be guaranteed. I don't think we have anything to be concerned about with these strangers. I have a good feeling about it all."

Hypsipyle, Katerina and the young girls of Myrina began decorating the palace in preparation for the feast. Seats were adorned with colourful cushions, flowers arranged in vases, pottery strategically placed where it could be seen and garlands of olive and oregano hung from any vantage point available. It was not well thought out, but Hypsipyle was happy with the outcome given such short notice. After the palace decorations were completed, the girls seamlessly moved on to running deliveries between their laundering mothers and the naked Argonauts.

Dressed in freshly laundered clothing, the Argonauts wandered away from the beach to explore the surrounding environment such as the port area and castle hill situated within walking distance from the palace. Some could be seen strolling through farm land and talking to the women working on the land.

Sunset came, and all roads led to the palace. Women from their farms, women from village homes, Argonauts from their meanderings and young girls, well, from everywhere, made their way to the palace. The anticipatory mood was joyous and light hearted.

Hypsipyle invited Jason to start the evening by making a small speech.

"All of you know that we are on a very important quest to find a most valuable fleece in Colchis. We also have another part to this quest, that we haven't told you about yet. You may have noticed the boat we arrived in. Its builder, Argos is here with us on the journey, to see how the vessel fares, and to make the necessary adjustments and repairs as and when they are needed. This is the finest boat ever built, and it is manned by the finest and strongest athletes and artisans ever assembled. In honour of Argos, the boat builder, we named this boat, the *Argo*, and we are Argonauts. We believe that all boats should have names, because to us, we feel part of it and it is part of us. It is alive, and we are its heart beat."

"Tonight, we are honoured to be your guests. We intend to stay with you for as long as necessary to help with any jobs you feel that we are capable of, since your own men have so disastrously vanished, never to be heard of again. We can appreciate how difficult this past year has been for you all. We are your humble servants. We are here to help."

You can imagine the roar of approval from all women at Jason's' final words. Now it was Queen Hypsipyle's turn to speak.

"As Queen of Limnos, I welcome you all to this special feast tonight, to honour Jason and his Argonauts, who are at the beginning of a very significant journey of discovery. We trust you enjoy the hospitality offered and that you stay for as long as you feel is necessary to prepare for what lies ahead. We have been without male company for quite a while now as has been explained to you, so forgive us if we seem overjoyed and just a little bit excited. I won't speak any longer, so eat, drink and be merry and enjoy the feast."

Before any ritual throat cutting of sacrificial animals, or any wine was consumed, Polyxo rose to speak.

"Jason. You can see that we are without men. Tragically, they were taken from us some years ago, leaving this island vulnerable to attack."

Hypsipyle looked straight at Polyxo wondering where she was headed with this speech, but allowed her to continue.

"But in the intervening time we have become strong. However, we also know that this life for us cannot go on much longer unless our young women produce sons. We are ready for a new beginning, and if you or any of your crew would like to remain here on Limnos, we welcome you."

It was as if the weight of the terrible deed had now been taken from the shoulders of each woman by the very one who initiated it in the first place.

Hypsipyle and Katerina were stunned. Happy of course, but stunned by Polyxo's response. The woman who convinced all other women to help murder each male was now clearly promoting a thorough reversal in thinking. She seemed to be offering the young women to the Argonauts.

Before Hypsipyle and Jason performed the commencement rituals, Polyxo whispered into Hypsipyle's ear.

"This is the new beginning the god Phoebus promised me in my dreams. Remember? She promised new marriages and that life would begin again."

Rising together, Hypsipyle and Jason undertook the usual feast rituals of animal sacrifice and wine libations and the celebration commenced. All Argonauts, with the exception of Hercules, lept into the spirit of the night immediately. Orpheus played his kithara, made up songs, and sang about anyone and everything. Although a captive audience, he was a sight for sore eyes and a sound for sad ears. Limnian women had heard music since the deed, but it constantly made them sad, in remembrance for their departed male relatives, but tonight definitely made them feel happy once again. Orpheus clearly had a gift, and that night, he shared his gift with Limnos.

After consuming glorious food and not-so watered-down wine, mixed in with music and dancing, conversation and laughter, and then more wine, the long-suppressed urges of women bubbled to the surface, and couples started to depart together.

Orpheus was playing to a dwindling crowd, but he didn't seem to mind at all. Soon, the only people remaining were some older women, the children, Hypsipyle and Katerina, Jason, Atalanta and of course Hercules who had stayed all night on the Argo. Hercules did have some food and wine brought to him by Komi, who then left him in peace and returned to serve food to others.

Atalanta lost sight of her fellow archer Philoktetes early in the night. She assumed he had wandered off with a local woman, but that was not the case. Philoktetes did wander off, but he was alone. He enjoyed his own company, and many times on the Argonauts journey after Limnos, he would be seen walking on his own and exploring the surrounding lands. Philoktetes had no idea at the time, but he was destined to spend 10 years on Limnos in the future. Perhaps he developed a deep affection to the island on this short visit as an Argonaut, but that is another story for another time.

Philoktetes returned to the feast before the night was over, and made a point of speaking to Atalanta about archery training planned for the morning. The two archers chatted for well into the night, talking about their lives, when they became interested in weapons, and who their mentors and teachers had been. Although from different geographical and cultural backgrounds, their lives had many similarities. There was a deep respect each had for the other, and before sleep took over, they bid a good night and settled down on the Argo for a well-earned night's sleep — separately!

Hypsipyle and Jason also sat together for a long time talking about many things. Hypsipyle felt that she could talk easily to him, and thought that the feelings were reciprocated. She calmly lied to Jason about the island's history and probably did love him from that moment, but it would take her some time to win him over. She didn't allow love or passion to cloud her judgement. She was calm, eloquent and relied on persuasion to gain his trust.

No one can tell with any confidence where each of the Argonauts slept that night, or if they did actually sleep. All we know is that Atalanta, Philoktetes and Hercules spent the night onboard the Argo and Jason curled up next to the weapons on the beach.

Sunrise the next morning saw some unusual activity in and around the village. All women archers were ready with their bows and arrow, firing at the same target Atalanta and Philoktetes had hit the day before. Aspasia was as excited as a cat playing with a mouse.

Philoktetes and Atalanta arrived with their bows and arrows and set up a number of targets, well away from the main beach, and closer to the castle at the top of the hill. For the rest of the day, a master class was given and both Argonauts enjoyed giving and sharing their advice. In years to come, these lessons helped the Limnian archers repel a number of small pirate raids and certainly added to their perceived and no doubt actual prowess.

Orpheus was sitting in the plateia outside Ambrosia's wine bar first thing in the morning, waiting for it to open. He wanted to let Ambrosia know that the wine from the previous night was the sweetest wine he had ever tasted. He probably was angling for a free drink first thing in the morning, but there he was, strumming his kithara and sitting quietly. Ambrosia opened her doors, and heard the music coming from outside.

Ambrosia always wanted to learn how to play a musical instrument and asked him if he could teach her something. Orpheus agreed, but said in quick response, that a wine would help him with the lesson. He got his free drink!

Orpheus could not have imagined, but that first lesson given by him to Ambrosia sparked an interest she had in music, and more importantly, having musicians regularly play in her wine bar. Ambrosia told him about a dream she had many years ago about travelling to many places she did not recognise, and immediately Orpheus began to try some words to accompany his strumming. He added to Ambrosia's idea slightly and ended up with a girl travelling to new and wondrous places. He called the song 'somewhere I've never travelled', which was about a girl dreaming about travelling around the world, and wondering what life would be like in these places. Long after the Argonauts left Limnos, Ambrosia set up a music school in Myrina, called 'Orpheus'.

Down at the water's edge, Hercules was still a lone sentry guarding the Argo. During one of his visual scans along the beach, he saw Argos return with one of the Limnian women, Anna. During the feast, Anna spoke to Argos and asked him many questions about his boat, and how much she liked the look of it. He promised to take her aboard the next morning to see more closely. But that night, she asked him back to her house to check for 'spiders'!

For many years, Anna has always liked fishing, boats, and all things to do with the water. Her ex-husband had a boat, but it was one of those boats in the port destroyed on the night of the deed. Until her husband became enamoured with his slave girl to work on their family farm, he would take Anna out with him fishing most days.

Always wanting to return to spending time on the water, Anna was resigned to being a farmer for the rest of her life, due to the lack of a boat. Now, her secret passion had been rekindled with this arrival of new life. She soon became interested in how the Argo was constructed, and on the morning after the feast, was seen with Argos inspecting the boat and asking a lot of questions. Argos could see that she had some knowledge and was pleased to explain anything he could to her.

Hercules also seemed at ease with the stranger on board, because Anna had bought a plate of fine food. Argos knew Hercules would be hungry, so he asked Anna to help win over the giant warrior with a plate of Limnos' finest fare. It worked.

Anna spent a lot of time with Argos over the next few days. So much so, that she asked him to build a smaller boat, in a similar construction style to the Argo, for use in fishing. Argos was thrilled to be creating a second, smaller version of his boat, and agreed to build it for her. He enlisted the help of 10 members of the crew with carpentry skills, showed them what wood to find, and then set about creating a new, smaller fishing boat for Anna.

So intently was Anna's observations of the skill of Argos and his builders, that she remembered each and every detail of its construction with precision. From that point on, Anna and Argos spent day and night with each other. Long after the Argonauts left Limnos, the boat Argos built for Anna which still survives and can be seen in the harbour.

Unlike the story that has been promoted for many years and told by people who were never there nor spoke to anyone who was involved, the women of Limnos did not only want to mate with these men. They wanted so much more, and this new beginning was a way to achieve it. Yes, mating with the Argonauts would guarantee a continuance of life on Limnos, but that was not to be achieved overnight.

Since the awful deed was carried out, women have thought about what it is that they truly wanted. Time spent without men had allowed their thoughts to ruminate on what would make them happy, and what was important to them. For some, it was as simple as wanting to stay at home and raise many children. For others, that was a part of their dreams, but they also wanted something else. The arrival of so many men aboard the Argo allowed each woman to find a man to help them learn new skills.

Stella was a woman who did everything her husband said. She stayed at home and raised children, but lost a husband and two sons when the deed was done. Since then, she and her two daughters struggled initially, but the sudden change in life circumstances had given women like Stella a new resolve.

On the night of the feast, Stella was in her element. She had always loved cooking and food preparation, and with her daughters, served their own food to many of the Argonauts. During the evening, Theseus asked if he could speak to the person responsible for food preparation. Stella spoke up and said that it was she together with her daughters and several of the other women.

At this time, very few Argonauts, and certainly none of the Limnians knew that Theseus was actually the future King of Athens. Obviously, Stella did not know this when she and Theseus started talking about food. Theseus was genuinely interested in the food quality, and the recipes Stella used. He had never tasted food like this.

Of course, Stella took Theseus back to her house that night, but all they did was to talk about food. Stella was not interested in Theseus as a man for sexual purposes, but was extremely interested in what he had to say about food.

The next morning saw a continuance of the previous night's food discussion, without any undue influence of wine consumption. Stella said that her dream now was to start a business whereby travellers could come to her shop and sit down to eat a meal, prepared by her, but a meal that reminded them of home. She knew this was a different idea, but it was something she always thought could be done. Many captains and crew from boats visited Limnos for trade, but all they could get at Ambrosia's tavern was wine, and fresh bread if lucky.

In her café, Stella asked Theseus if he could arrange for some of the Argonauts to help her and her daughters clear their land, and plant some seedlings. Theseus agreed and with the help of Laertes and five Argonauts, spent the next week clearing, planting, preparing, pruning, and general maintenance of their farm. The additional workers also repaired the dry-stone walls around the farm, and the wall surrounding the animal enclosures.

By the time the Argo departed Limnos, Stella had established her cafe next to Ambrosia's bar, in the port area. The two businesses complemented each other perfectly. One sold locally grown and produced wine with bread, honey and olives to weary travellers in the early mornings to mid-afternoon, and the other sold freshly prepared food in the evenings that reminded each traveller of home.

Laertes was the father of Odysseus, who years later would rise to fame in helping to bring about a solution to the Trojan blockade. During the week of hard work on the farm, Stella and Laertes were beginning to develop a very close and personal friendship. They were falling in love. It wasn't too long before he stayed at her home one night, and it would be fair to say, they were not discussing the next day's work schedule!

Allow me to digress here and jump ahead many years in time. Laertes was made king of Ithaca in his return from the voyage of the Argo. He had not been married at this stage and had met his future wife Anticlea only days before the voyage departed.

Towards the end of the Trojan blockade when neither side was winning, Odysseus visited Limnos to ask for Philoktetes' help in bringing about a swift end to the problem. Philoktetes had returned to Limnos to live a life of solitude after the Argo's voyage ended. Odysseus sought the help of local people in Myrina to find the missing and enigmatic master of arrow and bow construction, Philoktetes. Visiting Ambrosia's bar on arrival in the port, Odysseus asked Ambrosia where he could find Philoktetes.

Overhearing the conversation was Stella who entered the bar and said that she could help in the search for the missing reclusive Argonaut. Stella told Odysseus that her son knew where he lived and would take him there in the morning.

Before the night ended, Stella and Ambrosia, who were now very advanced in their years, couldn't help but noticing the resemblance between Odysseus and Stella's son Sophocles, who had just arrived after a long day in the field tending their sheep and goats.

After washing away the grime of the day's agricultural activities, Sophocles sat down with his young children and asked for a krater of Ambrosia's finest, while his mother prepared a meal. Sitting on the next table was Odysseus, who politely asked him if he could take him to where Philoktetes was.

"Sure. First thing in the morning, I'll meet you here, but when I say first thing, I mean before the sun comes up. We will have to travel for most of the day by donkey, and we won't get back until much later in the day."

Odysseus agreed. As the two men were talking about the logistics of the next day's travel, Stella and Ambrosia sat listening intently.

"If you don't mind Odysseus, could you tell me a little about yourself?" asked Stella.

The Greek army blockade of Troy was well known throughout the northern Aegean islands. To sate an entire army with its caravan of followers, Limnos had been selling wine and some food for many years.

"I am Odysseus. Son of Laertes and Anticlea. I am King of Ithaca."

Before he finished his rather short speech, Stella appeared to choke on some bread and honey.

"Are you alright Aunty", enquired the polite Odysseus. "Here, have some of this fine wine."

"Did you say Laertes, from Ithaca?"

"Yes. He is my father. Why do you ask?"

At this stage, Sophocles was busy devouring his meal, washing it down with Ambrosia's fine wine. He wasn't really paying any attention to the visitor. He was more intent on discussing what his children had done that day while he was out in the field.

"Was your father, by any chance, one of the famed crew from the Argo?"

"Yes, he was. How did you know that?"

"The Argo visited these shores many years ago, and I met your father then. Did he ever mention Limnos to you Odysseus?"

"My father talked about many things from that voyage. I seem to recall that he said he came here, but it was only for a few days. He said that they were very well looked after and cared for, and after a few days restocking the boat, left for the rest of their journey."

Clearly, Laertes had not told his son about how long they remained on the island. Clearly, he had not mentioned to Odysseus he had a half-brother, who was about to take him on another journey the next day to find Philoktetes.

Sophocles finished his food and wine and bid Odysseus a good night, blissfully unaware he was talking to his brother. Odysseus did the same and retired to the beach to sleep for the night.

Stella and Ambrosia were by now chuckling and smiling. After Odysseus had left, and just before Sophocles retired, he asked his mother why she was laughing.

"Sophocles, the visit from Odysseus reminded Aunty Ambrosia and I of the days the Argonauts visited here, that's all. We were young then and his visit today has jolted our memories. Our marvellous memories. Good night son."

"Good night mother, good night Aunty. See you in the morning."

Sophocles had no idea of the real story. He had no idea that he was the brother of perhaps one of Greece's most famous warriors. For the rest of his mother's life, she never revealed the truth. Sophocles and Odysseus were physically alike in so many ways, and each of them never suspected anything, even though they spent a day travelling together on the backs of donkeys to find Philoktetes.

Let me return now to the present tale.

There were many stories such as these where a Limnian widow together with an Argonaut spent intimate nights together, but later developed into something more substantial. To Polyxo's surprise, this new beginning went in a far better direction than she could have possibly imagined. Every crew member of the Argo helped at least one Limnian woman with a task, other than making them pregnant, that was to have far reaching positive ramifications for many years to come.

Even Hercules, the self-proclaimed Argo and weapons watcher had weakened a little and allowed himself to be taken away from the beach. One day while she was helping Anna prepare food to take on board to the hungry Hercules, Komi said she would take it herself. At this stage, Anna didn't mind, as she and Argos were busy constructing a new boat.

Komi came to the Argo each day to offer Hercules a plate of food, which he dutifully accepted. Komi didn't say anything for the first few days but gathered enough courage to speak to him on about the fifth day.

Komi had asked him politely to help with some house re-building, and Hercules surprisingly said yes. I say surprisingly because he had been so rigid and strict in his guarding of the boat, that he hadn't left its deck, apart for personal exercise or a quick swim in the sea to wash since their arrival. He would sit on the port deck, watching Philoktetes and Atalanta teach the archers each day, listen to Orpheus sing and make up songs at Ambrosia's bar, and watch the activity immediately next to the Argo on the beach where Argos and Anna were busily designing and constructing a new boat.

Seeing his comrades going about what appeared to be normal daily activities, he agreed instantly to Komi's request for him to assist in domestic duties.

Over the next few weeks, Hercules would be seen working on her house lifting large rocks into place to strengthen the walls and the roof. Komi knew she could not keep him, and Hercules did not promise anything he could not deliver. He never promised to return after the voyage of the Argo, and Komi understood, but those few weeks had an impact on Limnos more than we can possibly imagine. But it is true that Hercules did more with Komi than merely help with house construction.

Eight months after the Argo departed Limnos, Komi gave birth to a healthy baby girl, who she named Atsiki. As with all the women who gave birth, everyone knew who the fathers were, and no one was judged.

If it wasn't for Komi and her pursuit of Hercules, they would not have had a child, and I may not have known my life of story-telling. See what I mean? These events of years long ago are still being felt today. Now, after a slight detour I return to the story once again.

After killing her husband during the fateful night over a year ago, Magda was eager and keen to find an Argonaut who shared her passion for butchery. On the first night's feast at the palace, Magda bought along several lambs and goats to be slaughtered and prepared for eating. A number of the Argonauts offered to help in the slaughter, but were surprised when Magda quietly declined their offers, and proceeded to carefully and methodically kill, bleed, skin and carve each animal into portions ready for the ovens.

One Argonaut who offered to help was originally offended when his offer to help was rejected, but his feelings soon dissipated as he watched a master butcher apply her trade. Butes, an Athenian shepherd and warrior, was fascinated by Magda's skill and dexterity with a knife.

He introduced himself to her and asked if he could at least kill the last lamb. Magda reluctantly agreed and handed over her knives. It was the turn of Butes now to politely reject her offer and took out his own knives. Before Magda could say anything, the lamb was dead with its throat cut, and she sat back to watch Butes apply his talent. She too was amazed, and for the rest of the night, the two butchers talked all things knives, sharpening techniques, the slaughtering of different animals, and surprisingly, of cooking tips with succulent ingredients.

Over the following days and weeks, Butes and Magda were seen together constantly. After their first night, subsequent evenings conversations shifted to milking, cheese making and what to do with the fleeces of lambs and goats. It didn't take long for Magda to ask Butes to come back to her house so that she could show him her woollen blankets and woven rugs.

Sophia was one of the women who made constant trips to the beach on the first day to check on the Argonauts clothing needs. She was particularly taken by one member of the crew, Eribotes, who appeared to be different to the others.

On running back to the beach to give back Eribotes his chiton, Sophia slipped and cut her leg on a branch that was hidden just below the surface of the sand. She fell quite awkwardly, and also sprained her ankle in the tumble. Eribotes saw the accident and went to offer her his assistance.

Sophia was most embarrassed, not at falling over on a hidden branch, but because she had ripped Eribotes' chiton during her fall.

"Let me take a look at that for you" said Eribotes.

"I am so sorry that I have ripped your chiton. Let me go back home to fix it immediately."

"I want to look at your wounds, not my clothing."

Sophia was further embarrassed even more, as she was being

cared for on the beach by a stranger, a naked stranger who was now carefully washing and cleaning her cut while resting her ankle on his knee.

"Give me that chiton. It might as well go to good use."

He took the chiton from Sophia and began ripping it into strips. Each strip was then wrapped around the ankle to give it support. Some additional strips were used in cleaning the gash that had now almost stopped bleeding.

Sophia forgot about her naked medical assistant, and was feeling less embarrassed about her clumsiness, and his lack of clothing.

Surprised as his tenderness, Sophia enquired as to his past. Eribotes told her that he was a member of the crew because of his surgical skills. He then asked about her past and she told him she had a passion for making jewellery.

"My mother had the same passion, and she taught me many of her skills", said Eribotes.

For the rest of that first night at the feast, and long after Eribotes found some fresh clothing, they talked about rings, bracelets, necklaces, earrings, pendants, arm bands, diadems, and hair ornaments. Sophia told him about her own clothing she was designing, and the next day Eribotes paid her a visit. By the end of 10 days, Eribotes was the best dressed Argonaut in Myrina!

While all these liaisons were taking place, Hypsipyle and Jason were just as active. A surprising announcement was made 30 days after the Argo's arrival. Jason was so taken with Hypsipyle and living in Myrina, that he asked her to marry him. Hypsipyle said 'yes'.

The wedding was a different ceremony to the normal weddings of the day. With no mother, Hypsipyle spent the final few days in the company of Polyxo standing in as her maternal guide. Hypsipyle, Katerina and some of their closest friends took Hypsipyle's childhood toys to the temple of Aphrodite, to symbolically announce the formal end of childhood, and the start of life as a wife. Hypsipyle cut her hair, and on the day of the wedding, she and Jason bathed in holy water. Jason did not have his parents present, so no dowry could be offered, only promised.

A feast was held in the palace, attended by almost all Limnians. This was the first of several weddings between women and the Argonauts. Jason promised to return to Limnos immediately after his quest was completed, and Hypsipyle had no reason to doubt him. At this stage, Hypsipyle was probably pregnant, but she and Jason were unaware.

Over the next 30 days, many more weddings occurred. All grooms made promises to their brides that they would return on completion of the quest.

On reflection now, it was highly likely that most of the women who married, and even those who did not marry but still coupled with an Argonaut, expected their new partners not to return. They were aware of potential dangers with the voyage ahead and resigned themselves to the fact of a life with no man at home, and a new beginning through children born soon enough.

It had been 70 days since Jason and the Argonauts landed in Myrina, and now it was time to leave. Hercules was the one who reminded Jason and the others what their true purpose and mission was. After helping the people of Limnos with rebuilding their lives, it was time to move on to the next stage of their journey. Many storytellers over the years have tried to paint the visual picture of hundreds of crying women on the beach, as the Argo was re-floated. Nothing could be further from the truth. All women knew that one day soon these men would have to leave. In their brief time together, normal life had returned, and seeds were sown for new life to germinate and prosper. A new beginning had well and truly begun.

Before the Argo finally slipped effortlessly into the sea, Hypsipyle asked Jason to wait just a moment longer, as she had something to give him. Jason agreed.

Running back from the palace, Hypsipyle had a sword in her

right hand which caught Jason's eye, and a cloak in her left. He did not notice the cloak because his attention was firmly and squarely on the sword.

Hypsipyle offered the sword to Jason, saying that it once belonged to her father, King Thoas. This was not the sword Hypsipyle claimed as the weapon that killed her father. The gesture was not lost on the women of Limnos, who at that stage, still didn't know that Thoas may not have been dead, and that their Queen did not kill him. But to them, it was a symbol that the deed had well and truly been put to rest, and was now behind them, never to be spoken of again.

"Jason, this was my fathers. Please take it on your journey, and I hope it comes in handy for you one day."

Jason was delighted at this gesture from his wife. He knew the value of such a gift and thanked her for it. Hypsipyle gave something else to Jason. She handed him a special woollen robe, made from local cloth, and dyed purple. She told him to remember her each time he wore it.

Hypsipyle farewelled Jason. Jason promised to return, and Hypsipyle unconditionally believed him.

CHAPTER 10

Twins

Visually, life post Argo on Limnos appeared to be normal. Boats were loaded with exportable produce and boats were unloaded with imported necessities. But looks can be deceiving. Now, there was a different feeling in Myrina, a spring in the step of every woman, and an aroma of change.

Ok, I was just trying to be sensory with words, but you get the picture.

But there was a different attitude now. Women were carrying on their business with a sense of hope and purpose. Polyxo's new beginning had started.

As days passed, bellies grew. Older women fussed around the pregnant ones and planned for the imminent births. Polyxo had two impending births to contend with — Hypsipyle and the unmarried Katerina, who remained tight lipped as to the fathers' identity.

Hypsipyle's appearance looked different. Her belly appeared to be larger than other pregnant women.

"It is twins, I'm sure of it", said Polyxo.

"How can you be certain?"

"I just know. We older women know these things."

All Argonaut pregnancies were progressing normally. What a strange sight it must have been to see so many women pregnant at the one time, in the one place. News quickly spread to other islands about Jason and his crew impregnating a whole island of women, and like most stories, it grew into something far bigger than it truly was. The less subtle mariners who arrived and saw the growing bellies would say that Jason was just taking his boat around to islands and his men were having sex with as many women as they could. Rumours spread along the trade routes of the Aegean that this was the true purpose of Jason's quest. Limnos happened to be the first stop over.

It was inevitable these rumours could come back to Limnos via visiting captains and their unruly crews, but this did not seem to make any difference in how life was progressing in Myrina.

When a captain and his crew happened to mention this rather salacious and false aspersion cast in the direction of the Limnian women, Aspasia would appear with her weapons, and quickly mention to the captain that if he valued his testicles and having them attached to his body, it would be in his physical interest not saying those sorts of things again.

Aspasia and the other archers were not only now skilled in archery, but for their time spent in the presence of Philoktetes and Atalanta, they learned many other combat skills. One such incident did see a captain of a visiting trading vessel make some rather ill-timed comments after some fine Ambrosia wine about the Argo and Limnian women, only to have his manhood precariously hovering above a very sharp knife held by Aspasia, while another archer held his head back with her knife. He quickly withdrew his comments and on release of the knife-like grip, proceeded to then tell every mariner not to mess with the women of Limnos!

To this day, not one incident has ever taken place at the port of Myrina where a visiting captain, his crew, or any mariner has made any disparaging comment about Limnian women.

Hypsipyle offered the use of the palace as a place for any upcoming births should the mothers find it necessary. Polyxo and other older women started to plan for a rush of babies. The palace was transformed. Birthing chairs were put in place, with oils, herbs, and access to warm water all carefully planned. Normally, a village the size of Myrina might see a birth every thirty days, but this was to be something quite different. Nearly one hundred women were pregnant. If you consider that there were only 49 male Argonauts, and we know that some of them did not impregnate any women, some of the others must have been very hard at work. All women must have known the fathers of their children would never return.

Another strange event started to take place in Myrina at about this time. Over the past few years, prior to the visit from the Argo, some sailors had requested to remain on Limnos, but their requests were always refused. No reasons were ever given as to why this was the case, but it was most likely Polyxo's influence in not allowing strangers into their midst. But since the Argo left, some sailors did not take no for an answer.

One such sailor was a man called Stefanos, who came from Lesvos on an olive oil trading boat on a number of occasions. His boat would arrive from Lesvos with olive oil, and return with wine, honey and salted meat.

Stefanos grew up in the Lesvian village of Mythimna with his grandmother, mother and five older sisters. His father died shortly after he was born, so his entire life was spent growing up with and around women. Coming to Limnos did not seem at all different, or strange to him given the lack of men on the island. During the stopover while he waited for his boat to empty and restock with new produce, Stefanos wandered around the village and offered to help anyone he found who looked like they needed assistance. He had an affinity for the village and for the first time in his life, felt he belonged, even if he had only been there a day or two at the most.

Before the second trip to Limnos, he asked his captain if he could stay until the next time the boat visited with goods to trade. His captain agreed.

Stefanos first lived in the café with Ambrosia, but soon Polyxo asked if he wanted to live in the palace and work as a royal attendant, but not to be considered a slave. Ambrosia agreed, Stefanos agreed, and soon enough, he was living in the palace as a male servant. It had been a number of years since any males had lived in the palace, and Stefanos soon became indispensable. His skills with stone work, farming, butchery and of all things, dress making, were greatly admired. Growing up in an all-female family meant that he learned skills that many men did not possess. Although a novelty to women in Myrina, Stefanos did not see his garment making skills as anything different to his butchery skills, or his ability to repair houses and fences with dry stone construction.

It was apparent that his tailoring skills were better than Polyxo, Katerina and Hypsipyle combined. Even Sophia was impressed! Soon, Stefanos was loaned out to any family that required his unique set of abilities. He would often help with stone wall construction, make any repair work to roofs and house walls, and then work in the many gardens and farms outside the village.

When he was not working, Stefanos would ask Katerina to show him around, and introduce him to all her friends. Katerina, although heavily pregnant, became infatuated with him, and the feelings were mutual. Stefanos didn't seem to mind that she was carrying another man's child. He fell in love with her anyway. Polyxo was very happy with her only daughter, and equally with Stefanos. Hypsipyle liked him too.

Stefanos' captain returned one day from Lesvos, but he knew that he wasn't going to be taking back his young sailor. Stefanos had found a new home.

The example of other men like Stefanos coming to Limnos in trading boats, and wanting to stay, suddenly became a normal occurrence. Before the first of the Argonaut babies arrived, no less than 10 men did what Stefanos had done. Some of these men offered to work on farms outside the village, and some worked in the port area. The attitude of these men to Limnian women was one of complete respect.

Polyxo believed that the new beginning might take a generation or two to allow for babies to grow into men, but she could not have foreseen these new migrants coming to live on Limnos so soon. It was an unforeseeable yet fortunate variation on the new beginning theme.

In all this time, no-one seemed to mind, nor ask, why any Limnian men were not around. The myth grew, and before too long, became accepted as fact. All Limnian males were lost at sea, sold to slavery, or a mixture of both.

With the palace established as a birthing area, the first birth took place soon after Stefanos became a permanent resident. Polyxo and two of the older women, Sophronia and Kalliopi, set about their tasks to help with this first delivery. Kassandra had the honour of being the first mother to an Argonaut baby. Sitting in the birthing chair, Polyxo rubbed olive oil on her back while Sophronia waited for the baby to arrive. Kalliopi was the one who fetched anything either of the other women wanted.

It was a boy. The first delivery was a success with mother and son doing very well immediately. Kassandra named him Androcles. The second baby born within a few days was not so lucky. Soon after the birth, the baby began to have breathing difficulties, and died as a result. There was nothing anyone in attendance could do to save the little child.

Then the babies were coming at a rate of 2-3 per day. Polyxo, Sophronia and Kalliopi were beginning to feel the strain of being full time mid-wives, and had to enlist the help of some more women. At its height, there were no less than 6 women working as midwives in the palace. Fortunately, with the experience gained each time a new born baby arrived, deaths were kept to a minimum.

Katerina went into labour, and gave birth to a healthy boy, whom she called Alexander. Even though Stefanos was not the biological father, nor married to Katerina, he acted as the father and husband, as was as excited as anyone could be. He thought Katerina's choice of Alexander for her baby was a great name. Hypsipyle was also ecstatic at her best friend becoming a mother.

The palace was buzzing with excitement. Almost all non-essential farm work, house work and building repair work ceased during this time. The entire focus of everybody on the island was fixed firmly on each and every birth.

Around Myrina, the mood was one of joy and hope. Joy because a new beginning was finally a reality, and hope because of the future this new beginning promised. Music could be heard in the taverns by the port, and wine was flowing all day, and at all times of the day. During this birthing frenzy, there were new boats arriving with cargo. Before sailors were finished unloading their wares, kraters of wine were thrust into their hands in celebration of the latest birth. Some of these boats stayed longer than normal in port, which was hardly surprising considering the free wine on offer.

Hypsipyle went into labour early one morning several days after her best friend Katerina gave birth. Now it was to be Hypsipyle's turn to become a mother. Polyxo gave special attention to her needs and the result was a successful, incident free delivery of healthy twin boys. The whole process took most of the day, and by nightfall, Hypsipyle was exhausted. Her two boys were resting and in good care.

Knowing they were in good hands, Hypsipyle fell into a deep sleep. Early next morning saw most of the village excitedly entering the palace to meet the royal babies. Hypsipyle proudly named the first boy after her father Thoas, and the second boy Euneos.

The birthing tradition in Limnos and indeed on many islands was to decorate the houses of new babies according to sex. The birth of a boy saw a house decorated with olive branches, and new baby girl saw decorations of wool garlands. The palace had both kinds of decorations for 60 days due to the number of new babies.

It was decided very quickly to keep both sets of decorations up until the last Argonaut birth.

Never before, and never since had there been so many babies born in such a short time period on the island. Almost every house had a new baby in it, or at least, had people in the house who were helping family members with their new babies. Polyxo had her hands full at the palace with three boys, and two new mothers. Stefanos was a great help during this time not only with Katerina and Alexander, but also with Hypsipyle, Thoas and Euneos. Strangely enough, no one seemed to mind Hypsipyle naming one of her boys after her father. It was as if the past had been forgotten, and now, the residents of Limnos only wanted to focus on the future.

Standing at night in the middle of Myrina, it was possible to hear babies crying in all directions. Crying babies were simply more noises joining the already thick nightly sounds of the village. Visiting boat captains commented on the number of babies seen with mothers walking along the port area. Patrons at Ambrosia's bar were asked to be a little quieter because there were sleeping babies nearby. Keeping drunk sailors quiet is no mean feat, but many of these sailors were also fathers, so they knew to be respectful, even with a skin full of Ambrosia's fine wine.

After the final Argonaut baby was delivered, and home with its mother, the palace birthing area was converted into a childcare and drop-in centre for all the babies and mothers, to provide critical support and timely advice. Given there were no fathers undertaking the traditional masculine roles in parenting, Polyxo, Sophronia and Kalliopi organised as much support and advice as was deemed necessary. It soon became clear that various roles culturally assigned to males and females became obsolete, and all that was left were jobs to perform, regardless of gender.

For the next few years, the child caring services offered by the palace allowed many mothers to return to income producing farm work, port work and other work necessary to keep a family fed, clothed and housed.

One noticeably unusual ritual came about because of the work done in the port by new mothers. Returning sailors and captains were bringing in new and used toys for all babies from their own villages. Normally after unloading a boat laden with produce, sailors would head directly for the port-side bars and brothels for sustenance and personal pleasure. Now, they were making a bee-line for the palace to hand over toys as a priority, then proceeding to go about their traditional activities in the adult establishments adjacent to the port.

In the meantime, Hypsipyle adored her two boys, taking to motherhood with ease. Not having her own mother to assist and provide advice meant that Polyxo had an extra special bond with these two boys, as well as her own grandchild.

Life could not have been better on Limnos, in the village of Myrina than it was at this time in its history. From the depths of despair felt by women only a few years prior when their husbands abandoned them in favour of Samothrakian slaves, to now, where the past had been totally forgotten. Polyxo's predictions of a new beginning were a reality.

Remembering the comforting and sweet childhood memories of Queen Myrina singing to her as a child, Hypsipyle sang to her boys every day. Her mother sung one particular song more often than others, and was the one sung by Hypsipyle to Orpheus when the Argonauts were first on Limnos. Being an accomplished musician, Orpheus learned the song in no time and made some immediate changes and improvements to the words and melody. It was this new version that Hypsipyle now sung to her boys, and not the original version from her own mother.

Like many sets of twins, these two had their similarities, but there were some marked differences from birth. When Hypsipyle sang, Euneos enjoyed it more than Thoas. It wasn't that young

Thoas did not enjoy the sound of his mother's voice, just that Euneos loved it more than his brother did. Euneos learned to sing before he could talk.

The twins were identical in looks. Until they had their first birthday, it was impossible for anyone outside the palace community to tell them apart. Thoas was the first twin to walk, but Euneos talked first. Actually, he didn't so much as talk, but sang his thoughts. Thoas mumbled in baby talk, but Euneos always seemed to be singing. Apart from these differences, the boys were inseparable, not only from each other, but also from Katerina's boy Alexander.

The final Argonaut baby count saw a total of 96 women who had given birth to 100 babies. Of these births, there were only two deaths in child birth, which was a remarkable achievement. As well as Hypsipyle, there were three other sets of twins.

Hypsipyle lived each day hoping for news of her husband, but it never came. She would question each and every boat captain if they knew of, or had heard of Jason's whereabouts, but each time she was met with the same response — nothing.

In the interim, Thoas and Euneos, along with all other Argonaut babies were growing into normal, healthy and cheeky little people. The twins didn't speak of their father, as they had never met him, and by this stage, their mother had practically abandoned all hope of ever seeing Jason again.

But one day, quite suddenly, a boat captain did have some news for Hypsipyle regarding Jason.

But before I continue, I think I need to make room for more wine!

CHAPTER 11

A witless man

At first there was a sailor from Thessaly with news that a boat matching the Argos's description was seen in Iolchus. This was then corroborated shortly after through other sailors that the boat truly was the Argo, and Jason had returned with a special cargo.

When he left Limnos, Jason promised Hypsipyle to return as soon as his quest was completed. She may have felt that there was a small possibility that he might not return, but she nonetheless firmly believed that he would keep his word. After all, they were married!

To cut a very long and adventurous three-year story short, which is one of my other favourite epic sagas to tell people, Jason never did set foot on Limnian earth every again.

Hypsipyle had learned to be a single parent, and raising two boys was a difficult but not insurmountable task. She was not alone in this endeavour, and many of her friends were in the identical situation. If Jason had indeed returned to his home, she may have been able to forgive him if he chose to remain there, but news of the existence of a second wife was unforgivable.

Jason never did see Hypsipyle again, or hold any of their two boys. Hypsipyle never had an opportunity to look him in the eyes and say what was on her mind. But imagine if she did. What might she have said?

I heard that your ship has returned, with the fleece! Congratulations on a safe return, but a message from you to that effect would have been nice. Maybe the winds were not ideal, but then again, a message can be sealed and sent to Limnos in any weather. Where was my "Dear Hypsipyle" letter? I think I deserved one, don't you think?

So, tell me? How come you can tie sacred bulls to a curved yoke, plough a field sown with dragons teeth, watch while a crop of armed warriors grew, somehow have them all kill each other without you raising an arm, slip past a dragon who had miraculously taken a sleeping potion, and then steal the mighty fleece hanging from a tree branch? How nice would it have been to say to all those non-believers, nay sceptics, "Oh no, everything happened just like that because Jason wrote me this very nice letter!"

But do I complain? I would be most satisfied if I am still yours.

It is also rumoured that a witch came home with you, and now shares your bed? Didn't you once promise that bed to me?

You could say that these rumours were all lies, and all accusations against you were untrue.

But I just received a visitor from Thessaly who accidently let it slip. I asked him how my Jason was, and he suddenly became fixated on something on the ground, trying to ignore my eyes.

"How's my Jason doing" I screamed at him as I ripped the tunic from my chest.

"Is he alive?" Embarrassingly, he said "Yes, he is alive". I forced him to swear to Zeus, that what he said was true, and he did so. I couldn't believe it.

After I regained my thoughts, I began to ask him about you and what you had been doing. That is when I heard about the bulls, tilling the soil with dragons' teeth, the warriors and the sleepy serpent. Still, I asked if you were alive. With each story of your deeds, he was exposing all the wounds you have inflicted on me.

What has happened to your promises to me? Our marriage vows? The wedding torch is now better suited to lighting my funeral pyre. Our wedding was not some secret lovers' rendezvous. It was attended by Hera and Hymen, the Goddess and God of marriage. Or was it some blood soaked, infernal Erinys, Goddess of revenge leading the procession carrying those doomed wedding torches?

What business did I have with your Argonauts, or for that matter, your precious ship? What did you and the helmsman Tiphys have to do with Limnos? There was no magical golden fleece here, nor was Limnos a royal seat of the respectful Aertes.

My first thought was to turn back the foreign invaders on your ship with the help of my female warriors. We Limnian women know a thing of two about conquering men. We should have been protected by our reputation, but alas, I welcomed you into our widowed city, into my home and into my heart. And what did you do? You stayed for two months until you were called to complete your quest. But do you remember your parting words to me Jason?

"I am being taken away, Hypsipyle, but may fate reunite us. I am your husband, and I will always be your husband. However, I hope the child inside your belly lives to remember me. I hope we can both be parents together one day."

I seem to recall these were your final parting words. What a load of rubbish! Your tears flowed down on deceitful cheeks and you could not finish the rest. And in conclusion, you were the last to board the Argo!

With a favourable wind, you surged away with all oars. You looked on our island, and I looked on the endless ocean. I rushed up to the tower on top of the castle, where I could gain an unobstructed view of all sides, tears running down my cheeks and chest. But, through my tears, I could see clearly see further than normal. It was there I made a vow to be faithful until your safe return. Am I to keep those vows, so that your new wife can reap the benefits?

My rage goes from total heartache to overflowing love for you.

Should I take offerings to the temples because you are lost to me, but still alive? Why should I sacrifice an animal because I have suffered?

I was always insecure, always afraid of your father, who I thought would choose a wife for you from an Argive city. While I was afraid of Argive women, a barbarian mistress was my downfall. I didn't see that coming! I was wounded by this unexpected enemy.

Surely it wasn't her beauty or her help that has won you. No, she knows spells and understands how to use herbs of shocking powder cut with an enchanted knife. She can bring down the reluctant moon and bury the sun's horses in shadows. She can bring flowing rivers to a standstill, and move rocks and forests from their living place.

She walks through graveyards with hair and dress hanging loose, collecting bones from the still warm funeral pyres. She puts hexes on men from a distance and makes wax images of them through which she stabs sharpened needles into their suffering livers. She probably does other things to them, but I don't want to know.

It is wrong to seek love through these means. It should be won by character and beauty. How can you stomach embracing this woman? Left alone with her in a room at night, how can you possibly get a good night's sleep? Aren't you afraid?

Obviously, she has forced you to bear the yoke — just like she did for the bulls, and she has charmed you with the same spells she used on the savage serpents. She is now taking credit for all the things you and your Argonauts have done. She is taking all of your glory!

Others are saying that all your deeds weren't done by you, but done by magic from her. These rumours are starting to take over.

"Oh no, it wasn't Jason who did these things. It was the daughter of Aertes who removed the fleece".

Even your parents do not approve of her. Let her go and find a husband from her own lands. Jason, you are fickler and more inconsistent than a springtime breeze. No wonder your words lack their promised weight. You left here as my husband. Why didn't you return as such? Now that you are back, I should be your wife, just as I was when you left.

Is it high birth and titles you want? I have them. I am the daughter of Thoas, grandson of Minos. My grandfather is Bacchus, and his wife wore a crown. Her stars outshone all other lesser constellations. Is it land you want? I have Limnos as my dowry, a land that farmers say is most fertile. I am part of that dowry too.

I have given birth, so be happy for both of us Jason. My pregnancy was made sweet because it was given to me by the father. I was most fortunate, having given birth to twin boys. Children to bind us. If you were to ask who they look like, well, your physical features are to be seen in them, but they have not yet learned to deceive! However, luckily they have other traits of their father.

I nearly had them taken to you, to plead on behalf of their mother, but the thought of the savage stepmother stopped me in my tracks. I feared Medea. Medea is more than a stepmother. Her hands are suited to every crime.

Is this woman who can scatter her brother's body over the earth likely to spare my children? You are a witless man, Jason. Your judgement has been stolen by Colchian magic. This is the woman men will say you preferred to Hypsipyle's bed! This is the woman who shamelessly had her first romp with a married man!

Our marriage was chaste, that gave me to you and you to me. She betrayed her father, while I saved mine from slaughter. She abandoned Colchis, and I still live on my native Limnos. But what does any of this mean when a wicked woman has beaten a devoted wife, and her dowry is the crime by which she won her husband's affection? I do not condone the Limnian woman's crime Jason, but I understand it. Resentment will drive even the weakest to pick up arms.

What would have happened if the unfriendly winds drove you and your companion into my harbour, and I came out to meet you with the twins? No doubt you would have wanted the sea to open up beneath you. What look would you have given to see me and the children? What would have been a suitable death for your treachery?

I would have allowed you to live safely. Not because you deserved it, but because I am merciful. However, as for your mistress, I would have glutted my eyes with her blood. Your eyes as well, because she stole you with her evil magic. I would have been Medea to Medea! But if Zeus gives me answers to some of my prayers, she would grieve herself and lose at her own game.

Just as I, a wife and mother of two, may she be abandoned and robbed of her husband. May she lose him more miserably. May she be exiled and seek refuge throughout the world. May she be as harsh to her children and husband, as she once was a sister to a brother and daughter to a suffering parent. And when she has exhausted the earth and sea, let her try the sky. May she wander helpless, hopeless and bloodied by her slaughter. These curses are my prayers Jason. But if I am not answered, live on you two, bride and husband, in your cursed bed.

CHAPTER 12

Some bad news

Given her obvious disappointment, Hypsipyle soon learned to live with the knowledge that Jason would never return. She was not the only women in Limnos in this situation who had an 'Argonaut' child from an absent father.

Life on Limnos for all families after the substantial increase in natural population was as happy a time as can be imagined. In the palace, there was joy and laughter again. Not since Hypsipyle herself was born, was there so much life and hope for the future. The entire village was brimming with little children. As each child grew older, they would venture further away from their homes to the port area, the beaches, and sanctuaries — with their mothers not far behind. It was not uncommon to see a swarm of 30 children running around on the beach at any one time, with their mothers' and at times grandmothers in hot pursuit hand feeding them and attempting to keep them safe from imaginary dangers.

Life in the village and at the port of Myrina was bustling with activity. Every day, a new boat would arrive at the port bringing wonderful and much needed goods from other islands and the mainland, only to return laden with Limnian produce.

One day, a fisherman from an island no one at the port had heard about arrived in port to sell his salted fish. He also had some amphorae of wine. After unloading his goods, and then restocking with olive oil for the return leg, he took a moment to relax in the first café he saw, ordered some wine and fresh bread and began a conversation with Stefanos and Ambrosia.

Ambrosia had never heard of Oinoe, but Stefanos knew it was an island somewhere near Crete. The fisherman's name was Petros, and his story was a fascinating one. He told of his island, how it used to only be only known for its fishing, but lately, a new industry emerged — grape growing and wine production.

Ambrosia drank some of his wine, and liked what she tasted, so she asked him about it. Petros explained that the new industry happened only by chance.

"A number of years ago, a man washed up on one of our beaches, and said he came from Mythimna on the island of Lesvos, but had got lost in a storm. We looked after him, and nursed him back to health."

"Did you say Mythimna?" asked Stefanos. "That's where I'm from, but I do not remember anyone called Thomas from my home village."

Ambrosia was intrigued. "Can you describe him to us?"

Petros described the man, and Ambrosia felt uneasy. Firstly, she was alarmed that the man described by Petros was said to have come from a village where Stefanos was born, and secondly, his description seemed to fit someone she knew.

"Are you sure he said he came from Lesvos, not Limnos", asked Ambrosia. "It is an easy mistake to make."

"I am sure. He said Mythimna, in Lesvos."

Stefanos was confused by Ambrosia's sudden responses and questions. Why was she questioning a fisherman from Oinoe about where a man claimed he was from? Because Stefanos did not know this man from Mythimna, maybe Thomas was confused and disoriented after his ordeal, and his story may have been misunderstood by Petros.

He asked Ambrosia about her concerns, but she kept her thoughts to herself, and only said that this mystery man Thomas may be a person that she thought she knew, but could not be sure. Stefanos did not think much more about it, and within a few days had completely forgotten the story.

Petros enjoyed the hospitality showed to him on Limnos, and promised to come back again with more salted fish and more wine. Ambrosia asked him to come only to her, and not to speak to anyone else. Petros was told that she would pay him double what the goods were worth if he did one thing for her. Ambrosia asked him to tell Thomas that his daughter misses him and that she has given birth to twin boys, and one of them is called Thoas.

"When you tell Thomas this, make sure no one is listening, and please let me know what his reaction is. Have you got that? But there is one more thing. Make sure you tell him that you sold your fish and wine in the village of Myrina, on Limnos."

Petros did not understand what Ambrosia meant, but promised to do this for her. After all, he was about to get double the price for his goods if he did this, so he didn't question her intentions.

On the next available wind, Petros and his crew dipped their oars and sailed back to Oinoe. With favourable winds, he made it home in seven days, and set about to stock up his boat with the required goods as soon as he could.

When he had just about the right amount of salted fish, Petros visited Thomas and told him that he met someone on his last visit who wished to pass on a message. Thomas thought that Petros sold his produce in Lesvos, so didn't see what was coming next.

"A lady called Ambrosia says that your daughter is well and that she has twin boys, one of them is called Thoas!"

For a brief moment, Thoas' past life came flooding back to him. All those happy memories from a life in Limnos with Myrina and Hypsipyle. But then he remembered being set adrift in a boat and not knowing what was happening in the village. He smiled at

Petros and said that the lady he met must be mistaken, as he did not have a daughter.

"Are you sure that you visited Mythimna?"

"No Thomas. we got blown off course, and by pure chance, found our way to Limnos, and the village of Myrina."

Thomas could not believe what he was hearing. Inside, he was ecstatic at this news, but could not let Petros know of his real identity, so he had to pretend not to show any emotion. His daughter Hypsipyle was alive and now a mother, and they named one of the boys after him. What wonderful news.

Petros sensed there was something unusual with Thomas' response, but did not say anything, remembering that all he had to do was to report back to Ambrosia Thomas' reaction to the message. He did not try to analyse the situation any further, so he set about restocking and planning a return trip.

Four weeks later, Petros set sail for Limnos one more time, but this time he was carrying more than just fish and wine. He was taking back something that was worth all the wine and fish together.

Arriving back in Myrina, Petros sold Ambrosia and Stefanos all that he had. While Stefanos took the salted fish and wine into their port side café, Ambrosia approached Petros and asked him about the other information.

"He smiled at first, but then stopped the smile to tell me that you must be mistaken and that he has no daughter. I did not believe him at the time, but then again, I have no reason to believe or not believe him. Thomas has been very good to me and all the other fishermen families on Oinoe."

"If it wasn't for him, we would not be selling our wares this far from home."

"He married one of our young women and they had a baby together, but the mother died soon after childbirth, so now the boy and Thomas are inseparable and living and working to make this very wine. The boy is called Sikinos, and at his young age, knows more about wine making than many older people."

Ambrosia didn't want to cause Petros any anxiety, so she lied to him when she said "…forget about it. It must be someone different to the man I once knew. I'm sorry if I have caused any concern."

Ambrosia asked one more question of Petros, to throw him off the scent of her thoughts.

"Does Thomas have a scar down the left side of his face?"

"No. He has a scar on his right arm, but definitely not on his face."

Ambrosia set the trap, and Petros walked right into it. King Thoas was injured once in an accident at the palace where he was taking some sword fighting lessons with young men, and one of them accidently cut his right arm.

She was now physically shaking. Both Petros and Stefanos saw this, but she simply said that she was not feeling well, and needed to go for a walk along the beach.

Fuming inside, Ambrosia stormed up to the Temple of Aphrodite to gather her thoughts and to think of what to do next. Too many emotions and thoughts were competing in her mind for attention, and she was not at all sure how to handle any of it. She sat on the very rocks where the deed was carried out. The very rock where all those men and boys had been slaughtered. Hypsipyle has lied to us all along, she thought. Did Katerina also know of this? Did Polyxo know of this? Who else knew of this? How did King Thoas get away? How did he make it all the way to Oinoe? Hypsipyle came back with his bloodied sword? Whose blood was it? What do we do now?

She sat for a long time, and had calmed down considerably before taking the steps down along the path back to the café. Stefanos asked her if she was feeling better, and Ambrosia said that she was. "It must have been something I ate," she said. "I'm much better now. Much better."

Once again, Petros purchased more goods to load on his boat for the return trip. Happy with his windfall gain, he asked Ambrosia if she wanted any more things from Oinoe, and Ambrosia said no.

Two days later, Petros thanked Ambrosia and Stefanos for buying his produce and sailed for Oinoe, not knowing that he had inadvertently set about a chain of events that he could not have possibly imagined. Once back home, he quickly forgot Ambrosia's questioning and didn't give it any more thought. In Limnos, Ambrosia slept on her thoughts, and decided to speak to Polyxo in the morning.

After a troubled night's sleep where Ambrosia was conflicted in what she wanted to do, and what she thought others wanted to do with the knowledge that King Thoas lived, she knew that she must speak with Polyxo. What if Petros was mistaken, and this Thomas was a fisherman from Lesvos?

Polyxo was sitting on a stone in the courtyard of the palace when Ambrosia entered, looking rather perplexed. Polyxo normally awoke early each day to walk to the well for a bucket of fresh water for washing and cooking.

"This is an unexpected surprise this early in the morning Ambrosia. Is there anything wrong?"

"I don't know"', said Ambrosia. "There might be, or there might not be. I'm just not sure."

"Then sit down, and help me mend this basket, so that you can tell me what is on your mind."

Ambrosia took her time to explain the timeline of events to Polyxo, not leaving anything out, and making sure not to alarm anyone who may have been overhearing. Before she reached the part where King Thoas may have been alive, she asked Polyxo to walk with her to the well.

The main village well was a distance far enough from the palace, and far enough away from any houses, so it was unlikely anyone overheard what was said next. Many people came to the well for this very purpose. It was an ideal place to talk, and to listen. It was an ideal place to discover the secrets of others in the village. I am sure every village and city have a well just for this purpose.

Sitting together on seats carved into rocks at the well, Ambrosia continued with her story.

She explained how it came to be that the fisherman from Oinoe began talking, and talked about the stranger washed ashore there many years ago, and who claimed to be from Lesvos. She talked about the ruse she set in place for Petros to ask the stranger a few questions, and told Polyxo about what this person said.

By the end of Ambrosia's story, Polyxo was not visibly angry. She appeared to be rather calm, but what she said next explained her cool veneer of mixed and anxious emotions.

"Although I love her with all my heart, Hypsipyle must be punished."

That is all she said, Hypsipyle must be punished. Polyxo believed that Hypsipyle was guilty of deception and according to custom, had the choice to decide her outcome.

Together, Polyxo and Ambrosia walked quickly back to the palace to confront Hypsipyle immediately. They did not talk to any of the other women, and did not seek anyone else's opinion. They knew what had to be done. They were both extremely calm.

Like Jason never returning to Limnos, Hypsipyle also had the belief that the true story regarding her father's exit from the island may be discovered one day. She had no way of knowing if he was alive, just the faintest of all hopes that he was, and that he was safe.

Polyxo was first to speak.

"Queen Hypsipyle. Please sit, as we have one question to ask you."

Polyxo, Hypsipyle and Ambrosia sat at a table in a small room next to the larger throne room. This room was used for many purposes, but never before had the reigning monarch been subjected to this kind of questioning in the room where she was normally the one interrogating others.

"How do you explain to us that your father King Thoas is alive and well on the island of Oinoe?"

"What do you mean?"

"I will ask the question again, if you did not understand it."

Hypsipyle certainly understood the question, but chose a different approach to making a confession.

"I did not actually tell you I killed my father. Remember, I simply pointed out to sea at the larnax. You assumed I had killed him."

"But his sword was smeared in blood. If not the King's, then whose blood was it?"

"Not whose, but what blood was it. It was pigs' blood on the larnax, and I killed it, not my father."

"But we saw him drink the special wine. How come he was not affected like all other men?"

"I gave him some highly watered-down wine, not the tainted brew you put together. It was very diluted — about one to ten, so as not to cloud his judgement."

Polyxo did not ask Hypsipyle how or when she warned her father of the impending doom, but clearly, she had warned him.

"Why didn't King Thoas warn the men of their fate? He had the time."

"Putting him to sea was the best option, and that if he survived, he should start his life again. There was no time to develop an alternative plan. My father could have saved all the men by warning them, but if he did do that, then what might have become of all of you for planning it in the first place? Surely the men would then have taken their own retribution?"

Polyxo did not want to entertain those thoughts. All she could focus on at that time was how Hypsipyle would be punished.

"Hypsipyle, we are giving you an option. To put it simply, you have the choice to be sacrificed at the altar, or you can be ostracised, never to return to Limnos. You choose! Oh, and one more thing. You will have no further contact with your boys. They will be well looked after here in the palace by myself, Katerina and Stefanos. Ambrosia will help of course. Your boys are completely innocent in this saga, but you are not. You deceived us. You lead us to believe that you killed your father. Whether or not you killed him does not matter much anymore."

Hypsipyle was instructed not to leave the Palace, and not to talk to anyone. Ambrosia and Polyxo were not concerned that Hypsipyle would leave, because she had nowhere to go. She could not escape. Friendless and alone, Hypsipyle remained inside the Palace to await her destiny.

Hypsipyle knew that she could not remain on Limnos. She also could not face any woman who had killed their family members, when all along, they most certainly believed she had killed a King. She was fearful of facing any of them.

Ever since King Thoas was saved and set adrift, Hypsipyle understood the illusion of his death could be shattered at any time. She accepted the unescapable possibility that one day, her idyllic life with the boys could come to a shattering and sudden end.

She chose to be banished through ostracism. Hypsipyle understood that her leaving the island was the best possible outcome for all concerned, even though she was the one, over a lifetime, who would be most affected. Her boys were still young, and would soon learn to live without a mother, much like they had lived without a father.

No one outside Polyxo, Ambrosia and Hypsipyle had any idea as to what was about to happen to their Queen. Not even Katerina.

In port that day, there was one boat only, from the Peloponnese and about to return fully loaded with produce bound for Argos and Nemea. Ambrosia approached the captain, a man called Nemos with an offer he couldn't refuse. She explained to him that Hypsipyle would be given to him as a slave, and not to believe her when she complained otherwise. On arrival in Argos, he could on-sell Hypsipyle. To keep her from knowing the ultimate plan, the captain was not to reveal anything of this conversation.

Unaware of Ambrosia's deal with Nemos, Hypsipyle thought that once in Argos, she would be free to start a new life as an ostracised citizen, with the sole stipulation was she could never return to Limnos.

Many people since have asked me why Hypsipyle did not complain openly about her punishment at the time before boarding Nemos' boat. Quite simply, it was this. Just prior to Hypsipyle boarding, Polyxo told her that the boys' lives would be in danger if she did not leave peacefully. Knowing that Polyxo was capable of extreme violence, Queen Hypsipyle of Limnos boarded the vessel thinking only of her boys, and hoping that they were to be safe.

Polyxo and Nemos had a simple pecuniary arrangement. Upon reaching Argos, Nemos was to be paid when he sold Hypsipyle as a slave and that he could keep all money received. He readily agreed to the plan, and the boat set sail. In Hypsipyle's mind, once she was to reach land in Argos, she would become a free citizen, ready to begin her new existence, whatever that would be.

Before I take a small and well-deserved wine break, there is one issue here that has never satisfactorily been explained, and a possibility that events could have turned out very differently. By Hypsipyle warning her father of the planned crime, and King Thoas not relaying the news to Stelios and other men, both Hypsipyle and Thoas saved Polyxo and Ambrosia's lives. If the King chose to pass on this message, surely Stelios and the others would have taken revenge. Just a thought!

CHAPTER 13

Nemea

Nothing much is known about the trip from Limnos to Argos. The winds were extremely favourable and there were no complications or delays. Although very sad, Hypsipyle was quiet and seemed to be locked in her own thoughts. She had no way of knowing what would happen once on land. The whole trip took four days. By daylight, the little boat made its way within eyesight of land, and by late afternoon each day, pulled in to shore to spend the night on the beach. Hypsipyle continued to sit alone and by all accounts, she hardly spoke to anyone.

Finally at its destination, Nemos explained that he had a friend nearby who could help her start her new life, but she needed to be patient for the time being. He asked Hypsipyle to wait on board the boat while he made some inquiries.

A short distance away from the port was a slave market, with slaves from all over the known world for sale to the highest bidder. Captain Nemos approached the market place with an unusual request for the traders. He met with them and said that he had a particularly nice business proposition.

Instead of buying a slave, Nemos told the traers he had one to sell to them. They immediately said they were not interested, and if he wasn't going to buy any slaves, he should leave.

Not to be put off so easily, he said he would buy a slave only if they went with him to visit his boat, and if they did not like what they saw, he would gladly buy a slave.

One of the slave traders, a man by the name of Vaiyos, could see an easy sale, so he agreed to go with the captain to the port to view this precious cargo. In the meantime, Hypsipyle was still completely unaware of what was about to happen.

Vaiyos was an unusual man. A man in his early 40's, he had spent a life on the road, travelling all over Greece, finding jobs where he could. Although he was born in Argos, he never really felt that he belonged, so he left at a very early age, and started his life of adventure. An accident one day at a forge where he was helping a smith make swords and helmets, saw him lose an eye when hot metal flew from the anvil and into his face. Now, he was forced to wear a patch over the missing eye.

Before his accident and when he was a young man, he spent some time working on boats, and once visited Myrina. He remembered Hypsipyle as a young girl who often played at the port. Although he never spoke to the former Queen of Limnos on his one and only visit to the island, he certainly recognised her, but fortunately, she did not recognise him. Why would she? He was now 20 years older, had a patch over his eye, and walked with a slight limp.

In deep conversation, Captain Nemos and Vaiyos stood on the pier next to where Nemos' boat was moored. Hypsipyle saw them standing there, looking up at where she was, and immediately came down to see them, thinking that this was the man the captain talked about.

As Hypsipyle walked down the gang plank, Vaiyos couldn't believe his eye. He whispered to the captain that he had a deal. He must have thought that he could get back 10-fold what the captain was offering him when he sold her later.

Vaiyos paid Nemos and walked back to the slave market with his new purchase. Still Hypsipyle had no idea what lay ahead. Vaiyos the slave trader knew he could get top price for her because as luck would have it, the King and Queen of Nemea were looking for a nurse maid for their as yet unborn children. They gave Vaiyos some definitive physical characteristics of what was required, and he could see that Hypsipyle fitted the description perfectly.

Not wanting to scare Hypsipyle at this stage, Vaiyos said she was to accompany him to the royal palace in Nemea tomorrow and she could start her new life there.

Back at the port, Captain Nemos completed the unloading of Limnian cargo and together with his crew, headed directly for the nearest wine shop for some nectar of the gods.

On my many years of travels around the known world, one thing is the same wherever you go. Captains of trading boats are hard workers, and lead a dangerous life, transporting goods between islands and the mainland, battling severe weather conditions, dealing with questionable sailors and trying to avoid the ever-present threat of pirates every day. But once safely ashore, with their cargo unloaded, they all proceed immediately for the nearest wine seller to sample the local produce.

At the slave market, Hypsipyle sat in the shade under a large olive tree while a slave prepared a horse ready for the trip to Nemea. Once in Nemea, the slave was instructed to proceed directly to the King and to inform him that a suitable nurse had been found.

Hypsipyle still had no idea she was about to become a slave. Vaiyos believed that it would be in her best interests if she was not told the true nature of the transaction until she arrived at the palace the following day.

Vaiyos arranged for Hypsipyle to sleep in a room above an inn nearby. Knowing a woman was going to be spending an evening in this establishment on her own, and in wanting to keep his investment safe, Vaiyos paid the inn keeper to make sure no harm would come to her. That night, Hypsipyle slept intermittently, thinking of her boys in Myrina, her father who she now understood to be alive, and what the day would bring tomorrow.

Before dark, the slave on horseback arrived at the Nemean palace and asked to see the King. Lycurgus knew this slave, and asked that he be allowed to enter the palace to speak directly to him.

"Do you have any news for me from Argos?"

"Blessed King Lycurgus, my master has found your nurse, and she will be delivered tomorrow. My master says that she is just as you wanted, but probably better that he imagined. He hopes you will be happy with your purchase, and that he looks forward to working with you again in the future."

"Tell your master that he better be right, otherwise he will pay for his mistakes in ways I won't discuss with you."

"Until tomorrow my Lord."

With that quick discussion, the slave swapped his stallion for a fresh mare and began the return journey to Argos.

Let me tell you all about this event here. When a slave on horseback travelled in one direction for this distance, he used only one horse. It was not an overly long trip, but it would have been too tiring for the horse to return on the same day. So, by previous arrangement with the King, who had done much business with Vaiyos the slave trader in Argos, the slave would swap horses, leaving his horse behind and taking another. That way, he could ride back just as fast as he came, but with a fresh horse for the journey.

Next morning, Hypsipyle woke to the sound of horses outside her room. The travelling slave had three horses ready for what looked like a short trip. Hypsipyle knew she was going to Nemea, but did not know how far away it was.

The slave, Hypsipyle and Vaiyos mounted their horses and rode off following a well-worn track leading out of Argos. The trip was uneventful, and they managed to spend some time resting the horses, and watering them in a creek along the way. No one spoke much. Hypsipyle's thoughts were again far away. The slave thought of his own eventual freedom so did not say anything, and Vaiyos was mentally counting his gold before receiving it. He rode with a smile from ear to ear.

In the early afternoon, with the sun still high in the sky, the three tired riders arrived at the doors of the Nemean palace. Hypsipyle was amazed at its opulence. It was nothing like the palace in Myrina — it was so much bigger and much more magnificent than the palace built by her father King Thoas.

Two female slaves came out to greet them, one gathering the reins of each horse, and one offering each weary traveller a drink of water. Hypsipyle was most impressed with the slave's actions. The slave rider quickly disappeared behind the palace gardens, and Vaiyos together with Hypsipyle entered the palace with the second of the women slaves.

The female slave asked Hypsipyle to sit on a wooden chair and wait while Vaiyos followed her through a set of larger doors. Hypsipyle was nervous and excited at the same time. She still had no idea that she was now a slave.

After a few minutes, the doors opened and Vaiyos came through clutching a leather bag and holding it very close to his chest grinning even more widely than he was on the way to the palace. His one good eye was weeping. He couldn't believe his luck. Apparently, the slave girl told the king that the new slave was just what he had been looking for. Vaiyos was rewarded even more handsomely than he had expected.

On his way out, he wished Hypsipyle well for her new life, and quickly walked out into the afternoon sun to find his new horse for the journey home. For Vaiyos, it was the happiest moment of his difficult and troubled life. The leather bag contained enough gold to secure his and his families future.

King Lycurgus asked the slave girl to bring Hypsipyle in to see him.

"Hypsipyle, may I introduce you to King Lycurgus and Queen Eurydice?"

Before Hypsipyle could speak, King Lycurgus asked for all other slaves to leave the room.

Queen Eurydice studied the new girl now standing before them like she would do so at the market, before buying a goat, or a pig.

She leaned in to her husband's ear and said something like 'she'll do'.

"Welcome to Nemea. Welcome to our home. My wife and I hope you will enjoy your new life with us, and one day, maybe if we are blessed, you will be the nurse to our first born."

Hypsipyle thought that this conversation was a nice start. She still had no understanding what her role would be, but the mention of children made her feel happier.

"King Lycurgus and Queen Eurydice, if I said I was happy to be here, I would be lying. I too am a Queen, from the island of Limnos, where my twin boys live in the palace without a mother. I come to you after a set of very tragic circumstances."

"Yes, yes. I am sorry for your loss".

The King turned to his wife and said — "well, that was a different story to spin."

"No, really, I am Queen Hypsipyle from the island of Limnos."

"Yes, we heard. So why are you now standing in my palace, as the nurse to my children, or should I say so more exactly, my future children?"

Hypsipyle could not bring herself to say any more, knowing that one wrong word could see her precious boys murdered. She thought better of it.

"I am sorry King Lycurgus and Queen Eurydice. I will not burden you with my woes. I would not know where to start."

At this stage, King Lycurgus did not believe a word Hypsipyle was saying. Queen Eurydice was the same. All she could think of was how lucky they were to finally have a nurse.

"She will do!"

With those words, Queen Eurydice left the room and asked one of the female slaves to show Hypsipyle her new quarters. The King studied Hypsipyle a little longer than his wife.

"I have had many slaves in this palace, but none have ever told me they were my equal. That is indeed a variation on a theme! I think you have a vivid imagination Hypsipyle. If you want to remain alive, I suggest you never mention that fanciful story to anyone else. Do you understand me?"

Hypsipyle did not know what to think or say. She stood very still with her head bowed in front of the King.

"Did you hear me?"

"My lord, yes. You will never hear that story from my mouth again."

"Good, now go off with Helen here and make yourself comfortable in the slave quarters. You start work tomorrow."

With a clap of his hands, Helen, the older slave and Hypsipyle, now the younger slave, walked quietly out of the Kings room, through a set of long and dark corridors, into the slave women's quarters.

Frightened and alone inside the Nemean Palace, it was now abundantly clear to Hypsipyle that she was a slave. Although feeling angry that she had been tricked, she also knew not to complain as the life of her boys depended on her keeping quiet.

So began the next phase of her life.

CHAPTER 14

Orpheus

Hypsipyle had been sold into slavery, and was now starting a new life as the nurse to the King and Queen of Nemea. She had all but forgotten about Jason and his Argonauts and was oblivious to events outside the Nemean palace. What had become of all the people she had loved? She knew her father was alive, but nothing else. What had become of her boys? Was Katerina looking after them?

She did not spend much time thinking about Jason, but from time to time, she did wonder what he made of his life after the Argo returned. Indeed, what had become of all the men who arrived on Limnos with Jason? Where were they now?

But what of Jason? There are many stories I have heard about what happened to him, but most of them are without substance. Here is what I know. Without going into his life in detail, allow me to give you a brief synopsis of what happened after he came back with the fleece.

Jason returned to Iolchus to claim his rightful inheritance. At this stage, he did not know that his father, King Aeson had been killed by his own brother Pelias just after Jason was born. As far as Jason was concerned, his uncle was merely holding on to the kingship until Jason was old enough. But on reaching manhood,

Jason asked his uncle to hand back the crown, but Pelias had other plans.

Remember that Pelias, who killed Jason's father a long time ago and usurped the throne, said to Jason he promised to restore the throne to Jason if he undertook a fanciful adventure to find the mythical golden fleece in Colchis. King Pelias must have been laughing to himself, because he truly thought this quest was extremely dangerous and practically impossible to achieve. He must have known Jason would go for it, and secretly hoped he would die in the process. With the death of Jason, the crown would still be his!

Moving on several years, and after one mighty adventure, which is a story in itself, Jason returned, very much alive with a golden fleece.

If you would like, I can come back after I finish this tale to tell the full story of Jason and the Argonauts. But allow me to continue with the current tale.

Along with the fleece, Jason brought with him a new woman, Medea who turned out to be a deeply troubled and quite unbalanced individual. Jason was infatuated with her. They marry, and it is not long before Medea gives birth to twin boys. What it is with Jason and twin boys?

In the meantime, King Pelias and his daughters, who were not about to relinquish their privileged life as royals, realise a potentially monumental problem in allowing Jason to regain the throne and desperately want to change the King's mind.

By this stage, Pelias wasn't getting any younger. His physical abilities were waning, and he actively searched for ways to take magic potions to make him younger again. He tried everything, and nothing seemed to work, but one day, his daughters overheard Medea discussing a remedy from Colchis for regaining a youthful disposition. This was a sinister trick purposefully played by Medea on the daughters, as the remedy was a death concoction of herbs and roots. Medea wanted to make sure that Pelias could not possibly retain the crown. The remedy could have been similar to the brew made for the men of Limnos by Polyxo and Ambrosia, but this one did not make you sleepy — it killed in just two days.

Pelias' daughters made the special mixture, and tricked their father into drinking it. Within days, Pelias had died, and the daughters blamed Medea.

Although not yet the King, Jason sensed something was not quite right with his wife, and feigned a trip to Corinth to escape for a short time to escape his responsibilities. In Corinth, he met and what do you know — he fell in love with a Corinthian princess. Wanting to marry this new woman, he came home with secret plans to leave his wife and move to Corinth with the boys.

Jason never truly wanted to become King of Iolchus. After Pelias' unfortunate demise and prior to his trip to Corinth, Jason spoke to his cousin, Pelias' son Acastus, who was one of the Argonauts and a dear friend of Jason, if he wanted to be King. Acastus agreed.

Soon after arriving back in Iolchus, for some reason lost in the passages of time, Jason unintentionally informs Medea of his plan to leave her, take the boys and marry the Corinthian princess.

Medea does what every normal person would do in this situation. She kills her own boys, thus depriving Jason of his dreams. She leaves him and moves away, where she starts a new life for herself!

Jason is so distraught and inconsolable, he seeks refuge in the bottom of a wine krater, and commences his slide into a life of unhappiness and loneliness. He can only remember the not-too-distant past when his life looked so promising, and the one thing he truly loved was being in charge of the Argo. His last days were spent under the bow of the rotting vessel sitting in precisely the same spot it was beached on its return from the epic journey to find the fleece.

The palace had lost a potential king in Jason, a queen in Medea, and the former ruler of the land was dead from being poisoned. Pelias' son Acastus dedicated funeral games in honour of his father, which were attended by many of the Argonauts.

I know that I have skipped over much of this epic story, but to go down that rabbit warren, we could take days. So, let me quickly finish.

There is a reason for this. You see, Jason never knew he had twins with Hypsipyle. Remember, he left well before they were born. When he had twins again, this time with Medea, he honestly thought that they were his only children, and he loved them dearly.

For many years after his death, people criticised Jason for leaving his first children, but as I firmly believe, he never knew anything about them, although he did know Hypsipyle was pregnant, and should have returned to find out the outcome of her pregnancy. For this lack of action, he stands condemned. The boys certainly understood they had a father, but never actually knew him as a father or a man. As far as they were concerned, he was of little consequence to them, and they were not curious enough to seek his version of events.

But this part of my story is where we reconnect with one particular Argonaut again, Orpheus. He was Jason's best friend. In fact, it was Jason who got him the job on the Argo as a musician, when all about were advising him to add another strong rower. Against all odds, and seemingly endless advice, Jason totally ignored them and asked Orpheus to join the team.

All throughout the Argo's voyages, it was Orpheus who was the story teller, the singer, and the one who immortalised Jason and all the Argonauts with his songs. To this day, Orpheus' songs are still sung all around Greece.

After the Argo returned with the prized fleece, which was nothing more than a large woollen fleece of a lamb that once placed on the bottom a river, gold flecks would stick to it, Orpheus decided to stay in Iolchus, playing to packed audiences in wine bars! He hung around with Jason and Medea for a while, singing his friends praises, but Medea was becoming unstable, and quite mad. He could see the writing on the wall, and wanted to leave to find his own way in the world.

Orpheus knew of Hypsipyles' boys, but never told Jason. He couldn't bring himself to upset the current state of affairs. Letting Jason know would only complicate things, especially with that nutter of a woman now married to his best friend.

Orpheus decided to leave Iolchus. He couldn't bear to stay a moment longer. In the days before Jason died, Orpheus was asked to sit with him under the Argo's bow. This location had become Jason's safe place where he could feel normal. Sitting there reminded him of the adventures he had with his Argonaut friends. He had his best friend with him now, and wanted to give Orpheus something.

Jason said that he had a gift for him. Reaching behind his back, Jason brought out the sword given to him by Hypsipyle on the beach in Myrina all those years ago.

"This is yours my friend. Take it and return it one day to Limnos where it came from. It is of no use to me anymore."

There were many words spoken between the two men, but on no occasion did Orpheus speak of his final conversation with Jason to anyone after that day. Whatever you have heard, Orpheus never broke that trust between he and his best, and dying friend. He hinted at it in some of his songs, but the lyrics are too dark to actually comprehend and connect to that particular moment.

We can only imagine how sad Jason must have felt at that time. Sad and only days from death.

Carefully carrying the sword with him, Orpheus left Jason on the beach and did not look back. This was to be their final moment together, as Jason died a matter of days later.

Devastated at losing his dearest friend, Orpheus departed Iolchus. He had one thing in mind at that stage, which was to return to Limnos, find Hypsipyle and explain to her what had happened to Jason. Also, and perhaps more importantly, to take back the sword, and present it to the boys.

Orpheus didn't make it to Limnos immediately. One night while playing his kithara in a wine bar, singing the praises of Jason and all of the Argonauts, a young, beautiful woman sat in front of him on a log and listened intently to everything he said and sung about. Her name was Eurydice, and this was love at first sight for her.

I know what you are thinking. How come there are two Eurydice's in this story? I can't answer that, but there were truly two women of the same name, but they were most definitely, not the same woman. A mere coincidence!

It took Orpheus a little while to feel the same way, and not too long later, they were married. For a short time, Orpheus forgot about his sadness at losing Jason, and overlooked his promise to take the sword back to Limnos, because for now, he was deeply in love.

Orpheus and Eurydice travelled all over Greece together. They made a living from Orpheus' performances in any wine bar, private house or palace that would have him. His reputation was growing. His musical ability, already as good as anybody around, was getting better. His songs were less about the sadness of losing a friend, and more about finding that true love and being in love. It also helped him get work that he had such a beautiful woman by his side.

Still, his audience yearned for songs about heroes of the Argo, and Orpheus never let them down. A typical night of an Orpheus performance started with stories of his travels, moved to songs about love and sadness, and just as the crowd were crying in their wine kraters, reaching for anything to dry their tearful eyes, he would finish with some boys-own travel songs with tales of strong, virile young men on a faraway adventure. The crowds loved it and so did Orpheus.

Life could not get any better. Although Orpheus had not visited

Limnos to hand back the sword, he did manage one day to find a sailor in Piraeus who visited Limnos regularly as part of his normal trading routes. He asked that this sailor take some money to Myrina on his next voyage and give it to the twins, and to say that is was from a secret benefactor in Athens, but not to disclose his true identity.

It was a matter of trust, and at first, Orpheus did not know if he could trust the sailor. When the sailor returned one day to say that he had delivered the money, and to pass on the thanks from the twins, Orpheus knew that he had done something right.

As I said, life could not get much better for Orpheus and Eurydice. But like any story worthy of telling, things soon began to change.

After one particular night when Orpheus won over a new crowd in a wine bar in Piraeus, he went home early because Eurydice insisted on remaining there as she was not feeling well. By the time Orpheus returned home, she was very sick and getting worse by the minute.

He sent for a doctor, who came immediately. The situation was grim. Eurydice lasted for another few days, but died a painful death in the arms of her one true love. No doctor could say what actually happened, or what caused her death. It was a complete mystery to all concerned.

Understandably, Orpheus was totally devastated. For months after her death, he too found solace in the bottom of a wine krater. His performances became darker with songs only about death, dying, and lost love. His audiences soon faded away too, as they only wanted to be uplifted with his kithara playing and beautiful singing.

Performances were cancelled and soon Orpheus ceased performing altogether. His hair and beard grew long, and his personal hygiene suffered through a lack of washing. The only time he felt water was when it rained as he trudged along the streets of Athens! Like Jason, he was headed on a downward spiral with only one possible ending to his short life.

By chance, a young man by the name of Nicko, who was an artist for hire, and also down on his luck, met Orpheus in a wine bar one night. Both very drunk on cheap and unadulterated wine, Nicko invited Orpheus back to his home to sleep it off. The next day, Orpheus woke to a new set of clean clothes, a proper breakfast of honey, eggs, bread soaked in olive oil and fresh cheese.

"Time you got back on the donkey my friend", said Nicko as he stood over Orpheus, waiting for him to wake from a wine induced stupor.

"What do you mean, get back on the donkey? I hate the animals! All they do is fart, shit, eat grass and fart again. But then again, it is a nice lyric. It could easily be put to a melody."

"I mean it is time to stop killing yourself with wine, and get back to what it is that you do best."

"What would you know about sadness, pain and death...my friend?"

"Orpheus, I am an artist. All artists have suffered. It's what makes us who we are. There is nothing special about your pain. We all have it, now it is time for you to get over it, never forget, but move on with your life. You have so much yet to offer the world"

Or so the conversation went. Orpheus and Nicko had so much in common, they spent the better part of the next ten days, discussing who had suffered the most, who had drunk the most, and who was the saddest. Nicko too had lost a wife to a sudden and painful death, and spent a year wandering around Greece, wearing nothing but the one chiton until it fell off in the wind one day. Some say it disintegrated, and some say he did it on purpose, to be free of any clothing.

In Nicko's state, wandering from wine bar to wine bar in search of a reason to live, but found nothing but pain and misery. But he did have a skill. He could draw, so he combined his two favourite pastimes, which were drinking wine and drawing.

He told Orpheus of the wine bar they met the night before, and how Nicko had found a way to make a living. He drew the images of faces onto wine kraters, so all visiting patrons had their own, personal drinking vessel in the bar. People loved it so much that the owners of the wine bar let Nicko's skill be sold to the highest bidder so that people could come to the bar, hire Nicko to draw them a facial likeness on their own krater and then they were permitted to take it away from the bar if they so wanted. Nicko now had a paying job, and the wine bar grew in higher patronage, simply due to the skill of the new artist.

Nicko's fame grew so much that he had no time for drinking and only time for drawing. The bar sold wine in large kraters with an image of grapes and a vineyard, where customers could now take away the wine, for a price that is!

Orpheus was amazed at Nicko's story and decided one night to come to the wine bar to watch him working. After much convincing from Nicko, the two hairy artists walked together to the wine bar. They must have looked like twins, as both men had long black hair tied at the nape of the neck with a piece of leather, and long beards. Now I think of it, they probably did not look like anything out of the ordinary at all in Athens.

The venue of Nicko's new employer was a wine bar on the port at Piraeus, frequented by sailors, prostitutes, men conducting business and the odd respectable traveller simply looking for a good wine to drink.

Soon after the sun disappeared, Nicko commenced his work. There was already a line of new customers wanting to get their own krater. Orpheus sat in a corner and observed the situation. He hadn't noticed, but behind where he was sitting, was a kithara leaning against a stool. All around the beautiful instrument were painted images of Orpheus' life.

Knowing it had been carefully painted by Nicko over the last few weeks, Orpheus thought it was the most beautiful instrument he had ever seen.

While this was happening, Nicko jokingly told his employers that the new man in the corner was none other than the famous singer, kithara player and Argonaut, Orpheus!

Having seen Orpheus once a few years before, the man before him looked nothing like the image he had in his mind of the great singer and kithara player.

"My friend, that man you have brought in is not Orpheus. I have seen him perform, heard him sing and that is not him. I thought Orpheus died of a broken heart at losing his wife."

Nicko asked his employer "Can he sing and play the kithara quietly in the corner, while you make money selling wine and I make you even more money by drawing?"

"Go ahead. I bet he can't sing a note or even play a tune about sheep! I bet he will be so bad that it will drive all my customers away. I fact, if one customer leaves because of his singing, you won't be paid for this week's work."

Nicko was a cunning man. He immediately responded with a proposition his employer could not refuse.

"What if more customers stay longer and drink more wine because of his singing? What will you do then?"

"I doubt it, but to humour you, I'll pay him the same as you for one week."

"We are in agreement."

Listening intently in the corner, Orpheus wasn't too concerned about where this situation was headed. He must have missed his wife deeply, but at the same time, realised he had to do something to drag himself out of self-pity and deep anguish. Nicko had managed to do what many had tried in the past year. That was, to clean Orpheus up, and place him in a position to play music again. As his friend Nicko suggested, it was time to get back on the donkey.

Carefully observing the kithara, Orpheus could not help but wonder if this beautiful instrument sounded as good as it looked.

Nicko and his employer finished discussing the situation of the new musician sitting in the corner of the room, and then casually drifted back to their individual work. His employer served wine at the bar, and new customers sat while Nicko carefully constructed and drew their images on a wine krater.

Orpheus heard the wine bar owner doubt his musical credentials when talking about him to Nicko, so he did not admit to being who he was. There was no doubt many people in the bar that night who had heard him perform previously, but his longer than normal hair and beard hid his recognisable and quite distinctive facial features.

Orpheus picked up the kithara and began to sing a sad song about losing the one you love, and feeling that life was hopeless and heading nowhere, or something like that.

At first, he could not be heard over conversations all around the room. People were talking about mundane things, like how their vegetables were going, what trading vessels were arriving in port, current wind direction, the likely price of olive oil tomorrow, or some other tedious topic.

One by one, the wine bar crowd stopped talking, turned to the corner where Orpheus was sitting, and listened. So too did the wine bar owner. There is a story that the song was so sad, the wine bar owner, who was drinking from his personalised krater in one hand and serving customers in the other, dropped the krater due to how sad the song was.

He couldn't believe that a song could cause that much emotion. He must have thought that this singer was better than Orpheus! The wine bar owner began to cry, and wasn't alone. Many patrons did the same — cry that is, not drop their kraters.

By the end of the song, Orpheus was himself crying. He knew the song was sad, but he had never experienced such sadness himself while playing and singing. For many years, Orpheus performed the song with as much feeling as he could muster, but now it was personal. He had lost the one he loved, and he did feel that life was heading nowhere. He discovered a new element to his musical craft.

Physically drained and emotionally empty, Orpheus looked up to a sea of crying faces with tears enough to re-float the Argo. Normally, he would finish this song with a smile, but now, that gesture seemed highly inappropriate. He looked back at them with an expression that garnered more audience tears.

At once, he knew that he could perform these songs and give them the feeling they deserved. In the past, he was acting. Now, it was personal.

It seemed like an eternity, but it was Nicko who broke the sound of gentle sobbing. He too was wiping the tears away, as he remembered his own life and losses.

Thinking to himself, he knew Orpheus was good, but not that good.

"Orph......Orestes, that was good. Very good."

Orpheus then took the hint not give away his true identity, and spoke to the audience.

"My name is Orestes, and Nicko is my friend. He helped me to understand that life is worth living, and we can move on after immense tragedy."

"If you liked that song, I have plenty more, but now I would like to play a song an old friend taught me years ago. It was a song her mother sung to her when she was a little girl. He mother died soon after her 3rd birthday, and her father would then sing it to her every night so that she would not forget her mother. I think it went something like this..."

He didn't tell the audience that it was Hypsipyle who taught him the song. Orpheus had never sung this song in front of people before. He had filed it away in the dark recesses of his mind since Jason and he were sitting on logs of wood outside the palace in Myrina when Hypsipyle sang it to them for the first time.

Talented and gifted musicians like Orpheus can hear a song

once, forget it for years, and then retrieve it subconsciously at an appropriate moment. This was one such moment. But if you look and listen closely to the words, it fits neatly into a five-beat rhythm. This was one of the tricks used by Orpheus to remember tunes.

He sang this strange bedtime song for a little princess, and again, the audience cried, no doubt remembering their own mothers.

"I never knew what love was like my child. For love is like a flower in the wild."

By this time, the wine bar owner had filled every krater a second time, and Orpheus, or Orestes as he was now called, sang with such passion, tears were impossible to avoid.

The wine bar owner couldn't believe his luck. I don't really know if he knew that the famous Orpheus was the new singer, but he called him Orestes from then on.

That night, Orpheus sang for the first time in front of an audience since Eurydice died. He missed her so much, just as much as he missed performing. He now sung with raw passion. He sung with great joy. He sung like a god, and the kithara seemed to follow every word as if the two physically separate things were one.

He sang songs he wrote while on the Argo, and had never performed anywhere before, outside the crew sitting around campfires at the end of each day. These were songs about Jason, Hercules, Philoktetes, Atalanta, Laertes, Telamon and all the others. Over the next few months Orpheus appeared at this wine bar, he sung about all the Argonauts.

At the end of the night, Nicko had exhausted the supply of kraters to draw on. The wine bar owner had nearly run out of wine. So close was he to having a dry bar, he almost started to serve the good wine! He saved that for Nicko and of course, Orpheus. After all the customers had departed and gone home, the three of them sat around a table and opened a new wine krater, from the owners' personal stock. Words were not spoken for a while, and again, it was Nicko who once again broke the ice.

"Well? Can he stay?"

The wine bar owner looked Orpheus in the eye and said that he could stay as long as he liked.

Orpheus said that he would think about it and give him an answer the next day. Of course, the answer would be yes, but at this time, with three men sitting and drinking wine, life again seemed worth living.

Orpheus agreed to perform once a week at the wine bar, and while the owner was disappointed, he knew that he could make more on the night Orpheus was performing than the rest of the week combined, possibly more.

So began the friendship between Nicko and Orpheus. Nicko agreed not to reveal his true identity to anyone, and for the next few years, the two of them lived together in a new house Nicko purchased with the extra money he now earned. Nicko wanted to do more with his life than painting caricatures of people on wine kraters, so he started to work in marble, carving and polishing statues on request for wealthy new citizen clients of Athens.

Nicko seemed to have a different lady friend around at the house every night he was not working at the wine bar. He told Orpheus that these ladies were modelling for him so that he could form their likenesses in the statues he created for his affluent clients. He needed a different lady each night so that he could find the most perfect body form, or that was what he told Orpheus. Nicko conducted a lot of research into this pursuit. Orpheus admired his tenacity and dedication to his calling, but most of all, his virility!

Orpheus too dabbled in other pursuits, such as kithara making and teaching music. The two men set up their house so that Nicko had a masonry workshop, and Orpheus had a music school, which he cheekily named 'The Orpheus School of Music'. He liked his new identity, his new life and friendship, but there was one thing in his life that remained unresolved.

For these next few years, Orpheus sent money via his sailor

friend to Limnos so that the boys could follow their dreams and not have to worry about finances. In Limnos, the boys were making names for themselves, and were eternally grateful to their secret benefactor. He wanted to reveal himself to the boys, but could not decide when that time should be. For now, it was to be some time in the future.

CHAPTER 15

It's a boy!

Daily life for Hypsipyle had become repetitive and ritualistic. She woke at dawn, milked sheep and goats, helped the Queen choose what to wear for the day, gathered the royal clothes from the day before to launder, prepared food for the morning, cleaned the royal bedchambers, helped in the kitchen, worked in the garden next to the palace, and anything the Queen saw fit to ask her to do.

Hypsipyle, the former Queen of Limnos was now a slave to the Queen of Nemea. A long way from where she had been a year before, but the alternative was much worse. If she did not accept the banishment from Limnos willingly, her boys could have been killed, and she couldn't live with that. Despairing at her situation in life, Hypsipyle outwardly appeared calm and in control of her emotions, but internally, she was deeply upset with her new circumstances.

Although she completed these daily duties diligently and quietly, she did not forget her sons, or that they might one day be reunited again. From time to time, she would talk to her fellow slaves about her past life. They never told the King and Queen about these conversations, as all the slaves were someone else in a former life. They all harboured thoughts of returning home, but current circumstances did not permit this. The slaves had their own secret pact and freely conversed with each other when they felt safe to do so. Although captive inside a palace, their minds and thoughts were free to travel anywhere they desired.

Hypsipyle made friends with the other slaves in the palace. Humility was one thing her father Thoas taught her from a young age. In Limnos, Hypsipyle was more of a friend to all the palace servants than a princess or queen. When they were ill, she would help care for them. When they were carrying heavy loads, she offered to help. She did her share of the menial chores around the palace on a daily basis. To Hypsipyle, it was perfectly normal to do these things.

Life was gaining some degree of familiarity. However, one thing was not happening as planned. Queen Eurydice was not yet pregnant. No matter who was brought into the palace to try to help with the royal pregnancy, nothing worked. They tried everything. Lycurgus drank red wine tainted with a rabbit's womb, and Eurydice drank red wine mixed with rabbit testicles, and wine mixed with cinnamon and honey! Still nothing.

Many years passed with no change in the Queen's condition when suddenly, everything changed. Queen Eurydice was pregnant. King Lycurgus was overjoyed, but Hypsipyle encouraged him not to upset the Queen by becoming too excited and having unrealistic expectations.

Lycurgus agreed with Hypsipyle's suggestions, and quietly kept his enthusiasm at bay. When no one was looking, he beamed with joy at the prospect of becoming a father, and more importantly, Eurydice becoming a mother. In public, he held the same emotionless expressions as he had always done.

No one in the palace knew of the impending birth for many months, until it was abundantly clear that the Queen was carrying a child. Hypsipyle was quietly excited too, because her life would soon change if the birth was a success. She would be the full-time nurse for this child, and her daily life of chores would be replaced with the joy of caring for a little person, something she greatly missed. Her own life as a mother of twins was amplified with the births of all other argonaut babies so close to the palace, but still she was excited to be a witness once again to the miracle of child birth.

In the weeks leading up to the birth, she missed her own boys more than ever. Watching the belly of Eurydice grow each day gave Hypsipyle conflicting feelings. Desperately sad at the thought of not being with her boys, and very excited for the Queen, knowing how happy she would be at becoming a mother.

Each day Hypsipyle carried out her chores without fuss or bother, but before retiring for the night, she would sit alone and wonder about her precious boys. How old were they now? Did they miss her? What were their personalities like? What had Polyxo told them? Who was looking after them? Was she kind and gentle with them? Each night was the same. She sat and wondered about a life that must have seemed so far away, but never out of mind. Hypsipyle never gave up hope of seeing her boys again, but she also could not let this hope take over her emotions and thoughts too much.

Days, weeks and months went by very quickly until one morning, Queen Eurydice called out for Hypsipyle to come quickly to the royal bedroom.

"I think this is the day Hypsipyle. Quick, make all the arrangements for this birth, but don't tell the King just yet."

Hypsipyle sensed the birth was imminent, so she hastily asked Helen to bring all the birthing instruments, clean cloths and plenty of warm water. Even though Helen was the older slave, she had never taken part in a birth before, and Hypsipyle had all that experience from Limnos years ago. Helen was not a mother, and did not really know what was going on, or how to organise it all. She listened to Hypsipyle for the first time closely and followed instructions without hesitation.

Later in the day, Queen Eurydice gave birth to a healthy baby boy. King Lycurgus was sent for without haste, and on his arrival, with Eurydice, named the boy Opheltes.

Lycurgus was so exceedingly happy, he declared a feast in 30 days hence for all the kingdom, to be held at the palace, where everyone could pay their respects to the new prince. Invitations to the feast were sent by Lycurgus to friends, and dignitaries from neighbouring kingdoms.

Prior to the feast taking place, Lycurgus consulted an oracle to ask for advice on ensuring health and happiness for his child. The oracle suggested the child must never set foot on the bare earth until he had learned to walk. Lycurgus thought that this advice was a little strange but was not about to argue with an oracle. On reflection, he must have thought that not touching the ground was a small price to pay for guaranteeing his son gained the best possible start to his life.

Returning from visiting the oracle, Lycurgus told Eurydice of the advice, and said that she should instruct Hypsipyle to follow this instruction without fail. The next day, Queen Eurydice told Hypsipyle that under no circumstance should she leave the child alone, or to allow him to touch bare ground until he had learned to walk. Hypsipyle thought this an odd piece of advice but did not share her thoughts with the King and Queen. She dutifully followed her orders regarding Prince Opheltes, never letting his feet touch the ground, in case he crawled off too quickly for her to catch him.

Hypsipyle had her hands full from that day forth. Queen Eurydice was older than Hypsipyle, and not as agile as she would have liked to be. Eurydice continued to do all the royal duties a Queen was expected to do, and Hypsipyle became the full-time nurse to Prince Opheltes, whom she now loved as much as her own boys.

Her daily chores now centred around little Opheltes completely, with all her existing roles and responsibilities taken up by other slaves. She fed him, clothed him, put him to sleep, sang songs and only handed him over to the Queen in the evening or whenever the Queen requested, which was on rare occasions. Queen Eurydice spent the nights with her son but required Hypsipyle to be close by at all times.

Hypsipyle now had less time to spend alone with her thoughts as the needs of Opheltes and Queen Eurydice took up all waking and sleeping moments of each day. She now had precious little time to spend thinking about her own boys.

Over time, Hypsipyle would sing songs to Opheltes, imagining him to be one of her twins. Quietly, she would alternate each day imagining him to be either Thoas or Euneos. When anyone was in earshot, she reverted to calling him by his proper name, but when they were alone, she would pretend he was her own child.

Until the prince was able to walk, Hypsipyle carried him in a basket whenever they were outside the palace. All the slaves and palace attendees knew of the oracle's instruction, and Hypsipyle was not about to be caught disobeying this, for the punishment would most certainly be severe.

Life was finally becoming tolerable for Hypsipyle once again. The King and Queen were blissfully happy, Opheltes was growing and doing all the things her own boys did at that age before becoming independently mobile, and she was able to finally think of Thoas and Euneos without being too sad. Singing to the prince definitely helped in her transition from feeling like a slave to feeling like a mother again.

CHAPTER 16

Kratiras

Limnos has an excellent geographical set of natural conditions conducive to grape growing and wine production. Being an island, it is free of pests and diseases, has an excellent climate, well irrigated land with access to a constant underground water supply and enough sun in summer to produce succulent grapes. Wine from Limnos has been and will always be amongst the best quality in the whole of Greece.

During King Thoas' limited time as monarch, he introduced the idea for some local farmers to change their crops to grape production or at least to add grape vines to their land to see what they could grow. Thoas imagined economic benefits for Limnos in trade with other people throughout the Aegean and mainland Greece. After all, this was the reason he was sent to Limnos from Crete in the first place. However, he didn't really see the efforts of his labour, due to an unfortunate exit from the island before many grape vines bore fruit.

Vineyards set up by King Thoas were abandoned after Hypsipyle was banished. Too many people linked grapes with Hypsipyle and left their grapevines to rot and be overgrown with weeds. Polyxo thought this was a drastic response, but could not think of a way to solve the problem.

It was not too long before she had a solution. Given the years since Hypsipyle departed, young Thoas and Euneos were now active young boys, looking for an outlet for their exuberance. Polyxo thought they needed a hobby. Not just to keep them from remembering their mother, but a hobby that could bring prosperity to Limnos. At first, Polyxo had them clean up the royal vineyards by weeding, clearing the ground, repairing fences, planting new vines and pruning existing ones. But later, it turned into something more than a hobby.

Well after their mother had been ostracised, Thoas and Euneos began their journey into learning all they could about wine, how grapes grew, what varieties existed, what ones were conducive to Limnian soil, how water and sun affected their growth and anything else they could learn. From being two little boys pestering anyone who could answer any questions they had pertaining to wine, it is fair to say they learned a great deal in a very short space of time.

Convincing farmers to take up grape production again, Thoas and Euneos became known in Limnos as the 'wine twins', and Limnos was fast becoming known again as a producer of fine wine. Their mother and grandfather would have been proud of them. By the time of their 12th birthday, they had already sold wine to Crete, and bought wine from a number of islands nearby. Limnos and the twins were developing a burgeoning reputation throughout the Greek speaking world.

Every day a new shipment of goods arrived at the port, the 'wine twins' were already there to ask sailors what they had for trade but more importantly, if they had any grapevine cuttings. Many of the regular traders were expecting these questions, and came readily prepared for the immediate interrogation from a pair of 12-year-old boys. Sailors brought cuttings of new vines in exchange for other delights such as dried figs and kraters of Limnian wine itself.

By the time they were 18, news had reached Limnos and all the Aegean islands of a potential blockade at Troy. Polyxo and the boys didn't wait for an official announcement of a war, so they started amassing great storages of wine produced locally and coupled with wine purchased from traders. The 'wine twins' were suddenly in a position to make a lot of money supplying soldiers with wine given the proximity to Limnos of the city of Troy, if such a conflict were to eventuate. If not, they would simply recoup their investment and sell, bit by bit, their already expanding wine collection.

Should they stock up on wine on the chance that a war was imminent, or continue to learn as much as they could about making wine? If such a blockade were to happen, Limnians stood to gain a considerable amount from the sale of wine to a thirsty army.

News came to Polyxo of a wine festival in the Athenian port town of Piraeus. Athens was a small city with visions of grandeur eager to impress the world with its modern and rapidly developing culture. City officials thought it might be a good idea to showcase this culture with a new festival dedicated to the God of wine, Dionysus. Polyxo and the twins decided that it would be a good idea for them all to attend the Dionysus Wine Festival in Athens. This festival was the best possible place to meet others involved in the wine industry, to discuss ideas and learn new techniques of grape growing and wine production. Polyxo was getting old now, and told them that she should remain in the palace, so the twins were to attend the festival with Katerina.

Thoas and Euneos had never left Limnos' shores. They were quietly excited about travelling to Athens, and most of all, seeing what the world was like outside their island home. Passage for the princes was booked on a trading boat bound for Piraeus, due to depart in less than a week.

While preparing for the voyage to Athens, Thoas overheard something that profoundly disturbed him. One day, Polyxo and Katerina were talking quietly in the palace, unaware that anyone was listening to their conversation. Katerina was deeply upset at having to lie to the boys about Hypsipyle's departure from the island all those years ago, and wanted to tell them the truth. Polyxo managed to calm her and say that it was still best for the boys to believe that their mother went off on her own free will, therefore abandoning the boys. To tell them the truth would only upset them, so it is necessary for all concerned to remain silent on the matter.

Part of Polyxo's strategy was to gently remind Katerina how her brothers died. "I would hate for any accident to happen to you, Katerina!"

This was not the first time Polyxo had directly threatened Katerina. Understandably upset, Katerina went to the cave from where Hypsipyle sent King Thoas out into the water and eventually to safety. The cave was a place Katerina visited regularly to be alone and to remember what had happened, and to remember her friend. It became her sanctuary in the same way that other women went to the Temple of Aphrodite.

Thoas followed Katerina to the cave and asked if he could talk to her. She agreed and invited him inside. Thoas and Euneos often played in this very cave when they were young, but he had not visited there in many years.

Katerina began to cry and could not stop. Thoas thought he knew why, but asked anyway. She sat down next to Thoas and told him everything, from the women's idea to have a ten-day celebration without men interfering, the men returning with their boats filled with young girls from Samothraki, the decision to kill all males, the drugged induced sleep after drinking wine, his grandfathers' escape, and most of all, his mothers' role in the entire episode.

Thoas may have thought he knew why his mother left the island, but this talk with Katerina proved he had no idea of the reasons for her leaving. He was speechless. He was amazed with Katerina's openness. How could all this happen? So many people he had grown up trusting were guilty of the vilest crimes. How could Polyxo kill her own boys? What kind of women was she?

Although Thoas had many questions, Katerina sensed them and continued her story, anticipating any possible questions Thoas may have had.

Throughout Thoas' short life, he had been told stories of how the brave Limnian men were killed or kept as slaves after trying to take the farm girls back to Samothraki. What he and his brother always wondered, but never spoke of to anybody, was how it was possible that not one man had ever made it back to Limnos if the stories were true of them being sold to slavery. He and Euneos just put it down to all of them being annihilated in a battle either on Samothraki or on the seas between the two islands.

Surprisingly, Thoas was not upset with Katerina for keeping this terrible secret from him and his brother. When Katerina had finished, she was emotionally drained and physically exhausted. She let her head fall into her hands and rubbed her empty, dry eyes.

"I am so sorry Thoas, for everything. Please forgive me, and most of all, forgive your mother. She is the innocent one in this. She has done nothing wrong, and paid a very high price."

"I am sure she thinks of you and Euneos every day, and wants desperately to see you again."

Thoas had many questions, but asked only one.

"Do you know where our mother is Katerina?"

"Sweet child, I do not know where she is, but I think I know who you can talk to about this. The day your mother left our shores, she travelled on a boat to Argos with a captain who regularly visited our port from that city."

"He hasn't been to Limnos for many years, but I've heard that he has since died. However, a sailor who was with him all those years ago may know something, and he is now a captain operating a trading route between Argos and Piraeus. His name is Korelli, and when you visit Piraeus for the wine festival, you can easily find him. If anyone can help you, Captain Korelli is the one."

"The person who should know where Korelli might be operates

a wine bar in Piraeus, called Kratiras. It is a well-known bar, but I cannot remember his name, but go there, find the owner, and ask him to tell you how to find Korelli. He did say to us on a regular basis that when he was in Piraeus, he immediately went to Kratiras to quench his wine thirst, just like he did here with Ambrosia."

Thoas and Katerina sat together in the cave for a little while longer. Katerina told him of the time she helped his mother deliver the boys and how happy the household was that twins had been born. She went on to detail all the events in the boys' lives thus far. Thoas was amazed that she remembered things he had forgotten. Like taking the boys for long walks after Hypsipyle left the island, talking of anything other than their mother. There were many stories she remembered, but the ones Thoas was most interested in were those about his mother.

Thoas and Euneos felt for many years that their mother did abandon them, so in order to deal with that horrible situation, they simply tried to put her out of their sentient thoughts. It was easier for them both to imagine their mother had died. But this time spent talking with Katerina in the cave certainly changed that for Thoas.

After he left the cave, he went directly to his brother and told him of the discussion with Katerina. Euneos had always hoped their mother did not leave on her own free will, and that something caused her to go. Both boys were shocked at the thought of their mother being alive, but equally confused. However, their shock had to be kept in check as they could not let anyone know what they now knew of the circumstances of their mother's departure so long ago.

Now more than ever, Thoas knew what to do. He and Euneos had to go to Piraeus, find Korelli, and hopefully find their mother.

To hide the true reason of their trip to the port of Athens a secret from Polyxo, the wine festival excuse was the perfect ruse. After all, the wine festival idea was Polyxo's. The next day, Katerina and the boys took a walk up to the fortified castle walls opposite the sanctuary. It was a walk they had done together many times when they were young, when the boys would throw small rocks down the hill to an invisible enemy hiding behind larger rocks. She needed to talk to them both without the chance of palace slaves and or village gossipers listening to their conversation.

It seemed to be a perfect plan. Considering they were going to the Dionysus Wine Festival with the full blessing of Polyxo, Thoas, Euneos and Katerina prepared their things in readiness for a boat trip to Piraeus. Closer to the day of departure, Katerina would suddenly acquire a mystery complaint that would render her unable to travel. The boys would have to go alone.

Once they were well and truly far from Limnos, and on their way to find Hypsipyle, Katerina would confront her mother with the truth of the boys visit. She was no longer scared of Polyxo.

Until that day arrived, Katerina, Thoas and Euneos were to act completely normally. However, the twins were excited about both their reasons to leave Limnos. There was a hope that Hypsipyle could be found, and they were going to be attending the biggest festival of wine the world had ever known. What an adventure!

On the agreed day of departure to Piraeus, the plan began to fall into place. The trading vessel Polyxo had booked for three passengers was in port, loaded full of produce to sell in Athens, and ready to set sail with the addition of the extra passengers. Luckily, no other boat was in port at that time. Thoas and Euneos were nervously sitting on the dock, hoping Katerina had not suddenly changed her mind and informed Polyxo of the alternative reason for their trip.

Shortly after the final loading on board the trading vessel, Polyxo came to the dock and spoke to the captain. She appeared visibly upset and told the captain the three passengers would now not be coming onboard.

Thoas and Euneos looked at each other with a shocked

expression. Almost at this point in time, as if written in the script of the day's plan, Katerina arrived and said to her mother that the boys should go on without her, as she was too ill to travel. She told Polyxo the boys were old enough, and could learn so much from visiting the wine festival.

Polyxo disagreed and once again informed the captain to set sail without these three. While this now loud discussion was taking place, all other cafe owners entered the conversation. Ambrosia and Stella sided with Katerina saying their business would grow considerably with the additional knowledge gained by the boys.

Thoas and Euneos said nothing. They were riding the tide of emotion of staying on Limnos and not finding their mother, to going to Piraeus to commence the journey of trying to find their mother. Because they could not show their feelings, they had to let the discussion take its natural course.

With the added strongly worded advice from Ambrosia and Stella, Polyxo reluctantly agreed for the boys to travel without Katerina. The boys were elated, and without any delay, stepped over the guard rail onto the boat.

Katerina feigned her mystery illness right up to the moment of departure. But before she left to go back to the palace, she walked up to the boat and asked Thoas to come over to her.

"Here. Take this", handing Thoas a small package.

"What is it?"

"It is a golden vine ring, given to your mother by her father Thoas, your grandfather. It was given to him by his father many years ago. Your mother knows this ring and if you show it to her, in case she does not believe you, she will know instantly who you both are."

With tears in his eyes, Thoas quickly secreted the ring inside his tunic and sat down on the deck. Just the thought of holding on to this artefact somehow brought him closer to finding his mother.

Katerina stood on the docks with Polyxo, Ambrosia and Stella, watching her beloved boys disappear over the horizon, en route to

Piraeus for the wine festival, but knowing they could potentially come back with much more.

Once the boat disappeared from view, Katerina miraculously overcame her illness. Polyxo still did not suspect a thing. The first part of their plan was now completed.

Many men have visited Limnos since the Limnian deed was done. None of them had ever known the true story of why so many men and boys were missing from the island. In the years since, the population of Limnos has gradually approached the gender balance it had before the deed. Births of males, male migration and deaths of older women had done enough to restore this balance. After all, the population of Limnos had nearly 18 years to recover by the time Thoas and Euneos left for Piraeus.

Katerina woke the next morning smiling and happy. She went about her daily chores with an extra bounce in her usually steady gait. Polyxo was amazed at her instant recovery from what appeared to be a serious medical problem, rendering the younger woman incapable of travelling to Piraeus.

Polyxo was by now, an old woman of about 70 years. Her power and perceived influence over Katerina had finally ended. Katerina was trying to decide how best to break the news of the boys' true purpose of their visit. This part of the plan had not been thought out at all, and she had one chance to get it right. She chose a public place to talk with Polyxo, which was Ambrosia's cafe in the port.

Mid-morning was a time of high activity in the port area. Boats came and went with goods for sale and for trade, and many sailors were sinking their last cup of good wine before their next journey into the Aegean. It was the perfect place and perfect time for a confession.

Katerina asked Polyxo to join her for a unique treat in honour of the boys visit to Piraeus. She asked Ambrosia to prepare a special plate of dried figs, goats' cheese, olives from Lesvos, freshly baked bread, olive oil, and dried fish. The extra surprise was a wine Ambrosia had now perfected. It was the same wine used to drug the men and boys all those years ago, without the addition of poppy juice to send them all to sleep.

This wine seemed to be a Limnian speciality in Ambrosia's cafe, enjoyed by all sailors who visited. Whenever a sailor tasted this wine, they instantly enjoyed it. Whenever Ambrosia sold this wine, she could not forget what happened to the first people who tried it.

Katerina asked Ambrosia to prepare a watered-down version of the wine for this special mid-morning meal. Walking by the cafe at that exact time, were a number of Polyxo's old friends on their way to extract drinking water from the town well, so Katerina invited them all in to share the special meal. They put down their amphorae, and joined Polyxo and Katerina.

Katerina did not hesitate. She immediately steered the conversation to the delicate topic at hand as soon as the women drank their first mouthful.

"Thoas and Euneos know everything. They know their mother did not voluntarily leave them. They know their grandfather could very much be alive. They know how and why all Limnian men and boys were killed. They know how you drugged them, how they died, and most of all, they are on their way to find out if their mother is still alive."

"In case you are wondering, they will attempt to find their mother, and may not return for a long time, should their quest be successful. You cannot change this now. It is fate. It is in the hands of the gods. You cannot stop them. You cannot get word to them to change their minds, and you cannot silence them. They know everything."

I am sure this speech by Katerina was much longer than what I have just outlined. I am also sure there were many attempts at questions from all women at that table, but Katerina kept her voice quiet, yet confidant. Normally, Katerina spoke loudly and very forcefully, but not this time. Choosing a public venue was a wise move on her part, as none of the women who were major figures in the planning and execution of the Limnian deed could speak out loud. There were too many witnesses.

Either none of the sailors heard what was being spoken about, or they simply kept quiet, but Polyxo could not afford to question each and every one of them as to what they just heard.

Polyxo was stunned, Ambrosia was relieved, Stella was sobbing, and the other women were also crying. In a way, it was a massive relief for them.

But Katerina had not quite finished.

"The boys do not blame you for what you have done — for what we did all those years ago. They do not seek to gain retribution. All they want is to find their mother and see what comes of that."

"Also, they really do want to learn about wine, so going to the festival in Piraeus is not a complete smoke screen as to their core purpose."

Polyxo should have been livid. She had finally been exposed, but she now felt relief too. She was also proud of her only daughter Katerina for having the courage to speak her own mind. She wasn't angry because deep down, she must have known the truth would eventually emerge, and they would have to live with the consequences.

"Mother, I love you very much, but the time has come for truth to prevail. No more lies and deception. No more threats. You can't change this now. We cannot change the past, but we can learn how to live in the future."

No one knows for sure what happened next, as the principal characters in this story had differing memories. Some say that Polyxo and Katerina embraced each other, and left Ambrosia's cafe to walk back to the palace together. Some say Katerina left and went to the cave alone. Some say Polyxo, Ambrosia and Stella sat together for the rest of the morning. Some say all the women sat all day in the cafe and got drunk. Over the years, stories told many times develop multiple endings, depending on who is telling them. Maybe what I am telling you now never happened like I say it did, but no one can ever say one way or another. You will just have to have faith in me that I have done my homework.

Either way, what we do know for sure is Polyxo went to bed that night, and did not wake up.

CHAPTER 17

The Dionysus Wine Festival — part 1

Thoas and Euneos survived the trip to Piraeus, but only just. Not accustomed to long distance sea travel, the boys were violently ill for the first two days, but had vastly improved for the final day's travel. Before their vessel had even tied down in port, the boys paid the captain, and jumped onto the pier.

Not knowing where to go, Euneos asked the first person he met to seek directions to Kratiras' wine bar.

"Just follow the crowd. See, straight down there...."

Before the kind stranger had time to finish his sentence, Thoas and Euneos were running in the direction of the crowd. Within no time at all, they were standing in front of a sign over a shop door that said 'Kratiras welcomes all to the Dionysus Wine Festival'. A smaller sign under the large one read 'Tonight, the Great Orestes'. Euneos suggested to Thoas that they should go inside, sit, drink a wine and methodically plan their next move. It was just before their first mainland sunset, and Thoas agreed to his brothers' idea. They walked inside, found a small table by the door, and ordered a krater of wine.

Serving the boys was a young girl of about 16 who said her name was Ambrosia. Not lost on the irony of the situation, Thoas asked her to tell them what was in the wine as she brought it to the table.

"Wine", she said.

"Yes, I know that", said Thoas, "but how was it made?"

"From grapes."

"We seem to be getting nowhere. I know wine comes from grapes, but can you tell me anything about this wine? What are its characteristics? Is it a special wine for the festival?"

"Oh, I see. Yes, I can tell you."

Ambrosia told them how the wine was made, where it came from, what kinds of grapes were used and how old the vines were. As it turned out, Ambrosia was as knowledgeable as the twins in wine production, and much younger. The boys were in love!

Cheekily, Euneos broke the ice with a follow up question.

"Do you have a sister?"

Not many people who met Thoas and Euneos suspected they were twins. Although they were born identical, at this stage in their lives, they only shared some visual and obvious physical characteristics.

"You are not going to believe this, but I am a twin", said Ambrosia.

Thoas fell backwards off his chair.

"Are you alright? Is the wine too strong for you?"

"Not at all", said Thoas as he clumsily picked himself up from the dirt floor, wiping dust from his chiton.

Thoas looked at Euneos and smiled. Euneos had the composure to ask another probing question.

"Is she here?"

"Yes, she is. That is her over there talking to Orestes."

The boys looked in the direction of Ambrosia's sister, who was talking to a man holding a kithara.

"Who is he? Is he the one mentioned in the sign outside the front door?"

"Haven't you heard of Orestes?"

"No," they both said in unison.

"How long have you two been in Piraeus? Orestes is the greatest singer and kithara player in the whole of Greece."

"We have been here for only a few hours. We arrived from Limnos late this afternoon, just before sunset. I am Thoas, and this is my brother Euneos. We're here to learn as much as we can about wine production."

It was this stage that Ambrosia had to serve some more customers, so she left but promised to return soon. In the meantime, her sister Helen came over.

"I heard you are from Limnos. You must stay tonight for Orestes. He sings a song from Limnos, or so he claims. It is a song he says a friend from that island taught him many years ago. You will have to let us know if it is a song you know too."

Thoas and Euneos briefly forgot why they had come to Piraeus. Here they were in the biggest wine bar they had ever seen, far bigger than Ambrosia's in Myrina, drinking some sweet wine and eating freshly baked bread, being served by two beautiful girls, who happened to be twins, and who were about to be serenaded by some mysterious singer with a song from Limnos. The gods were truly smiling on them.

Euneos walked over to Orpheus, and introduced himself.

"My name is Euneos, and that love sick man there is my twin brother Thoas. We are from Limnos and just arrived today. We're here for the festival, but we'll stay tonight to hear you. I too play the kithara, but I am not very good. My brother says I play like Orpheus, but I don't think I am very good at all."

Orpheus was thankfully sitting down at this stage. For the last 18 years, ever since he heard about the twins' birth, he has sent money to Katerina to help with their education. He had never met them, and did not know what to do on the day he was to meet them face to face.

He just sat there and smiled at Euneos. "What did you say your name was again?"

"Euneos, and he is Thoas."

"From Limnos you say?"

"That's right. Where are you from?"

"Oh, I'm from everywhere. My life is too complicated for such a short conversation."

It was at this time Orpheus realised who this young man really was. He had an idea, but could not have been sure if it really was one of Hypsipyle's boys.

"Would you happen to be about 18 years old?"

"Yes, how did you know?"

"Just a wild and lucky guess."

"Anyway, if you can tell us where we may find a room for a few days, we would be very grateful."

"Young man, you and your brother are more than welcome to share with me and my house mate Nicko. You'll meet him later. I think you'll like him."

"You are so kind Orestes. Thank you very much. One more thing, Ambrosia said that you play a song from Limnos. What song is it?"

Orpheus was sitting in front of the son of the lady who taught him the song about 20 years ago. He had no idea if Hypsipyle ever sung this song to her boys, but he was desperate to find out.

"You will have to come back tonight to hear that song. I am sure you will know it."

"Ok. By the way — how much do we owe you for the room?"

"Consider this my gift to you both."

Orpheus was shaking with anticipation. Instantly, he could see Jason's characteristics in Euneos, and for the first moment in a very long time, wished his old friend was alive to see what he could see.

Euneos left Orpheus and went back to his brother, and told him of their good fortune in finding accommodation for the night.

Ambrosia returned with her sister Helen, and explained where they were from, and why they were in Piraeus.

"We are from Samos, and our family is involved in the wine business. We have been visiting Piraeus since before we can remember, and we work here in Kratiras while our brother Nicholas, and our father and mother go about their business," said Ambrosia.

"Nicholas should be coming any time soon. He is a few years older than us and will be visiting the festival for the first time this year. Normally, he stays home to tend the vines while we come here."

"We've heard of your island, and know of its reputation for wine. We too are here for the festival. Perhaps when you get time off work, you can show my brother Thoas and I around this city."

Helen chipped in and instantly agreed on behalf of her sister. The boys had not met anyone like these girls before, and were instantly attracted to them. At the same time, the girls had every man and his friend asking the same questions of them — that is to show them around. Every time, they had the excuse of work. The wine bar owner was very protective of these two young girls, and quickly removed any patrons who were getting too friendly when it was not appreciated.

Helen said that they could talk after Orestes' performance later on that night. The boys didn't know, but the girls were as interested in the brothers as they were in the sisters.

Thoas and Euneos left their bags containing fresh clothes and Euneos' kithara with the girls and asked if they could put it away until they returned later on that night. The girls agreed, and just as the sun set, Thoas and Euneos walked out into the night air. They had a few hours to wander around, clear their heads, and discuss what to do next.

Euneos suggested that first thing tomorrow morning, they ask around the port area if anyone knew how to find Captain Korelli. Thoas approved of his brother's updated plan, and the two newly established wine merchants from Limnos checked out as many of the festival's activities as possible, which included a lot of wine and food sampling. After agreeing to ease up on their wine tasting for a while, they returned to Kratiras.

Orpheus went back home, lay down on his bed for his customary afternoon nap, but could not sleep. He heard Nicko arrive with a new model, and ran to see him.

"Nicko, I must talk to you immediately. Something amazing is about to happen, and I don't know how to begin to explain it to you."

Nicko could see that Orpheus was highly excited. He recognised that look in his friend's eyes. It was the look he had when he was performing. Sometimes as a performer, singers are completely lost in their thoughts and words. Time appears to stand still and all problems are put on hold at that moment in time in front of that particular audience.

"Sit down, tell me, but slow down. You are not making any sense."

For the next hour, Orpheus told Nicko everything. From the time Hypsipyle taught him the song, to his final days with the boys' father, to wandering around lost until Nicko found him.

He explained also that there were to be two young men staying the night, and they might bring with them, two girls. That last bit claimed Nicko's attention. Orpheus told him it was the twins from the wine bar.

Apparently, Nicko had asked the girls to come back to the house and model for him on many occasions, but they refused every time. His reputation had spread to all corners of the world of his willing 'models' and their value to Nicko, the great sculptor.

"Should the girls come back to our house tonight, you must promise to not ask the girls to model for you Nicko. I know you. They are not the modelling kind. Do you agree?"

"Reluctantly, dear friend, I agree. I know how important it is for you to have Euneos and Thoas here. I will do as you ask. Would you believe me if I said that I had asked these girls to model for me before — only for modelling?

"No."

"Really! I honestly do want them to be models for me. They have perfect bodies for imaging in marble. Now I know who they are to you and your boys, I promise to behave."

Back at Kratiras, Thoas and Euneos had secured prime seats and a table near the stage. They had no idea that Helen requested the wine bar owner to save this table for some special guests, or they would quit. He immediately agreed and set up the table with a sign on saying that this table was 'not to be used by any customers'.

Sitting at the reserved table, Thoas couldn't take his eyes off the girls, going about their nightly work. And Euneos couldn't help noticing the kithara sitting on a chair in the corner.

A short while after they sat down, Nicko offered them a free wine Krater with their names on it. Thoas had no idea what he meant, and after Ambrosia stopped laughing, she said "Can you see all those kraters on that shelf? Customers who come here regularly pay Nicko to draw an image of them on a personalised wine krater. It is an honour for the great artist to offer you this for free. Take his offer!"

"We accept," said Thoas. Euneos did not hear any of that conversation, as he was still staring at the instrument.

"It is beautiful, and just like the one I brought with me, only better of course."

All Euneos' life, he had never questioned why he had a kithara at the palace. It always seemed to be there, and can never remember a time when it wasn't. He was told it once belonged to the great Orpheus, who left it behind when he and the Argonauts departed Limnos. Whatever its true heritage, he loved it, and played it as often as he could. Staring at this instrument on stage, he couldn't help but wonder about the similarities between them both.

Thinking the similarities between kithara's were nothing but a mere coincidence, Euneos settled in and ordered a wine from a freshly painted krater with his name and face on it. Thoas did the same, and the girls brought each wine out individually for them. Too distracted by their beauty and their own naivety, the boys couldn't see the girls had similar feelings.

The wine bar was now crammed full of customers. A good proportion of them were here for the festival, but there was still a sizable contingent of regulars, down from Athens for the entertainment. Orestes and Nicko had a reputation spreading the length of the mainland, and now it seemed, to many islands.

Following the usual entrance procedures, Orestes walked in the front door, greeting each and every customer he met with kisses on both sides of their cheeks. On the attractive ones, he actually kissed the cheeks and not the usual air kisses now so prevalent in this part of the country. Some were meeting him for the first time, hearing of his singing and storytelling capabilities from friends. His resurgent fame was growing daily.

Nicko had arrived earlier by a rear entrance and set up in his customary position, close to the bar, where he had all his equipment necessary to draw faces and names on new wine kraters. This specific work area was raised so that he could watch Orpheus perform. Otherwise, he would be at a level where he could not see anything. His line of eager new customers was already at approximately twenty.

All along the front section of the wine bar, the temporary walls were removed, and the audience had expanded considerably by the addition of more seating outside. Anyone inside the perimeter of Kratiras were served by the Ambrosia and Helen and some other young girls, and outside the perimeter were catered to by various wine sellers from many parts of the country. All regular festival activities were suspended for the evening, as Orestes singing was the main event in town. Even other cafe and wine bar owners were part of the expectant crowd.

Sitting directly in front of the stage, at their reserved table, were Thoas and a highly excited Euneos. The atmosphere was one of freshly poured wine, body odour, food from within the wine bar's kitchen, and outside where dozens of street vendors were cooking anything from roasted meat, fish, vegetables, roasted nuts and a whole assortment of food no one seemed to know what it actually was. But with a krater of wine, convivial company, grossly animated conversation, surrounded by like-minded people, the expectation of Orestes and his songs, these people would have eaten anything!

It was impossible to imagine a more perfect summer night. The sun had retired for another day, the moon was full, and the air was still with anticipation.

Orestes completed his audience greetings, and carefully made his way to the front of the crowd. He observed Euneos and Thoas, noticed they were being attended by the girls, and then stepped up to the stage.

As if it was pre-ordained, the entire crowd stopped talking. Water could be heard gently lapping the shores of the port area, and Orestes began.

Picking up the kithara that had been sitting on a lonely chair just off stage to the left, Orestes moved the chair to centre stage, sat down, and began to talk.

"Tonight will be special for many reasons and for many people. I guarantee you a wonderful night ahead, but for two very extraordinary people, their lives are about to change forever. My life will change forever tonight, as you will soon discover."

"For a number of years, I have been playing here, relating stories, singing songs, and even writing new ones while on stage. Many years ago, I came here a broken man, but my good friend Nicko picked me up, dusted me off, gave me a good listening to, made me wear new clothes, cut my hair, but most of all, became by best friend."

Nicko was oblivious to the crowd adoration, but sensed that something powerful was about to happen.

"There is one person here tonight that almost guessed who I really was on the first night I performed."

"I knew it," yelled Michali the wine bar owner as he spat out a mouthful of recently ingested wine.

With this revelation, Michali hushed the patrons both inside and outside. Instead of a quiet 'ssshh', he yelled "shut up the lot of you," at the top of his voice.

Sitting at their front row table, Euneos and Thoas were quietly demolishing some bread and fish, washed down with a second krater. They sensed something was about to happen, but could not have possibly imagined what it was exactly.

Orestes leaned over the stage and spoke to Euneos directly.

"This young man has been playing the kithara for many years, but has never played it in public before."

Euneos choked on a piece of bread and wiped his mouth with the back of his hand. Little did he know, Helen mentioned to Orestes about a kithara Euneos had brought with him from Limnos. Orestes asked Helen to secretly bring it up on stage, where he hit it under a blanket.

This particular kithara was one of the first pair Orpheus ever made. In the year prior to the Argo's departure, Orpheus had worked on many styles of kithara, but could not settle on a final version. Jason begged him to finish as quickly as he could, as he needed his musical friend to be the story teller and singer on the voyage. Orpheus completed the task in time, and spent the final few days perfecting their look and feel.

Both new instruments were taken on the maiden voyage of the Argo, as Orpheus wanted to have a spare in case one became damaged. This particular instrument now in Orpheus' hands one more time had been played on the Argo, in front of Jason and all the Argonauts en route to Limnos.

For reasons only known to one man, Orpheus decided to leave one of the instruments with Hypsipyle and take the other one with him for the remainder of the voyage.

On the Argonauts last night in Limnos, and as such, the last night Jason and Hypsipyle spent together, Orpheus declared that he would leave the instrument with her, to pick it up another day some time hence. When Hypsipyle learned of this gesture, she asked Orpheus if she could teach him a song her mother had sung to her as a child and later, her father sung when her mother had died. It was a song to sing for very young children at night so they would slip peacefully into a night of deep sleep.

Orpheus quickly learned the song, made some minor improvements, and played it just the once on Limnos for Hypsipyle and her husband Jason. He could not have known at the time but Hypsipyle was pregnant with twin boys. This instrument was special to Orpheus in many ways.

Close to twenty years later, Orpheus was once again reunited with his old kithara. As he bent down to pick it up, a thousand mixed emotions ran through him all at once. He did not know how to feel. His fingers trembled and his eyes searched the room for Euneos and Thoas.

Euneos said aloud "That's mine. Look — that is my kithara. How did he get it? What is going on here?"

A hushed silence came over the crowd in anticipation of a night to remember. Orestes spoke quietly, but all patrons at the venue could hear with ease.

"My friends, new and old, those who have been here before and especially to those here for the first time: Welcome to Kratiras. Normally at this stage of the evening, Nicko has finished his paintings and is now well and truly into his second krater of fine wine."

"I normally say who I am, followed by you all loudly cheering."

At this moment, the crowd erupted into a loud cheer.

"Tonight, I am starting, or restarting my musical career, as myself."

Regardless of where they were seated, inside or outside, the audience were somewhat perplexed and certainly confused at the meaning of this last statement.

"Sitting in front of the stage, down to my right, are two fine young men all the way from the island of Limnos. They are here for the festival, they want to learn about wine, but they are about to get much more than they could have possibly imagined."

"Many years ago, about twenty to be precise, a group of my friends, who happened to be the finest, the fittest and most of all, the best looking young people in the whole of Greece, set sail in a boat that was named the 'Argo' on a voyage that was truly epic."

"You all know the stories. People like me have been telling them through songs for years now."

Orpheus hadn't said anything new at this stage. The crowd were quietly murmuring yet listening intently.

"I know I have said that many times before, but I neglected one tiny detail. I was on that boat! You see, dear friends, my real name is..."

"Orpheus. I knew it" yelled Michali the wine bar owner. He could not contain himself.

"From the first night you performed here, I knew I had heard you before."

"He is right. My name is not Orestes. I *am* Orpheus, and if it wasn't for Nicko and you Michali, I would be still be lost in a tragedy of circumstance beyond my control. I have been hiding in plain sight as Orestes, but now, it is time to be myself once again and for all time."

The crowd did not know what to think. Thoas and Euneos were stunned. Michali was crying tears of joy and so too Nicko.

"The first stop over for our little expedition was on the island of Limnos, where we received the best possible hospitality in the whole world. I will never forget that joyous time in my life. We were all beginning to know each other, and after two full days of rowing, a beautiful island came into view."

"Strangely, the island seemed to be over populated by stunning women, with no men in sight. The Queen told us the story of how all men and young boys went to a neighbouring island to help the local people deal with pirates, but never returned."

"Limnos was an island where women had suffered terribly, but were getting on with life, and doing everything for themselves, without the help of men."

"There were 49 men and one woman aboard the Argo at that stage of our journey, and we stayed on Limnos for over 60 days. We helped the women and children rebuild their city, and their lives. We also helped re-vegetate the island, and many of the male Argonauts planted some very special seed."

"On our last night in the capital city of Myrina before we resumed our journey, the young Queen of Limnos, who had been recently married to Jason, our leader, taught me this song."

"After she taught me the song, I made a few minor changes and sang it once in front of Queen Hypsipyle and Jason. After perform-ing it this once, I told Hypsipyle that she could keep my kithara, to remember me. I told her I would come back one day to play the instrument again, but it was now hers to keep forever."

Euneos was still stunned. He couldn't think of what to say. He simply sat there with his mouth wide open in a strange sort of smile. He did manage to say something. "That's my kithara, but you can play it Orpheus!"

"Sitting down here is the current owner of this instrument. I hope you don't mind if I borrow it for the night. It has been a while!"

"What many of you may not know is that this young man and his brother sitting next to him are the sons of Queen Hypsipyle and our leader Jason. May I introduce Euneos and Thoas?"

CHAPTER 18

The Dionysus Wine Festival
— part 2

Sikinos was excited about leaving Oinoe for the wine festival in Piraeus, but at the same time, equally terrified about leaving the island. At only 17 he was an established and successful wine producer and merchant with his father Thomas, and could have easily have slipped into a comfortable life on Oinoe with all he had achieved.

However, his father could see that his son was not going to be content with being merely comfortable. After all that Thomas had experienced in his life, he could see the need for Sikinos to learn much more. The Dionysus Wine Festival in the port of Piraeus was to be the perfect first trip to learn as much as possible and to bring back that knowledge to Oinoe.

The Athenian wine merchant explained to them both that the first place to visit would be a wine bar in the port area owned and operated by Michali, called 'Kratiras'. It was this place where young Sikinos could first make contact with other wine producers and sellers, mingle with the crowd, and generally have a good time. He told them that all the people who could help him with advice would meet at this wine bar on the first night.

Sikinos embraced his father and kissed him on the cheeks in

a farewell that brought tears to many eyes. After sharing some private and brief words with his father, Sikinos and the wine merchant stepped aboard the sailing vessel and made a good start with favourable winds for Piraeus expected for at least two days. Thomas was happy that his boy was in good hands, and was not in the least bit sad or unhappy about his leaving.

Unused to travelling by boat, Sikinos was quite sick for the whole trip. The only time he felt well enough to stand up was when the port of Piraeus was in sight. Once the boat docked at the pier, the wine merchant paid the captain, pointed Sikinos in the direction of 'Kratiras', and bid him a farewell.

"The wine festival will last for about a week, and then we'll commence the return trip to Oinoe. Enjoy the week lad. If you can't find any accommodation, you can always sleep on the boat. The captain won't mind."

With those parting few words from the wine merchant, Sikinos slung his bag over his shoulder, tightened his leather belt and headed in the direction of the wine bar known as 'Kratiras'. On the way, he met another young man called Nicholas, who was also going in the same direction. Nicholas had been in port for an hour longer than Sikinos, and was from the island of Samos.

"We are from Samos, and this is my first time here", said Nicholas. My sisters and parents are already here. How about you Sikinos?"

"I'm from Oinoe, a very small island just north of Crete. I work with my father there, but he sent me here for my first time to the festival, while he tends the vines."

"I'm not sure where mum and dad are, but my sisters work at 'Kratiras'.

"What do you know. That's where I'm going."

The two young men became friends immediately, and talked non-stop as they made their way to the wine bar. Just walking to a wine bar, even one as popular as Kratiras, was not easy. Along the way were many wine producers offering samples of their produce and food vendors presenting many local delicacies to hungry festival participants. Sikinos and Nicholas decided to arrive at the wine bar later in the evening, but thought a stomach full of food would be best option before sampling too much wine.

It was easy to forget time on a night like this. Both Sikinos and Nicholas, first time festival attendees and experienced wine producers in their own islands, lost track of time and arrived at Kratiras too late to score an inside table, so settled for a spot on a table well away from the music.

Too late to speak to his sisters, who he could see were busy, Nicholas suggested that they should stay on an outside table until he could get them closer. Sikinos agreed, and looked after their belongings while Nicholas went in search of his sisters.

It was only a matter of moments until Ambrosia saw her big brother in the distance, walking towards her through the crowd. The two siblings embraced immediately.

Ambrosia said that she was busy and would talk later to him, and Nicholas managed to quickly get out the words that he had met a friend and they had a table far away, and asked whether she could get them closer to the entertainment.

"Wait here", said Ambrosia as she pushed through the crowd to Euneos to ask if would be alright if two more young men joined them.

"Before you get any ideas, one of them is my brother, and I don't know who the other one is. Can they sit with you?"

"Sure. The more the merrier."

Nicholas negotiated his way through the maze of tables and chairs back outside to where Sikinos was sitting patiently, and said that they could move closer to the stage as he secured them a prime table near the entertainment.

Picking up their bags, Sikinos and Nicholas moved towards the front of the venue, much to the annoyance of many other patrons as their bags inelegantly banged into heads and bodies. They made their way to a table in front of the stage, where Thoas and Euneos were sitting drinking wine and waiting patiently for the singer to start.

Standing up around the small table, introductions were made, and the four young men quickly resumed their seats. Ambrosia hurriedly arrived with two fresh kraters of wine for her brother and his new friend, while Helen refilled the Limnian twins' drinks.

Standing on stage, Orpheus saw the new arrivals at the table, and gave a slight nod of his head to them all.

"What many of you may not know is that this young man and his brother sitting next to him are the sons of Hypsipyle and Jason. May I introduce Euneos and Thoas?"

Before I continue with more of the story, the twins had always known of their father, Jason. Hypsipyle had never hidden this from the boys. Jason's adventures were hardly ever mentioned on Limnos because there were many other Limnian sons and daughters of Argonauts who had also never met their fathers.

The twins sheepishly stood and accepted the congratulations from all in attendance.

Sikinos and Nicholas were immediately impressed at both their new table so close to the entertainment and how the entertainer seemed to know who their new friends were.

"As I said, Queen Hypsipyle of Limnos taught this song to me, and I will now play it for you."

Knowing how the audience had previously reacted to this particular song, Orpheus had an idea that any new people who may not have heard it prior to this night, would love it too.

Orpheus started singing with Thoas and Euneos adding to the wine-soaked choir. Euneos could not believe his luck. Not only had this song meant so much to him and his brother as little boys, it reminded them of their mother, who they had not seen for many years. Emotionally charged via good wine and now this song, Thoas and Euneos shed a tear or two at hearing the great Orpheus sing their mother's song.

Members of the audience who had been at the wine bar before, also joined in the singing. But there was one other member of that audience also singing along, albeit with slightly different words. Sikinos!

Nicholas was the only member of the table not singing. He asked Sikinos, who he had known for a matter of hours, how come he knew that song. Sikinos replied that his father would sing the song to him when he was a baby, to help him sleep. Sikinos simply thought the song must have been a popular tune and didn't think anything of the song at all.

The twins noticed Sikinos singing and thought he had been in 'Kratiras' before. After Orpheus finished, they asked Sikinos how he knew the song.

"My father taught it to me. What's the big deal?"

"That song was taught by our mother to Orpheus many years ago when the Argo was in Limnos."

"What's an Argo, and where is Limnos?" asked Sikinos.

Sikinos had lived a very sheltered life on Oinoe. His father had told him precious little about his life prior to being washed up on the beach, but always thought that one day he would tell his new son about his previous life, but that moment didn't ever seem appropriate. Sikinos never thought to ask his father about any of it. Few boys by the age of 17 ask their father about their past life. Their father is simply their father. All Sikinos knew was that his mother died soon after he was born, and his father was little more than a farmer who knew something about growing grapes.

"Limnos is an island in the northern Aegean, and the Argo was a famous boat that landed there 20 years ago on its first of many stops as a part of a much larger adventure."

To Sikinos' credit, he could not have known anything about that time as his father had left Limnos, and even the former

King Thoas did not know any details about the Argo and its adventures.

While the twins and Sikinos were busy talking, with Nicholas listening, the girls were busy serving wine and made sure they regularly came past the boy's table to replenish their empty wine kraters. Orpheus had sung more songs, but this was all oblivious to three young men on the front table. They were in deep discussion about many things. Nicholas continued to listen to them but was paying much more attention to Orpheus.

At the end of Orpheus' set of songs, and after he said it was time to take a break to enjoy some wine, he sat down at the table of young men and joined in the conversation.

Orpheus had noticed Sikinos singing Hypsipyle's song at the start of the evening and asked him how he knew that particular song.

"Like I told these two, my father taught it to me when I was a boy. He would sing it to me to help me sleep — or that was what he told me. I have remembered it to this day."

Orpheus replied "but that song comes from Limnos. How come your father knows it? Has he been here in Piraeus?"

"Not that I know of. Isn't the song a popular one?"

"I doubt it, but the boys' mother could have taught it to other people."

Euneos by this stage was intrigued by the conversation.

"Wait a minute. Orpheus — you claim that our mother taught this song to you 20 years ago. Is that right?"

"That is right."

"But you Sikinos, say that your father taught you that song around the same time. Is that correct?"

"I guess so."

Thoas asked Orpheus if he had sung the song to anyone since learning it and appearing at Kratiras' bar recently.

'No. Definitely not."

"Thoas. Remember after our mother left, our nurse Tinker would sing the song to us? She kept it up until we were nearly ten years old. She often told me that she sung that song as it helped us go to sleep."

"That's right. Tinker left the island soon after our 10th birthday, and we never did see her again. Maybe she sung it to other children after us. Who knows?"

Nicholas was perplexed at all of this.

"Sikinos — how old is your father?"

"He's much older than normal fathers. He is about 60 now, but in very good health."

"That settles it", said Nicholas, speaking after far too much wine.

"Your father Sikinos, is the father of the twins' mother. You are all related. He taught the song to his daughter, who then taught it to Orpheus. Your mother then sung it to you Thoas and Euneos and now your father Sikinos taught it to you."

Nicholas could not know how accurate his conclusion to the puzzle was and everyone laughed uproariously at the ridiculous proposal he made — especially because they had partaken of so much of Kratiras's sweet wine.

The only one not laughing was Orpheus. He had noticed the similarities between the twins and Sikinos but could not draw any plausible conclusions. Nicholas' story was incredible, but was there any element of truth in it?

Orpheus returned to playing his old kithara and entertaining the crowd with more happy songs this time. Gone was his melancholy of past nights, and his joy of performing happy songs was returning.

The night ended, and all festival participants departed to their homes, or wherever their beds were for that evening. Nicko had finished his krater painting, and had convinced a young lady to go back to his house for some modelling work. Ambrosia and Helen helped Michali clean the tables and sweep the floor, while Nicholas and the twins were also getting ready for a night's well-earned sleep.

Orpheus too was tired, both physically and emotionally. He was outside talking to many different people, accepting their adoration and promising to remember them next time he performed. Of course, he never did, but that didn't stop him from making false promises. On his mind was what Nicholas said about the situation. How could all these people be connected? How was it that a song taught to him by Hypsipyle 20 years ago be known by seemingly unrelated people? He was beginning to sense that somehow, all these young people might be related.

Leaving the bar together, Thoas and Euneos walked past Orpheus and wished him a good evening.

"There is no need to give us a bed for tonight. We'll stay on our boat. We have so much to do first thing in the morning."

Orpheus said he understood and would see them again the next day and that they had much to talk about.

"Tomorrow, we have to find a captain called Korelli. We believe that he knows where our mother might be."

CHAPTER 19

Captain Korelli

Korelli was from the island of Sami, near Kefalonia on the western coast of mainland Greece. He operated his boat from Sami to Piraeus, but for many years before the festival, he worked as a sailor for other captains. One of these captains had a regular route from Samothraki and Limnos to Piraeus and Argos.

In the months prior to the festival, Korelli had been busy transporting wine from Sami, Kefalonia and Ithaca to Piraeus, and returning with all kinds of common goods for trade such as olive oil, figs, honey, salted fish and meat. As well as these agricultural goods, his latest cargo was people, eager to partake in a wine festival dedicated to the god Dionysus, and keen to see how the new city of Athens was progressing.

Day two of the wine festival saw many new arrivals of people and cargo. Korelli arrived from Sami with a boat packed full of wine in specially marked amphorae. He had arrived early, unloaded his goods and was enjoying a relaxing moment on the deck of his boat, curled up against a pile of ropes and canvas sail.

Euneos and Thoas returned around midday to Kratiras to find Michali setting up tables in preparation of the day ahead.

"Michali — do you know where we can find a captain of a trading boat by the name of Korelli? We need to speak to him urgently if he is in port."

"I don't know if he is in port, but if he is, he will be down there by the warehouse. See down at the end of the port area, there is a large stone warehouse that is built right up to the water's edge?"

"Yes, I see it" said Thoas.

"If Korelli is there, his boat will be just past the warehouse. Look for a boat with a large wooden carved ram on the bow."

"Make sure you take a gift for him. Here, take this krater of wine, and tell him it is from his old friend Michali. Remind him that he owes me for his last visit, but this wine is on the house!"

Thoas and Euneos took the krater, careful not to spill any contents, and proceeded to look for the captain. The spotted the carved ram, and saw a man sleeping under its shade, curled up on a pile of old rope.

Not in a deep sleep yet, Korelli woke to find two young men standing above him, holding what appeared to be nectar from the gods.

"Are you Korelli?

"I might be. Who are you?"

"Someone who has some free wine for you if you can help us with a small request."

"Then I am Korelli. How can I help?"

Not knowing precisely what to say, Thoas said "We are looking for our mother, and we heard that you might be able to help us."

"Is this some sort of a joke? Do I look like I am in the lost and found mother business? Get off my boat! Go away and look for her yourselves."

This time Euneos spoke. "Let me try to explain our problem in another way. Our mother was Queen Hypsipyle, and we believe you may remember the captain of the boat who took her from Limnos many years ago, and where she may be right now."

At the mention of this, Korelli sat up, grabbed the krater and drank a long mouthful to quench his parched lips.

Euneos could sense Korelli knew something about their mother.

"Thanks for the drink. I remember Limnos. I used to travel between there and here many times, but I was not a captain back in those days. I worked for a captain Nemos, a bastard of a man who would sell his grandmother if there was a piece of gold to be gained. Come to think of it, he did sell his grandmother one time. Or was it his mother-in-law? I can't remember!"

"Can you remember carrying our mother or not?"

"Listen. Back in those days I did what I was told and didn't speak to any passengers. Only Nemos spoke to them. But I do remember a woman from Limnos one trip. She kept to herself and seemed scared. I can't remember her name, but when we arrived in Argos, Nemos spoke to a slave trader called Vaiyos."

"Where can we find him?"

"I will tell you something. I remember best when I have had two of these fine kraters of wine."

"Oh yes, the wine comes from Michali, but he says that you owe him for last time, but this one if free."

"If you want my memory to improve, I suggest you go back to get another one. Tell that sheep-shagging bar owner to add it to my account."

Thoas ran back to the bar and asked for another krater from Michali.

"Another one?"

"Never mind — I'll pay for this one Michali."

"You tell him that he still owes me."

With that, Thoas took a fresh krater of wine, and once again, trying hard not to spill any, returned to Korelli's boat.

"Thanks lad. Where was I? Oh yes, Vaiyos. A rather sad old man. He once lived on Limnos for a while if my memory is any good. He left many years ago to work for Nemos just like me, but we never worked together."

Getting angry now, Euneos asked again slightly more forcefully. "Where can we find Vaiyos?"

"He worked as a slave trader out of Argo. He specialised in finding slaves for wealthy clients. Finding specific slaves to special orders if you like. If a rich merchant wanted a particular kind of slave, say a young woman of child-rearing years, then he would find one. If they wanted a more mature woman, to look after children, he would find one. If they wanted a strong man to work in the field's, he would find one."

"But you will need to go to Argos. It isn't far, and I will help you find the next boat to be travelling there. Let me ask around today, and if you come back here by sunset, I should have an answer for you."

Thoas and Euneos decided to wait until sunset, but not waste the day. They hurried back to Kratiras, changed clothes, and mingled with other festival participants, swapping stories of wine production and anything else to do with wine.

Korelli sobered up enough to ask around if any of the other captains were headed to Argos in the next few days. It wasn't long before he had success. One captain he knew from his early days working in the Aegean told him that a boat from Argos was due in later that night. This particular captain knew for certain this would happen because he was waiting for some items on that boat to buy, and he also had some items of value to sell.

Pleased with his efforts, and now fully sober, Korelli began loading for the return journey to Sami, a process that would take most of the day to complete. After he was finished, and ready for a drink, he thought it would be a good idea to go to Kratiras to settle his account with Michali, and of course, to drink some more of his fine wine.

CHAPTER 20

The King of Athens

After his days aboard the Argo, Theseus returned to his home village of Athens, ready to take on the most important role of monarch. Athens had not had a king until Theseus assumed the responsibility. At the time of his ascendency into the royal role, Athens was possibly the smallest kingdom in the whole of mainland Greece. Theseus believed his village could grow to be an important city one day, due to its natural geographical advantages and climate.

On top of the acropolis high above the town of Athens, Theseus built a palace for his wife Phaedra, and their son Acamas. It was always a palace in constant renovation, never ever being totally finished. People would always ask when it was to be finished, but Theseus could not give an accurate answer.

For the next 20 years, Theseus worked tirelessly to build Athens into a much bigger and important metropolis. Not yet having reached city status, his plan for the village was that one day it would be a grand city, developed around and underneath the acropolis that his palace now occupied.

It was Theseus' idea to have a wine festival at the port area in Piraeus, a short distance from Athens, and a fast-growing port of significance in the region. Keeping to himself, he did not attend the opening night, but promised his wife they would go along to visit the stalls and bars on the second day.

To celebrate the first Dionysus Wine Festival, Phaedra secretly commissioned a statue to be made of her husband, and arranged for a local sculptor to commence the work. The sculptor was Nicko, and the process of sculpting the work of art began a year prior to the festival opening. After visiting a number of times throughout the year to check on the progress, Phaedra also asked Nicko to make another one of her. He agreed, and now had two very important statues to complete.

Word reached Phaedra of Nicko's completion, and she visited him a week before the festival to personally witness the finished product. She was amazed at the likeness of them both and paid him handsomely for his work. Before taking possession of the beautiful art work, which had to be taken up to the palace from his workshop below the acropolis, Phaedra asked if Theseus could come and view them.

Nicko of course agreed, and the day for this royal visit was the second day of the wine festival.

Staying at Nicko's house that night was both he and Orpheus, and of course the young girl he had taken home the night before, for some modelling!

Nicko had innocently forgotten the visit and was busy in his workshop in his usual sculpting attire — a loose chiton with bare feet covered in marble dust, when a slave entered to announce the royal party. The young girl from the wine bar quickly disappeared to get dressed, leaving Nicko no time to change clothes, standing in the workshop ready to receive the King and Queen of Athens.

Theseus and Phaedra entered with Deanus, a royal engineer, who was given the task of removal and installation of the statues at a later date. He was there on this day so that he could begin making plans.

Nicko apologised for his lack of suitable clothing, but Theseus told him not to be concerned. Immediately, Nicko uncovered the two statues, and waited for the king's reaction.

"Nicko, I have heard so much about you from my wife lately, it is a pleasure to meet you in person. These statues are excuisite."

The royal party and Nicko talked and touched the statues for a long time, with questions and answers coming in all directions. The King and Queen were asking about how he got started in the artistic world, what he liked about it, and from where he gained his inspiration. Nicko answered as honestly as possible, even to the extent of explaining his love of the perfect female body form.

From his bedroom, Orpheus overheard the excitement in Nicko's workshop and thought it was a group of Nicko's friends visiting. He thought it would be a good idea to go to see them, because he knew most of his friends, but these voices did not sound familiar.

Walking into the workshop, Orpheus first saw the two uncovered statues, then saw Phaedra, the engineer Deanus, and finally Theseus. The two men stood, like statues (ok, that was a small joke) and just looked each other. Nicko did not know what to think, and Phaedra had no idea of who this new person was. Deanus was still working out how he was going to remove the stone statues, and completely ignored the two human statues.

Theseus was the first to move. He held his arms out, walked over to Orpheus and the two men greeted each other for the first time in over 20 years. No words were exchanged. In each other's embrace, there were tears of joy, cheek kissing, back slapping and hair ruffling.

Nicko was the first to speak.

"Ok, you two obviously know each other. Spill the beans. How, when, where?"

"Phaedra, this is my old friend from the Argo, Orpheus. I have told you about him so many times, you probably forgot most of those stories."

"Nicko, this man standing here is the King of Athens."

"I know that," said Nicko.

"Not many people knew I was an Argonaut" said Theseus. "I certainly don't go out of my way to mention that part of my life."

"Why not?" asked Nicko.

"Let me try to answer that. The voyage of the Argo was a time in our lives where a group of young men and one woman set off to search for an object, but we found much more. We found sadness, death, loneliness, despair, friendship, and love. That journey was the end of some of our colleagues. Just look at what happened to Jason's life after it finished. Look at how his life turned out."

"While we were away, the world changed, and we changed. I returned and started my life's ambition to build Athens into a great city."

"I came back, and nearly ended my sad life. I watched my best friend die, and I stopped doing the things that I loved."

"But look at us now, King Theseus."

"Indeed Orpheus. Look at us now."

The two men had not untangled their embrace, and finally when they parted, they sat down together, looking up at statues of Phaedra and King Theseus.

Wiping away tears in his eyes, Nicko could not have been happier. He completed the statues to the royal satisfaction of King Theseus, and saw his new friend embrace an older friend. He somehow knew what this meant to both men and kept a respectful distance.

Orpheus asked the King and Queen to be his special guests at Kratiras later on that night. Accepting his offer, King Theseus said that it would be his honour to pay for all their drinks.

Deanus finally looked up, oblivious to all the surrounding chatter, and stated that he had calculated the angles, and worked out how to move the statues for installation outside the palace.

Laughing at this comment and apologising profusely, Theseus said he had to return to the palace to meet some foreign dignitaries and bid Orpheus and Nicko a good afternoon.

CHAPTER 21

A short life

Hypsipyle was oblivious to a serious situation unfolding on the doorstep of Nemea. In the years prior to Prince Opheltes birth, neighbouring city states of Argos and Thebes had been long term enemies of each other, but in recent times, they were at least on speaking terms, thanks to the work of King Theseus of Athens.

Since the return of the Argonauts journey, Athens and Nemea were seen as neutral cities in this dispute, over which the original causes had long since been forgotten. No one really knew why these two cities were enemies, but at least tensions had been temporarily cooled. But all that was about to change.

In Thebes, King Oedipus found himself in a spot of bother. He had exiled himself because he discovered he accidently killed his estranged father and married his biological mother.

Let me go back a bit here and explain this to you. Given how difficult it is for people to hear of news from other parts of the world, you may be hearing this for the first time from me. One more thing — this story is also in my repertoire of stories. A most fascinating tale if I do say so myself!

Where was I? Oh yes, Thebes.

Oedipus was the first and only child of King Laius, and a young woman named Jocasta. A year before Oedipus was born, Laius consulted the oracle at Delphi who informed him any son born would kill its parents. Soon after, Jocasta became pregnant and gave birth to Oedipus. On remembering the oracle's prediction, King Laius took the infant and handed him over to shepherds, ordering them to leave the baby in the fields to die. Unable to perform this gruesome task, the shepherds handed the baby over to King Polybus and Queen Merope of Corinth, who were childless. They adopted Oedipus and raised him as their own. For the next 20 years, Oedipus lived in blissful ignorance of who his natural parents were because he had no reason to doubt his current situation.

Later in his life, a seer from Corinth told Oedipus that Polybus and Merope were not his real parents, so he went to the oracle at Delphi to seek further clarity on this upsetting situation. On his way there, he met King Laius, quite by chance. The two did not know who the other was and became embroiled in a dispute as to who had the right of way on the road both were travelling. Laius was also on his way to the oracle.

The dispute quickly escalated and turned violent, resulting in Oedipus killing Laius, not knowing that he was his biological father. Oedipus was close to Delphi, and took the body of Laius with him, so that he may return him to Thebes for a proper burial, after consulting the oracle.

The oracle of Delphi told Oedipus he would kill his father and marry his mother. Still believing that Polybus and Merope were his parents, Oedipus was totally confused by the prophecy and headed for Thebes to allow Laius to be buried according to custom.

On hearing of the circumstances of his brother-in-law's death, Jocasta's brother Creon assumed temporary control of the kingdom as a regent King. Creon bore no ill feeling towards Oedipus surrounding the circumstances of the death and said that the right thing for him to do would be to marry the dead king's wife.

Unknowingly, Oedipus was about to fulfil the oracle's prophecy, without fully understanding it at the time. Oedipus dutifully accepted Creon's offer and married Jocasta, not knowing who she really was. Together, they had four children, Eteocles, Polynices, Antigone and Ismene.

Many years later, a messenger from Corinth came to Thebes with news that King Polybus had died. Oedipus was overcome with grief at this news, but the messenger said to him that there was one more piece of information he had to pass on. He told Oedipus that King Polybus and Queen Merope were not his real parents, and that he as a child had been adopted by them, after being saved from death by a shepherd.

On hearing this news, Queen Jocasta ran from the room, because she knew than that her husband was actually her son, and this son killed his father.

Oedipus realised after a few moments that his wife was not in the room with the messenger from Corinth. Oedipus then instructed his slaves to find his wife and bring her back.

Shortly afterwards, two slaves came back into the throne room to inform the king that Queen Jocasta had been found dead in her quarters.

Shocked at this sudden turn of events, Oedipus ran to find his wife, only to discover her personal slave crying over the dead Queen's body. On realising the shame and guilt she must have felt, Jocasta stabbed herself, but not before explaining to the slave why she had to die.

The slave told the king of what Jocasta had said, and Oedipus grabbed the blade and stabbed himself in the eyes, causing immediate blindness.

Oedipus had just realised the full meaning of the oracles' prophecy and that he had killed his father and caused his mother's death as well. Together with Antigone, he fled Thebes for Athens, and sought out his old friend Theseus. Oedipus and Antigone were welcomed into the Athenian king's palace, and immediately considered themselves in exile.

Oedipus had news taken to Thebes that while in exile, his two sons would share the king's duties, one year at a time, starting with Eteocles, who was the oldest son. Eteocles and Polynices agreed, and Eteocles assumed the throne immediately.

All was going well until the end of Eteocles' first year-long tenure as king. He refused to hand over the role to his brother Polynices and had him banished from the kingdom when the younger brother disagreed with the latest arrangement.

Annoyed and very angry with his brother, Polynices left for Argos to seek assistance in raising an armed force to help him take his rightful place as the king for a year. Polynices fully intended to only remain King for a year as per the original decree from his father, but Eteocles was in no mood to accept this latest request. He wanted to be King forever and was not about to relinquish the role and title to his younger brother.

On hearing this news in Athens, Oedipus died, and Antigone returned to Thebes to be with her sister. Antigone disagreed with her brother's hold on the role and told him to remember their dead father's last request. Eteocles told his young sister that it was none of her business and he would stay on as king whether she approved or not.

By now, you are probably wondering why I am telling this story. Stay with me, as you will soon learn why this story is relevant.

Polynices managed to gather some support in Argos from a group of unlikely comrades. First was King Adrastus of Argos. Polynices was assured of gaining his support because he very quickly married Adrastus' daughter Argea.

Then came Tydeus, who himself was in exile in Argos from his native Calydon, where he had married Deipyle, another of Adrastus' daughters. Tydeus' crime in Calydon was that he had been accused of murdering one of his relatives.

Next to be included in the warring party was Hippomedon, who was Adrastus' sister's son, and by this stage, a local chieftain.

Hippomedon was a large and powerful warrior, who did not hesitate in joining the group.

Another nearby chieftain Parthenopaeus from Arcadia could see the benefit to his territory if he joined the group. Like Hippomedon and Tydeus, the three were considered the most experienced warriors in the new group.

Capaneus was a friend of Parthenopaeus and Hippomedon. His ability lay with his enormous strength and size, but more importantly, his skill as a charioteer.

The last of the eventual seven leaders was the most reluctant entrant to the group. Amphiarus was one of the three kings of the kingdoms of Argos. His wife was Eriphyle, sister of Adrastus. Like Adrastus, he was considerably older than the others, but most wise. Amphiarus was a seer, and a returned Argonaut. He was extremely hesitant in joining the group because he could only see bad omens in its mission.

However, Eriphyle convinced her husband to join in what soon became known as the 'Seven Against Thebes'.

Polynices convinced the other six leaders to help him raise an army with the sole purpose of restoring him to the throne. There was to be no looting, raping, sacking or taking of slaves. The mission of the seven was purely to restore Polynices. It was this idea that finally convinced Amphiarus and Adrastus to join, as neither man was young any more.

With the help of neighbouring kingdoms who all had a hatred of powerful and arrogant Thebes, an army was raised and trained.

Setting off for battle from Argos, the enormous army struck immense difficulties in finding sufficient water and food along the way. What is normally fertile ground with enough running water, the army found the going very difficult.

On reaching Nemea, the leaders decided to rest the army in shade while continuing ahead to the Nemean King in the hope of receiving some assistance.

King Lycurgus had been approached to join the group previously but declined the offer due to his new family situation, and that Nemea was still seen as being neutral in any wars or conflicts regarding Argos and Thebes.

On the way to King Lycurgus' palace, Amphiarus and the other six leaders came across a slave walking in a forest next to the palace, carrying water in a jug, and holding a baby.

Hypsipyle was startled to see seven men approaching her in full battle attire. She sensed these men were desperate for water and not a threat to her or Prince Opheltes. Hypsipyle must have looked like a goddess when she spoke to these desperately thirsty men, but she did not feel like one.

Stopping short of explaining her life story, she did hint that she had a regal upbringing, but declined to say much more. She told them that she now was the Queen's nurse for the little Nemean prince.

Amphiarus did not recognise Hypsipyle at all, and neither did she recognise him. After all, it had been many years since they had met under very different circumstances. Hypsipyle had grown into a middle-aged woman and Amphiarus was a slightly older man wearing full battle regalia.

Polynices asked her if she could show them where a running stream was so that the army and pack animals could quench their thirst.

"I can tell you where to find the stream, but I have to remain here with the prince."

"My lady, if you could show us, that would save a lot of time looking for it."

"But I cannot leave the prince alone."

"Just rest him here on this flower bad, and show us. Please. We are desperate for water."

"We are in the middle of a very difficult drought, and water is scarce, but I can show you where to find sufficient water", said Hypsipyle.

Hypsipyle innocently lay the sleeping Opheltes down on a bed of soft flowers, thinking she would return well before he would awaken. She believed this act would not be in violation of the prophecy, as the prince was asleep.

She indicated to the men where to find water in a well camouflaged river, close by in the forest. Overjoyed at this find, Polynices sent a runner back to the army to come quickly. Soon, hundreds of soldiers, horses and mules arrived at the hidden river, drank sufficiently, and then filled all water jugs and containers.

Thirsts quenched, the leaders told Hypsipyle that if they were successful in their quest to restore Polynices to the throne in Thebes, they would return to pay respect to King Lycurgus and to treat her to a celebration worthy of the gods.

Not long after this was promised, the group heard a scream near where Opheltes was laid to rest on the bed of flowers. They returned as quick as possible to find a lifeless baby being crushed by a large snake.

Hippomedon did not hesitate and killed the snake to rescue the baby from its clutch, but unfortunately, the infant had died.

Overcome with grief, Hypsipyle pleaded for them to strike her dead right there as she did not want to go back to face the King and Queen. What had only minutes before been a scene of joy at drinking the life-giving water was now a scene of utter despair and grief.

Hypsipyle had to be helped along as she was too distraught to walk alone. Polynices carried the dead child, and the other leaders accompanied the sad procession of death back to the palace.

At the palace, Lycurgus came outside and could instantly see that his precious son had perished. Not knowing the facts of the matter, and himself overcome with grief, he demanded the slave women to come forward to accept her fate.

Raising his sword above his head ready to strike Hypsipyle, who by this stage had resigned herself to her imminent demise, Tydeus stepped forward banging his sword on his chest plate and said "Stop this now. Don't be a fool."

"Speak up and tell the truth for once, and put an end to the constant lies about your royal life and confess to the death of my son."

All other leaders stepped forward with their swords ready to strike King Lycurgus if he carried out his threat. Realising his own possible death, Lycurgus' resolve to kill Hypsipyle had waned, and he backed down, placing his sword on the ground.

CHAPTER 22

Visitors

Before I move on with this part of the story, I need to go back in time a few weeks, to the Dionysus Wine Festival and a certain two young men seeking passage to Argos.

Korelli had settled his account at Kratiras, and Michali was happy. With a gut full of good wine, and some delicacies from nearby food stalls, Korelli made his way back at sunset to find the boat and captain bound for Argos.

It wasn't long before he spotted his old friend docking and unloading his cargo. The two old sea dogs talked for a while when Korelli asked him if he could take two young men to Argos on his return trip.

"What is in it for me?" asked Davidus, the captain of the now fully unloaded boat.

"Remember your days working out of Myrina?"

"Yes, what of it?"

"Remember the Queen at the time."

Davidus thought this was a trick question, as there was no Queen when he lived there.

"There was no Queen. Just an old lady called Polyxo, her daughter and granddaughter, and two princes. If didn't really know them, as most of my days were spent on the great green, travelling between islands and the mainland."

"My main memory of Myrina were the great taverns in the port. Never seen, tasted or smelled anything like it since. Women seemed to operate everything. It was as if men were invisible, or never came into the village."

"I remember this one time when a drunken sailor had too much to say to the owner of one tavern, and before he knew it, his balls were precariously hovering over a sharp knife used for slaughtering sheep. I soon learned not to mess with that particular lady. I think her name was Ambrosia. One more thing I do remember was the wine she had. Never had anything better, although I would put Michali a close second to her."

"Do you ever hear what happened to the prince's mother?"

"Not really. I do remember something about her leaving in a hurry."

"I heard that she ended up in Argos, where a slave trader called Vaiyos picked her up from the port. That is the last anyone knows of her whereabouts."

"Vaiyos. That name is familiar. He no longer does any slave trading I'm told. He's still in Argos, but a respectable business man making pots, children's toys and ceramic objects. I think I know where he lives."

"The princes are here now and want to find Vaiyos, because they need to ask him about their mother. Can you help?"

"Normally, I would say no, but I did like my time on Limnos, and the princes, who were very young when I was there, were nice to me. They would come down to the port and ask me hundreds of questions. Very inquisitive little boys they were. I always wondered how they would turn out."

At that very moment, Thoas and Euneos arrived to see Korelli talking to Davidus.

"Is this the man who can take us to Argos?"

"I am that man. If you can wait until tomorrow morning, I leave on the first available wind after sunrise. I won't wait for you if you aren't here, as the winds can change in a heartbeat."

"We'll wait on your boat if that is OK", asked Thoas.

With that, the deal was agreed to and Davidus and Korelli returned to the festival to taste some more of Michali's fine wine.

Thoas and Euneos were nervous and hopeful that they could finally discover some news about their mother soon. After almost fifteen years of not knowing, and being so close, they were cautious not to raise any false expectations. First, they had to find Vaiyos and survive another stomach-churning trip by boat.

Morning came, and Davidus was awake early to set his boat ready to sail to Argos. He woke the boys and asked them if they could row. Although a favourable wind was brewing, they would have to row out of the harbour to catch it far from port.

Sunrise, and the little trading boat set sail with Davidus, his crew of sailors, and the two guests. Four oars rowing, with a sail up, Davidus was pleased and the boat made good progress.

During the morning after all four made good time with their oars, Davidus told the boys he remembered them from Myrina. He told of the times they would ask him questions, but they had no memory of it. After all, they were only about five years old at the time, and they asked questions of any boat captain that visited their port.

Davidus spent the rest of the day under sail and thought longingly about his time in Myrina all those years ago. Just before sunset, the port of Argos was in sight. Arriving at the dock area, Thoas and Euneos helped Davidus and his sailors unload, and by the time they were completed, the boys were utterly exhausted.

Helping them find a room for the night, Davidus advised them to get a good night's sleep and to meet again in the morning when he would take them to Vaiyos' house. After a quick meal helped along with watered down wine, the boys fell asleep immediately. You could say that they were asleep before their heads hit the straw.

A knock on their door first thing in the morning saw Davidus standing in front of the waking twins with a man wearing a patch over one eye.

"Come on you two. Time to get a move on. Get dressed and we'll see you out front of the tavern in a few minutes."

Not really thinking, the boys got up from bed, stretched their muscle-weary arms, splashed some water in their faces, and stumbled out into the bright sunlight of Argos.

Before they could gather their thoughts, Davidus was waving good bye, and they were now in the hands of a strange, eye-patched man with three donkeys ready and packed for travel.

"Who are you?" asked Euneos.

"I'm the man who is taking you to your mother. My name is Vaiyos."

Gathering their possessions, Euneos and Thoas mounted their donkeys, while Vaiyos walked next to his. After this slow procession reached the edge of the village, Vaiyos straddled his animal and the three men began their journey proper.

"Where are we going?" asked Thoas, as he settled into a rhythm on his donkey.

"Your mother has entered the services of the King and Queen of Nemea. That is all I know, and that is where we are going today."

Excited at the prospect of at last finding their mother, Thoas and Euneos attempted to hurry along their donkeys.

"Whoa. What are you doing?"

"We want to get there in a hurry. What is the problem?"

"What is the problem? If you try to ride these beasts at that pace, you will kill them, and then we'll all have to walk, so in fact, you will take much longer to arrive at the palace. Just let me dictate the pace we travel at. OK."

"OK. But can you tell us about our mother, or should I say, about the King and Queen of Nemea? What else do you know?" asked Euneos.

"Like I said. I simply went with your mother and with my slave to take her to Nemea — to the palace. It is my understanding that she was to commence her employment there. Honestly, I have heard nothing of it since then. I have never been back to Nemea."

"If you don't mind me asking Vaiyos, why have you not been back to Nemea since then?"

"Listen boys. I don't know how to tell you this, but your mother was sold into slavery. I was simply the last and final person who negotiated the transaction between someone on your island who wanted to get rid of her, the boat captain, and eventually the King and Queen."

"You don't need to tiptoe around the topic with us" explained Euneos. We know why our mother had to leave us."

"Then you know something I don't know. All I know is that she was to be sold into slavery for something she had done. I made it my business never to ask any questions of my employers, or more politely, the people who were going to pay me. I just happened to be in the right place at the right time."

"Vaiyos. Are you sure you don't know the reason why our mother ended up here with you, on the way to Nemea?" asked Thoas.

"As sure as I am sitting on this ass talking to you both. I don't know what she did. You don't have to tell me if you don't want to."

"You said that you once visited Limnos."

"That's right. Many years ago. I do remember you both, but we never did speak. You were very young, and I was only there the one time. Your mother was the Queen, and you two are princes — am I right?"

"Correct. We are princes, and our mother is, or should I say, was the Queen."

Thoas took a quite a while to inform Vaiyos on everything he remembered from Katerina and what Polyxo told them both over the years. Especially the details Katerina explained to him. Euneos remained hushed during this time, and Thoas didn't leave anything out. Vaiyos was stunned into silence. He must have thought to himself 'what a fanciful story'.

"I am sorry for your loss boys, but I had nothing to do with that."

"We don't hold anyone responsible Vaiyos. All we want is to see our mother again, and to take her home if we can."

"Look. King Lycurgus is a prickly sort of man when it comes to slaves. His wife even more so. There is a very good chance that you mother has been sold on to someone else. Please don't get your hopes up."

Vaiyos was genuinely upset now. After he delivered Hypsipyle into the hands of Lycurgus, he was paid most handsomely. The reason he never did go back to Nemea was that King Lycurgus paid him so much, he could afford to leave the slavery trading business and go into a more legitimate and honest form of trade.

"Listen boys. We need a plan for you when you arrive at the palace. You can't simply walk into a palace, claim a slave is your mother and then walk out again! That isn't going to happen. The King and Queen of Nemea purchased a slave in good faith, and you have no right to take away their property."

"Ok Vaiyos. I understand — I think" said Thoas.

"What do you suggest we do?" asked Euneos.

"When you arrive at the palace, tell them you are travellers on your way to Sparta and you require a bed for the night. Don't say you are from Limnos — in case your mother has said something. While at the palace, walk around and talk to the slaves, but be careful that you don't declare the true reason why you're there."

"I won't be there with you. I'll take my donkey and wait in town for you for two days. It is better that we are not seen together. Many at the palace still remember me as the slave trader who sold them to the royal family. Do you understand my predicament?"

"Perfectly well Vaiyos" said Thoas. "That sounds like a good plan."

With their plan now somewhat established, the three weary travellers and their donkeys approached Nemea late in the day.

Vaiyos found a place for him to stay and told the boys where to find the palace. It was not far, just a few more stadia to travel.

Thoas, Euneos and two very tired donkeys walked slowly towards the palace and before they could dismount, a slave woman came out to greet them.

"Welcome to the palace of the King and Queen of Nemea. What are your names and the purpose of this visit?"

Thoas and Euneos were even more tired after this day's travel than their previous trip onboard Davidus' boat.

Thoas spoke first. "We are two brothers on our way to Sparta. My name is Thoas and this is my brother Euneos. Is it possible that you can feed and water our donkeys and allow us to stay the evening?"

"I don't see a problem with that, but let me inform the King first."

The slave woman walked back into the palace, Thoas and Euneos slipped gently off their donkeys and massaged their rather sore backsides.

At that moment, King Lycurgus came out to greet them.

"Welcome to the palace of Nemea. I am King Lycurgus and welcome to my home. Please rest a while and join my wife and I for some food and wine before you enjoy a good sleep. You look like you need it. We'll talk later. Helen here will look after you until then."

Helen took pity on these two young, tired, and bum sore travellers. She motioned to another slave to take the donkeys to a nearby stable, and for yet another slave to take the boys to their room, where they could rest and bathe before dining with the King.

Too exhausted to disagree with the arrangements, Thoas and Euneos let the young slave girl take them to a room. Desperately keen to begin their search, both boys thought it would be better to wait until after dinner.

"You look dirty and tired. Please allow me to prepare a bath and to wash your clothes. Take them off and leave them here once I have your bath ready."

The young slave girl was most impressed with the latest visitors and went directly to the bath house to prepare a bath. She instructed another male slave to warm up some water and to pour it into the bath.

Once it was ready, she returned to the boys' room and lead them towards the bath house — without clothing! Thoas was too tired to be embarrassed at this, and Euneos was most impressed with the hospitality shown towards them both.

Inside the bath house, the boys gently entered the warm water and two other young women came in to wash their dirty bodies, and then gently rub oil into their skin. Two clean and aromatically perfumed chitons suddenly appeared, and two clean travellers dressed into their new attire, all with the help of the two latest young slave girls.

"Thoas — this is something we must do when we get back home."

"What do you mean brother — get some slave girls to bathe us and then to rub oil all over our bodies?"

"No, I mean get a bath house. This is fantastic. Much better than pouring water over our heads standing on cold stones in a courtyard next to a well!"

"I agree, but can we also get some slave girls to wash us too?"

"If you insist."

"Come with me" said the first slave girl who had shown them to their room. "You must now eat and drink wine with the King."

Thoas and Euneos were led into the banquet hall where the King, two other men and a woman were sitting around a table.

King Lycurgus clapped his hands twice and magically, food and wine appeared on the table from different directions, brought in by slaves.

"Now boys. What brings you to this city?" asked the king.

Thoas spoke first. "We are on our way to Sparta to visit the young King Menelaus."

"What is the purpose of the visit, if you don't mind me asking?"

This time, Euneos spoke, because he thought Thoas would not be able to tell lies quickly enough, and to be convincing. "We have just finished visiting the Dionysus Wine Festival in Piraeus, and we were told that Sparta was an excellent region for growing wine. We are from the island of Imbros, and we want to start planting grape vines there."

"I have never heard of that island before. Where is it exactly?"

Thinking much quicker than his brother could possibly have done, Euneos responded, "Near the island of Tenedos, just across from Troy."

"I hope your visit to Sparta is successful. Now, you must share some of this fine food and wine with me, but very soon, I have some important business to attend to with these people", indicating the other three seated at the table.

Thoas, Euneos, King Lycurgus and the other three house guests then shared some fine food and drank some fruity wine. After a short while, the boys asked if it would be impolite if they asked to be excused, as they were very tired. Lycurgus said no, it would not be impolite, and excused them, thus being able to return to his important discussions with the other three people.

Back in their room, the first slave girl appeared as soon as they arrived and asked them if she could do anything else for them.

"There is one thing we would like to do before sleep takes a hold on us" said Thoas. "We would like to go for a walk around this beautiful palace in the gardens if that is allowed."

"That is certainly allowed" said the slave girl, as she took them out a side entrance into a garden. "Remember to come back through this door when you re-enter the palace."

Thoas and Euneos waited for the slave girl to disappear, and then proceeded to stroll around the palace grounds. They met many slaves, but not the one they were looking for.

Dejected and by now very tired, the two princes retired to their room and drifted off into a long sleep.

That night was the best night sleep the boys had had since leaving Limnos. Perhaps it was the nervous anticipation of potentially discovering some news about their mother, but they were not getting their hopes up too high. It had been nearly 15 years since they last saw her. Would she remember them? How much had she changed? Perhaps she had forgotten them. Would they remember her if they saw her anyway? Most certainly, they must have wondered if she was even here.

Next morning, the roosters crowed to welcome and introduce the new day. All around the palace, the sounds of a household waking were heard. Dogs barked, roosters continued well after sunrise, and donkeys brayed. They heard footsteps on stones, water slushing in buckets, and conversations of slaves doing their daily chores. These were the sounds of a typical morning they were accustomed to. Was one of them their mother?

The slave girl came to visit them and said that their donkeys would be ready by about midday and asked them if they could wait until then to continue on with their journey. The boys agreed, as it gave them more time to search for their mother. She also left them their clean clothes from the day before and told them they were more than happy to accept the chitons from the night before as a gift from the King.

This time, bathing was as they were used to — a bucket next to a well and a handful of water splashed into their faces. Just as they were freshening up, they noticed a slave woman carrying a baby in a basket walking out the front gate and heading off to the wooded area just a short distance from the palace.

Thinking nothing of it, they continued to wash, then put on their own clothes and started their search again. The slave with the baby was now out of sight.

After an unsuccessful walk around the palace, they were starting to meet slaves for the second and third time. Convinced that their mother was not there, they retired to their room to pack and get ready to return to Vaiyos to plan their next move.

CHAPTER 23

The Golden Vine

Hypsipyle did not know what to think. Was Lycurgus going to kill her? Was this going to be the last few moments of her sad and lonely life? Would she never see her sons or father again?

Queen Eurydice by now had been informed of her son's death and she ran outside to face Hypsipyle.

"What have you done? What have you done to my precious little boy?"

Hypsipyle prostrated herself in front of the Queen and waited for the sentence of death. Not wanting to hear any excuses and seeing her son lifeless in the arms of Helen, who had now taken the little boy away from Polynices, Eurydice picked up Lycurgus' sword and held it in both hands above her head over the neck of Hypsipyle.

All seven leaders stepped forward to wrest the sword from Eurydice.

"What are you doing? This slave killed our son, and she must die."

Amphiarus stepped forward to speak. King Lycurgus and Queen Eurydice knew him well and did not try to stop him.

"My lady — we all saw what happened. Your slave is definitely not to blame for the death of the young prince."

"We were on our way to Thebes to help restore Polynices to the throne and stopped to ask your slave if she could help us find water. We begged her to help us as we have not seen any water for several days and our soldiers and animals were desperate."

"Your slave here helped us by pointing out a hidden river that we could not find ourselves. She only lay the child down in a bed of flowers on our instructions for a few short moments when a snake came out from behind a rock and struck the child. Hearing its cries, we rushed forward to help but alas, we were too late."

"If anyone is to blame here it is us, as we forced this slave to change her routine, only for a few moments. It was an accident."

"Is that true Hypsipyle? Is that what happened?" asked Lycurgus.

"Hypsipyle? What an unusual name. I once knew a lady by that name a long time ago" said Amphiarus.

By this time, Hypsipyle had stopped crying, and was standing in front of the Queen who had also stopped crying. She looked directly at Amphiarus now and remembered him. Wiping tears from her cheeks, Hypsipyle spoke in a soft voice carefully choosing her words.

"Your name is Amphiarus, and you were aboard the Argo with Jason. I remember you."

Lycurgus was confused. How could she possibly know one of the Kings of the kingdom of Argos.

"Hypsipyle. Speak now before we pass sentence on you."

At that very moment, Thoas and Euneos walked around the corner of the palace with their donkeys, ready to leave the palace grounds and find Vaiyos. In the distance, they could also see hundreds of soldiers and their animals walking towards the palace, along the track next to the forest where the hidden river is located. The boys were looking for the King to thank him for his hospitality, before they departed.

It must have looked a bizarre sight, with hundreds of warriors marching towards the palace, seven strange warrior leaders dressed in their full battle regalia holding swords, and a dejected looking female slave standing in the middle of all the commotion. Hypsipyle did not see the new entrants with their donkeys, nor the hundreds of soldiers walking her way.

"King Lycurgus and Queen Eurydice. I am so sorry for your loss. It was an accident. A tragedy that no one could have foreseen. I understand the loss of a child. I have lost two children, never to see them again. The pain never leaves you. The sadness is deafening and the loss of hope is blinding, but life does continue."

Thoas stopped his donkey with Euneos and walked towards the ever-increasing crowd gathered around this lady. By now, all soldiers had come closer, behind their individual leaders. Euneos had to muscle his way in to see what all the fuss was about.

"Where do I begin? I have never lied to you. I told you who I was, and you did not believe me."

"You are Hypsipyle, Queen of Limnos, aren't you?" asked Amphiarus.

Thoas and Euneos could not believe their ears. Could this slave actually be their mother? How many Hypsipyle's had they ever heard of before?

"I am Queen Hypsipyle of Limnos, or rather I was Queen Hypsipyle from Limnos. I was exiled many years ago for a crime I did not commit, but for an incident I did sanction, and will regret for the rest of my life."

"Amphiarus here was a younger man then. He and 49 other Argonauts came past Limnos and stayed with us, helping to rebuild our devastated island. We were an island devoid of men. Two years before their arrival, all men on Limnos were slaughtered for their part in the crime in abandoning their women for young slave girls from Samothraki."

Hypsipyle spoke of the deed at length and didn't spare any sordid details. She told of young women being held captive on Limnos by the men, the special celebration with special wine, the death of each male and the supposed killing of the King, which she admitted was a lie as he was set free. Not knowing whether her father was still alive, she expressed her life of sadness to all the gathered people around her.

She told them of the Argonauts, of Jason and how much the men helped rebuild and repopulate Limnos with children born to the finest athletes in the whole of Greece. Amphiarus smiled at the thoughts he now had, as he too left his seed on Limnos all those years ago.

"That is right. Your hospitality was most appreciated and many of us did not want to leave."

"Jason was their leader, and he and I loved each other very much. I know he left me behind, but he did not know he left behind his unborn twin boys. Had he known them, he would surely not have left, or at least, come back after his journey concluded."

Thoas cautiously stepped forward with Euneos just a few paces behind. He did not recognise his mother at first, but now, with her story being told like this, he knew she was his mother.

Ignoring his own sadness, Lycurgus looked at his perplexed and devastated wife and said "I told you she was different."

Thoas stepped into the tight ring surrounding his mother and faced her for the first time in nearly 15 years. He asked her what present she gave to her first-born child.

Hypsipyle described a ring, made of gold in the shape of a vine.

Not knowing how he felt, or what to say, he simply stood motionless for a few brief moments looking her in the eyes. Something was welling up inside him, but still he did not know what to say. Euneos stepped forward, he too looking into the eyes of this woman, and asked Thoas to show her the ring.

Fumbling with his clothing, Thoas reached into an inner satchel strapped under his chiton and withdrew a small cloth, containing a ring. Hypsipyle looked at both boys and started to cry.

Thoas took out the ring and asked her if she recognised it. By now Hypsipyle knew these were her boys and rushed forwards to embrace them both. All those present could see that Hypsipyle could not possibly have known this unless she was the boys' mother. She took the ring and held it in the air for all to see.

"This ring was given to my father, King Thoas of Limnos, by his grandfather King Minos of Crete. See — it is in the shape of a golden vine."

As you can imagine, there were many tears, hugs, laughter and much joy at this long-awaited meeting between mother and sons. All seven warriors were equally impressed at this rather unexpected turn of events. Amphiarus was annoyed at himself, not recognising Hypsipyle. He could see that the King and Queen of Nemea were still upset, but he tried his best to allay their fears and concerns.

"King Lycurgus, I don't know how you and Queen Eurydice feel right now but let me say again — this woman here did no harm to your beautiful prince. She did what any caring and thoughtful nurse would do. She gently laid down the sleeping prince on a soft bed of flowers and offered succour and hope to thirsty and weary soldiers. If she is to blame in his death, then so are we all. If you decide to punish her, then you must punish us all. Everyone dies, but we bear it."

Until this time, Polynices had remained silent. He spoke.

"King Lycurgus and Queen Eurydice. Do not blame this lady for the unfortunate death of the prince. If it wasn't for all of us searching for water, none of this would have happened. I agree with the wise Amphiarus. If you want to punish her, then you must punish all of us as well. Placing an innocent sleeping child down on a bed of flowers is not a crime. I will gladly give up the Theban throne to my brother Eteocles if I could bring your child back."

One by one, all of the remaining generals said the same. Each took off their battle garments, laid down their weapons at the feet of Queen Eurydice, and offered their bare chests for sacrifice.

Queen Eurydice could not speak. Her emotions were bursting because although she felt extreme sadness at the loss of Opheltes, she was now becoming convinced that Hypsipyle had not caused his death. King Lycurgus stepped forward in front of Hypsipyle, who by now was kneeling on the ground and weeping tears of sorrow and joy.

"Hypsipyle. It is clear to us now that you did not intend to kill my, our son. Your actions were those of a nurse who loved him very much, and you are not to blame in his death. To have these fine men speak on your behalf is evidence enough that you are now exonerated of the death of Prince Opheltes."

Queen Eurydice nodded in agreement, as she still could not speak. Amphiarus spoke once again.

"In honour of your son, we will immediately commence a contest in his name. Athletic events where men will compete from all over Greece to desire the great prizes of the Nemean Games. We will build a great tomb so that his name will live on. Come my Queen, dry your eyes for we will have a great festival in his name."

CHAPTER 24

Athens

Hypsipyle, Thoas and Euneos spent the night camping under a canvas tent close to Amphiarus and his soldiers. Amphiarus understood how important it was for the boys to be with their mother, so he allowed them the time and space necessary to reconnect again after so long. It was their first night together in nearly 15 years.

Arising before dawn, Amphiarus and the other six generals laid down plans for a great tomb, but more importantly, for the games that would eventually be as important in the whole of Greece as other major athletic tournaments. Later in the morning, soldiers gathered to clear land and to construct areas appropriate for each event. The games plan was for foot races with and without armour, boxing, horse races, discuss, wrestling, pentathlon, spear throwing and archery.

Waking up that particular morning, Hypsipyle could not have possibly imagined how the day would unfold. Everything was happening so fast. She had dreamt of the day she might be reunited with her boys again, but now that it was a reality, those dreams were now a distant memory. There were far too many emotions competing for her attention, she didn't know what to think. Although extremely happy to be with her sons again, she was also very sad at losing Prince Opheltes. She was sad for the King and Queen, who although had been her captors, she knew how they would be feeling at the possibility of facing a life without children.

This particular morning saw Hypsipyle arise at the usual time out of habit. For the past 15 years, she had a daily routine of servitude and specific chores to perform, and now she had none of these obligations. Amphiarus left the other generals discussing tombs and athletic games when he saw Hypsipyle was awake. The two old friends sat and talked for a long time while soldiers and two young men slept nearby.

Hypsipyle had never learned of the Argo's voyage after it departed Limnos. She had many questions for Amphiarus, and he was glad to talk about it because it reminded him of a time long ago when life was so much less complicated. Hypsipyle also wanted to know about Jason, and what may have happened to him.

Amphiarus spoke at length. While he and Hypsipyle were in deep conversation, Thoas and Euneos woke and sat with them, listening to stories about their father. They too asked about Jason, the absent father they never knew. Amphiarus was only too happy to speak positively of his old friend.

Hypsipyle was permitted to return her room to collect her meagre possessions and then asked to leave immediately. She was not permitted to say good bye to any other slaves who had been her close friends and family for so many years.

Sleeping soldiers soon gave way to waking workers who immediately joined the other generals and their soldiers to commence work on clearing land in readiness for an athletic stadium. Hypsipyle, Amphiarus, Thoas and Euneos remained at the campsite and talked for most of the day.

Amphiarus explained to Hypsipyle that as far as he knew, Jason had fallen on misfortune after returning from his time leading the Argonauts. He could not be certain if Jason was alive or dead because he had heard unconfirmed stories of both possibilities.

Deliriously happy being with her boys, Hypsipyle listened to Amphiarus talk of the ever so slight chance of Jason being alive.

After spending the best part of a day hearing of the Argonauts adventures and journey to find a golden fleece, Hypsipyle and the boys chose to leave Nemea immediately, and travel to Athens to spend some time deciding what to do next. They wished Amphiarus well with his quest to restore the rightful Theban king to his throne. Hypsipyle could not thank Amphiarus enough for saving her life, and had no way of knowing that this would be the last time they would be together.

Athens seemed to be a safe option for them as they knew no one there and could be reasonably anonymous. With the two sad and ageing donkeys loaned to them recently, they made their way back to town to find Vaiyos. Perhaps he could help them once again.

Vaiyos was waiting for Thoas and Euneos to return. He had heard what had happened, so wasn't surprised to see them with Hypsipyle. It had been 15 years since Hypsipyle and Vaiyos spent some time together. Now, the circumstances were very different.

"Before you say anything, I had no idea you were a Queen. I am so sorry for what happened to you. Please accept my deepest apologies."

"Vaiyos — I know you were only doing what you had been paid to do. I suspect all women in my position told you they were Queens, or princesses, or of noble birth. You were not to know my true story. I don't blame you for what happened to me."

Relieved at this rather potentially awkward situation, Vaiyos accepted her words, and offered to help them in the next leg of their journey.

"One thing you may not know my Queen, but I left the slave trade immediately after you. You were my last customer. I'm now an honest business man and I have made something of myself since then. I have a wife, and two beautiful children of my own now. If there is anything I can do to help you, just ask."

Thoas thought of travelling to Athens, and asked Vaiyos if they could borrow better donkeys to assist with that passage. Vaiyos agreed, and further added that they could keep the donkeys, potentially selling them if they needed to, after arriving in Athens. Hypsipyle accepted the kind offer, and asked to meet his family before they departed. Vaiyos was very happy to oblige, and introduced them to Sofia his wife, Vasilius his son, and Georgia his daughter. Vaiyos was very proud of his children and could see how important it was that Hypsipyle was now with hers.

After arriving in Argos late the next day, Vaiyos and Sofia insisted they spend the night before travelling to Athens. Hypsipyle agreed and fell asleep as soon as she was shown her bed. Thoas and Euneos talked to Vasilius and Georgia, and immediately became friends, promising to meet up again one day in the future.

The next morning, Sofia noticed that Hypsipyle was in desperate need of some clothes, so offered to help her. Hypsipyle refused the offer, but Sofia would not take no for an answer, saying that the new clothes were to be considered a loan, only to be repaid if they would ever meet up again in Argos. For the last ten or more years, Hypsipyle had only worn the rough clothing of a slave woman. Giving in to Sofia's polite insistence, Hypsipyle agreed to the kind offer of help.

On the morning of their third day in Argos at the home of Vaiyos and Sofia, Hypsipyle, Thoas and Euneos set off on three donkeys for Athens. Euneos thought it would be a better idea if they went first to Piraeus, at least to see if the wine festival had finished, and for him, maybe he could see Ambrosia and Helen at the Kratiras wine bar one more time.

Travelling slowly with their four-legged transport and stopping for rest when needed, the excitable boys told their mother as much news as they could remember. From their earliest memories of Hypsipyle, growing up with Katerina and Polyxo in the palace, entering the wine business and the multiple reasons why they had come to Piraeus, then finally to more recent times in meeting the twins from Samos, Michali the wine bar owner, Nicko the artist, Sikinos their new friend, and Orpheus the musician.

Hypsipyle drunk in her boys' stories like a thirsty traveller parched from a long walk in the sun taking a well-earned water break. In return, the boys asked Hypsipyle many questions about her life before having them. As you can imagine, they had a lot to share, and no topic was off limits. I won't go into details here, but it is safe to assume that there were no quiet moments on this donkey trip to Athens between a mother and her twin sons after an absence of 15 years.

However, there is one topic of discussion from this journey that is deserving of a special mention. Hypsipyle was most interested in hearing about Orpheus.

Logistically speaking, their trip was uneventful, and they arrived extremely tired with very sore backsides at the port of Piraeus and made a beeline for Kratiras. Michali welcomed the weary travellers and offered for them to stay the night to rest and wash. Too tired to argue, the three fell into a deep sleep, but not before having some of Michali's best wine and some fine food.

Immediately prior to sleep overcoming the travellers, Michali explained to Euneos and Thoas that they had just missed the girl's departure to Samos by a matter of days. With the crowds departing and life reverting to some form of normality for Michali, both Orpheus and Nicko also decided to return to Athens. With the conclusion of the wine festival, Orpheus decided to take a break from performing in public for a while, and take a well-deserved rest.

Next morning, Michali told Hypsipyle where she could find Orpheus in Athens. Michali was so happy to finally meet Hypsipyle, after hearing about her from Orpheus for many years in the songs he sung, and the stories he told. Hypsipyle was equally happy and excited to hear of Orpheus, and what had become of his life since they were last in each other's company.

Michali also mentioned to Hypsipyle that King Theseus and Orpheus were friends, and maybe she should go to the palace first, considering that she was once a Queen. Hypsipyle asked Michali how old King Theseus was, and when she was told, she knew it must be the same Theseus who was also one of Jason's crew. Theseus told Hypsipyle many years ago of his intentions to make Athens a mighty city, and now she was about to visit his city for the first time.

Hypsipyle and the boys continued their journey along the goat track leading out of Piraeus directly into Athens, a relatively short distance of only 60 stadia. Her mission was to seek out not one, but two friends from the Argo. With the donkeys refreshed and rested, the group of three made good time and arrived in Athens in excellent time.

King Theseus was going about his normal morning routine of planning for the day ahead when one of his slaves entered his private room to inform him that there were some unexpected visitors waiting in the courtyard. The King was not expecting anyone this particular day and was most eager to see who had come to visit.

"Who are they?" asked the king.

"There is a lady about the age of our Queen and two young men."

"Tell our guests I will be with them shortly."

After completing his preparations for the day, King Theseus and the slave walked into the courtyard to greet the guests, whereupon Hypsipyle recognised him immediately. Forgetting normal protocol, the two old friends warmly greeted each other with the usual hugs and cheek kisses, leaving a stunned pair of boys, and an equally dumbfounded slave. It was some time before Hypsipyle introduced her sons to the King of Athens.

"Are these the sons of Jason?"

"Yes, we are. This is my brother Euneos and I am Thoas."

Hypsipyle quickly told Theseus that her sons have never met their father, and the King retorted that they looked just like him.

"I can see a resemblance."

Without being asked, the slave quietly dispatched a young slave girl to instruct the kitchen slaves to prepare a small welcome feast in honour of the guests. Theseus was joined by his wife Phaedra, and following some quick introductions, he instructed his man slave to cancel all appointments for the rest of the day, and to organise rooms and a bath for the guests.

"You must stay with us for as long as you need. Our house is your house", said Phaedra.

Hypsipyle could hardly believe her current reality. Only days ago, she was living in a palace as a slave for a Queen, now she was being invited by a different Queen to stay in another palace as a guest.

Theseus called on one of the young male slaves to run and fetch Orpheus and to command him to come to the palace immediately, but not to give him a reason for the unexpected visit.

"And tell him to bring his kithara!"

The young man scarpered away as fast as his sandals allowed and returned sometime later with a rather perplexed musician, concerned at being awoken at this ridiculously early hour. Let me add here that the hour was close to midday — early for a musician!

Before Orpheus arrived, Theseus asked Hypsipyle and the boys to hide behind a nearby statue, as he wanted to play a trick on his old friend.

Orpheus entered the courtyard and was offered a wine by Theseus.

"A bit early for this don't you think?"

"Never too early for wine Orpheus. I'll join you as well."

Theseus clapped his hands together twice, and more wine was brought out in some of Nicko's finest kraters.

"Orpheus, I want you to play that song Hypsipyle taught you all those years ago in Myrina. The one that you played at Kratiras a few weeks ago where the whole audience listened and cried with you."

Perplexed at this rather strange request at such a time of the day, Orpheus agreed and started to play his kithara and sing.

Behind a large statue of Aphrodite, surrounded by plants, and just out of sight of Orpheus, Hypsipyle, Thoas and Euneos sat waiting for their cue.

As Orpheus commenced strumming notes and singing, he could hear others singing in the background, but could not see them. Hypsipyle could not contain herself anymore and emerged from behind Aphrodite.

Singing the song she had taught Orpheus, which was given to her by her own father and mother, she walked slowly towards the singer with tears in her eyes. Orpheus stopped playing and just stared at her.

At that moment, Thoas and Euneos emerged from behind Aphrodite and stood next to their mother. They too were crying. They could sense the importance of this moment. Orpheus stood and embraced Hypsipyle for the first time in nearly 20 years.

"Please, finish the song Orpheus."

Somehow, he did. He picked up the instrument and recommenced. This was a song he had sung in public many times, and when people heard it for the first time, they cried. He had become used to its impact on people, but never forgot that first time he heard it. He now sung it like it was the first time for him again.

There was not a dry eye in the courtyard. Theseus and Phaedra embraced each other, crying like hungry babies, Thoas and Euneos once again heard that song, but this time, their mother was there too. They cried as well. Hypsipyle could not believe that that song had given so many people so much pleasure. She cried. Orpheus cried. He cried like a new born baby thirsty for its nightly feed, but managed to finish the song in-between his tears of absolute joy.

After the royal command performance, Orpheus told Hypsipyle and the boy's stories of Jason, about what they did during and after the voyage of the Argo. Theseus also listened as he had never really heard what became of their friend after the voyage ended.

Orpheus could not explain to Hypsipyle why Jason never kept his promise to return to Limnos. He could not explain it because he didn't know the answer. He told Hypsipyle that Jason did not know about his sons. Although Orpheus knew of the boys, he could not bring himself to let Jason know of their existence. Jason's mind was tormented enough, he told Hypsipyle.

It was now time for Orpheus to make another announcement.

"Boys. For many years, Katerina has been given money by a secret benefactor to help with your life. Did you know that?"

"Yes, we did know that someone was helping us, but we were told never to ask, so we didn't. How did you know that Orpheus?"

"That is an easy one. It was me."

Once again, the boys, Hypsipyle and Orpheus cried. When that finished, Orpheus and Theseus returned to regaling the twins about Jason.

Thoas and Euneos were extremely grateful for these stories about their father. Growing up, they did not care much for him, as they never met, but now they were hearing stories from his best friend Orpheus, from an old friend in Theseus, and now from their mother, they were beginning to understand him a little. Jason was a dreamer who could not settle down in any one place. His claim to fame was the voyage, and since that concluded, his life seemed rudderless.

The twins were learning that their father Jason was a deeply flawed character, but could love easily, and was loved by all who met him. They were beginning to like him.

Orpheus sang many more songs in the palace's courtyard later that night. It was perhaps his most outstanding performance of all time, attended by only a handful of people, but those people were the most important individuals in his life. Later in the evening, Nicko arrived and joined in the fun. He immediately liked

Hypsipyle and could see where the boys got their personalities from. He offered to make a new statue of her to leave in the royal palace, and Theseus agreed to fund the artistic endeavour. Hypsipyle was once again speechless.

In the clear light of a new day, Hypsipyle asked Theseus if she could remain in the palace until she could secure some more permanent lodgings. She didn't want to travel to Limnos with the boys at that moment because she could not be sure of the welcome she would receive. She also wanted to find her father, to see if he was still alive, and she wanted to spend more time talking with Orpheus. Theseus gladly accepted Hypsipyle's request and offered a room for her to remain in until she decided it was time to leave.

I should mention something about the three donkeys that accompanied Hypsipyle and the boys from Argos. The donkeys were not sold but given to King Theseus to keep in his stable. Quite by chance, Vaiyos visited Athens shortly afterwards to see his children, who by now were living there. Walking in the area near the palace, Vaiyos noticed a slave taking a donkey out to get some sacks of grain. The donkey recognised Vaiyos, and gave a rather surprised man an affectionate head butt from its rather large head.

Where was I? Oh yes, in the palace of King Theseus.

Life was looking optimistic again for Hypsipyle while in Athens, but she knew that her boys had to return to Limnos soon. After one week with their mother, Thoas and Euneos sailed back to Limnos on one of the many boats carrying cargo up, down and across the Aegean. Thoas agreed to see if it would be wise for his mother to return with him at a later stage, but first, he had to determine if she faced any danger or threat if she returned.

The day before Thoas and Euneos left for Limnos, they told their mother about a new friend they met in Piraeus at the wine festival recently, and how he had invited them to visit him and his father on Oinoe. Hypsipyle didn't think anything of this particular story at the time, but soon had reason to follow it up herself.

Sometime after the boys left Athens, Hypsipyle and Orpheus were sitting with Michali at Kratiras, and the men were discussing the success or otherwise of the wine festival. Hypsipyle listened to the two friends talking about all that happened, and how they were both looking forward to the event in a years' time. One thing Orpheus said caught her attention. He told the story of how this young man from Oinoe one night joined in the singing of the song Hypsipyle taught Orpheus that night in Limnos.

"Was that the young man Thoas and Euneos mentioned to me?"

"Yes, I think it was. The three of them became very close, and I remember Sikinos inviting the boys to visit him on Oinoe so that they could learn how they grew wine there."

"But you said that he knew the words of the song?"

"He did indeed."

Hypsipyle was most intrigued at this. How could a complete stranger know the words of a song only taught to her by her father? She knew that Orpheus had sung that song many times at Kratiras, so maybe a sailor had learned it there and then visited Oinoe. That was a possibility!

"Orpheus. We need to go to Oinoe. I have to find this young man and ask him about the song."

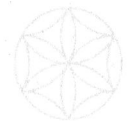

CHAPTER 25

Oinoe

Michali negotiated a passage to Oinoe for Orpheus and Hypsipyle. A boat was leaving in a few days' time, and Orpheus agreed to sing songs featuring the captain in return for two fares. The captain agreed instantly as he always wanted to be remembered in song by the great Orpheus.

Captain Thanasis made room for his two additional passengers in between kraters of olive oil, nuts, salted meat, various tapestries and dried figs. Leaving Piraeus some days later, Captain Thanasis beamed brightly at the possibility of being immortalised in song. On board his boat were ten strong rowers, and as soon as they were clear of the harbour, Orpheus instantly began improvising songs in the same manner as he did aboard the Argo all those years ago. Not ignoring the crew, Orpheus also included them in his lyrics.

The voyage lasted several days and having a singer on board somehow made the trip appear to pass much quicker. Orpheus was in his element.

The voyage to Oinoe was an eventful one for Captain Thanasis and his crew. Never before had they been entertained by someone as famous as Orpheus. On arrival at the main and only port in Oinoe, Captain Thanasis helped his customers ashore, and set about unloading his own cargo. Orpheus and Hypsipyle thanked him for their trip and proceeded to walk to the nearest tavern. This wasn't hard to find, as there was only one tavern in the port.

Many sailors and traders stayed in this tavern, and on this night, Orpheus managed to secure some more free accommodation with his offer to play songs for the owners and the crew of Thanasis' boat, who were due to be staying for a few days until they had sufficient cargo for the return journey.

Orpheus played his kithara and sang many songs that night, especially some of the ones he had just written. Word quickly spread around the island of the famous singer plying his trade, and quickly, there were about 70 patrons there to listen to the great Orpheus.

The owners of the tavern had their most successful night in memory that evening. In port were two more boats, and with Captain Thanasis, his crew, Orpheus, and a sprinkling of local people, more wine was drunk in that one night than the island produced in a year! Or so it seemed. Anyway, why should we Greeks let truth stand in the way of a good story!

Together with wine, a feast was prepared with the usual varieties of local produce to accompany the roasted lamb. The tavern owners were so pleased with Orpheus, they asked him to remain for another ten days with as much food and drink he could consume. He politely refused their most generous offer, stating that he would be back soon if their trip proved successful. He explained who he and Hypsipyle came to visit, and the owners said the person was not far away, working a vineyard at a distance of about half a day's donkey travel.

Next morning, Orpheus and Hypsipyle left the port on two donkeys, with instructions of how to find Sikinos and Thomas.

Sikinos had been home now for some months since visiting the wine festival. He returned enthusiastically to his father with numerous new ideas for grape production and wine making and began his new ideas at once. He and his father helped other farmers clear more land, which was difficult as Oinoe is not a flat island and has much of its arable land on the sides of mountains and hills.

It was the middle of the day when Orpheus and Hypsipyle arrived at the farm, but no one was home. They saw a well nearby and gave their donkeys a drink from a bucket attached to a long rope, sat down under the shade of some old vines growing adjacent to the house and ate some bread and olive oil brought with them from the tavern. They also found some feed for the animals, who were happy to be resting, eating and having a drink.

Guessing that Sikinos would be coming home shortly for an afternoon rest, Orpheus and Hypsipyle slipped into a light sleep. Soon after, Thomas and Sikinos arrived home to find two donkeys eating their feed, and two people sleeping under the shade of their vines.

Sikinos recognised Orpheus immediately and called out his name.

"Orpheus, is that you?"

Orpheus stood and embraced his new young friend. At this time, and when Thomas saw that his son knew the visitors, or at least one of them, he went inside to find a stool and some food for himself and Sikinos.

In the meantime, Hypsipyle had woken up, and Orpheus introduced her to Sikinos as the mother of the boys he had met in the wine bar. Pleasant introductions were made and Sikinos sat down, saying that his father had gone inside to wash himself and collect some food for their midday meal.

Thomas, now cleaned and refreshed, came out with a plate of food to share with his son and his new friends. Hypsipyle did not notice him at first and had her back to him. Thomas sat in the shade on a small stool and opened a cloth with some bread and cheese. He spoke to Orpheus and welcomed him and his friend to their home.

On hearing his voice, Hypsipyle turned around and peered lovingly into the eyes of the man who she had not seen for such a long time.

Thomas dropped his bread and wiped his eyes on the back of his hand in disbelief at what he was seeing. Hypsipyle rushed towards her father and gave him an embrace she had been dreaming about for 20 years.

Sikinos was now very confused. So was Orpheus.

"Son. This is your sister. My daughter, Hypsipyle."

Thomas, instantly reverted to being Thoas again, and said to Sikinos "I think I need to tell you something I have never told you. I need to explain to you who I really am, our family, and who you really are."

"What do you mean by saying you need to tell me who we really are?"

"It is a long story, and I am sure we will try to answer any and all of your questions in time."

"Sir, I am Orpheus, story teller and singer. I met your son at the wine festival in Piraeus recently, and I have known your daughter since I was on Limnos with Jason many years ago."

Perplexed at the last part of the comment, Thoas asked "Who is Jason and why were you on Limnos?"

Hypsipyle by now had gathered her thoughts and emotions and spoke directly to her brother.

"There is so much to talk about Sikinos, and what I am about to say you must promise not to blame your father for perhaps deleting certain parts of our family story. I don't know what he has told you over the years, but today, you will understand, I hope, who we all are."

Until sunset, Sikinos listened intently, to his father, to his sister, and to Orpheus. By now, he realised that the twins he met recently in Piraeus are actually his nephews. Sikinos found this so perplexing but so much of what he heard that afternoon was perplexing.

Hypsipyle attempted to explain how and why all males from Limnos were killed. Thoas said that he knew something was not quite right and blamed himself for not doing anything about the situation early. How could he let this happen? After all, he was King.

Orpheus also listened to this particular part of the story as he never actually knew the truth why Limnos was devoid of males at the time of Jason and the Argonauts arrival. He had no reason not to believe the tale of how men went to help a neighbouring island fight off pirates, and never came home.

Sikinos asked about Jason. Why was he there? This time, Orpheus had something to offer, and explained how the Argonauts were chosen, the original purpose of their quest, and who their leader was. Because he was very close to Jason before, during, and after the journey, he could talk at length about the man, his short-comings, but his strengths as well.

"The voyage of the Argo was a simple story. We heard that a particular type of sheep's fleece could be placed on the bottom of a river, and as water cascaded over it, specs of gold would attach themselves to the fleece, thus creating what appeared to be a Golden Fleece. This particular sheep only existed in a part of the world named Colchis. We know this because over the years, travellers from that region also visited parts of our country and talked about the wonderful qualities of the fleece. No one from Greece had travelled to Colchis, so King Pelias of Iolchus offered his kingdom to the person who brought back the mysterious fleece. Pelias quite possibly believed no one could achieve the impossible, and thought his offer was safe, but Jason had other ideas."

"Jason asked a friend to build a large boat to take 50 oarsmen on a journey to locate the fleece. The boat was built, and in honour of the maker, Argus, the boat was named 'Argo'. A search was conducted to find 50 strong men to row, and in time, 49 men and one woman were chosen."

"One woman?" asked Sikinos. "Why was she chosen?"

"Perhaps I can answer that," said Hypsipyle. "May I?"

"Of course."

"Atalanta was perhaps the best archer in the whole world, or she appeared that way to us. Her skills were the match of any man, if not better. She and another archer Philoktetes were Jason's personal body guards if you like, because of their archery skills. Both Atalanta and Philoktetes trained our women and made them vastly improved archers while the Argo visited Limnos."

"That's right. On the journey to Colchis, the skills of Atalanta and Philoktetes were necessary many times. We were attacked by pirates on a number of occasions, and if not for Atalanta's accuracy, we perhaps would not have come back alive."

"What became of them?" asked Hypsipyle.

"I don't know about Atalanta, but I am certain Philoktetes always wanted to go back to Limnos after the journey was over. He liked the solitude of the island, and I heard from King Theseus, that Philoktetes did eventually go back to live on Limnos. In the time since leaving the Argo behind, he became a master bow maker, and I believe people now travel to Limnos just to purchase his bows."

"I am guessing that the men you travelled with Orpheus, did more than repair the boat on Limnos?"

"Much more."

Apart from one local sailor who was blown off course and landed on Limnos by mistake, former King Thoas had not heard any news regarding Limnos since he left. He did not know about the Argonauts and did not know what happened to Hypsipyle after it was discovered she had not killed him. Hypsipyle told Sikinos and her father what happened after Thoas was sent adrift in the larnax.

While explaining the sword smeared with pig's blood, and how Polyxo assumed it to be the blood of King Thoas, the sword became a symbol of liberation from the yoke of man and was hanging on a wall in the palace until Jason arrived. On his departure from Limnos, Hypsipyle gave the sword to Jason and asked him to return it one day.

While this part of the story was being told, Orpheus quietly slipped away to get a special object from a bag tied to his donkey.

Hypsipyle continued.

"Many Argonauts laid with Limnian women, and to my knowledge, none of them ever returned to see their children. At least until I was ostracised, I never saw any returning Argonauts. Jason and I were married and I had two boys — twins in fact. Sikinos, you know who they are. They are named Thoas and Euneos."

At hearing this from Hypsipyle old Thoas wept again.

"I need to meet my grandsons. Sikinos, tell me all about them. Now you know they are family, I hope you don't feel differently towards them."

At that precise moment, Orpheus returned with a blanket wrapped around the item he took from the bag. No one noticed he had even gone and paid little or no attention to the blanket lying at Orpheus' feet.

"After Jason died, the possibility of him ever seeing his boys vanished, so a chance meeting one day with a sailor who visited Limnos regularly, agreed to accept some money from me to send to the boys. Now they are men and making their own way in life, I no longer need to do this, but I will always love them like a distant father figure."

At that very moment, Orpheus picked up the rolled purple blanket and gently put his hand on the hilt of the sword.

"Jason was dying, and in the final few days of his life, he and I lay down on the beach together, underneath the bow of the Argo, a place he felt most at home. The Argo was a rotting hulk then, and has most likely fallen into total disrepair by now, but it offered some shade and comfort to a dying man."

"He and I talked of many things, but his one last request was this.

He asked me to take this item to Limnos one day, to the home it came from, to the people who rightly owned it."

He then drew the sword out of the blanket and gave it to Thoas. "I believe this is rightfully yours."

If Thoas had cried before, by now he could not see for the torrent of tears. Hypsipyle too was crying, because she had never expected to see this object ever again. She never expected to see her father again, and most likely never expected to meet her little brother!

Thoas carefully took the sword as if he were handling it for the first time. He caressed it as if he were cradling a newborn baby.

"This was my father's sword who received it from his father. Sikinos, the sword belonged to King Minos of Crete, my grandfather. Now, it is yours."

"Are you telling me that King Minos….is my great grandfather? Can this day get any better?"

Thoas handed Sikinos the sword, and like Thoas, gently stroked it as if it were the most precious object the world had known. He stopped asking questions and marvelled at its exquisite craftmanship.

"Hypsipyle. Do you remember what else you gave Jason, apart from the sword?"

"Yes, I do. I gave him a robe, made of local fabrics and dyed purple. I asked him to remember me each time it was cold and each time he wore it. The other ladies and I wove many stories into the robe."

"Jason kept the robe and wore it almost every day on the voyage with us. After we returned, and he learned that King Pelias would not give him what was promised, he put the robe away, never to wear it again. Or so he thought. When he was dying, I noticed his possessions in a satchel next to him. Wrapped up in a blanket, or what I thought was a blanket was the sword. But the blanket was faded purple in colour, threadbare, yet still intact. I asked him about it, and he told me that it was the robe you gave him. I didn't recognise it at first, but he kept the sword wrapped up in it all those years. This is yours I believe!"

Hypsipyle looked at the robe in complete disbelief. The gift to Jason, made from her own hands, was now unexpectedly in her hands again. She held it to her face and smelled its fine fabric. It was something to remember him by, and she thanked Orpheus for saving this precious relic of their friendship.

"Before the Argonauts left us, I asked Polyxo and Katerina what I could give Jason as a farewell gift. They asked other women, and the answer they finally told me was to give him something to remember me by, but also to remember his time on Limnos. It was suggested that we weave some stories into the garment, and I can't remember what we did, but the one I do remember was a ram of golden fleece. After all, he told us that the main purpose of the journey was go find some mythical fleece that attracted gold flakes in a river bed."

Hypsipyle tried to recollect the other stories woven in the robe but could not remember them all. Holding and smelling the blanket seemed to jolt her memory.

"I remember we had seven scenes woven into the fabric. One was of course a golden ram, one about a chariot race, Aphrodite holding a shield, a Zeus thunderbolt, and I think there was one about building a new city. The others I forget."

Thoas now tried to explain his son's true identity. He knew this moment would eventually come one day but had no way of knowing when it would be, or what he would say. He started slowly.

"Many years ago, King Minos of Crete sent my brothers and I to different Aegean islands to shore up trade routes from the Hellespont, all the way through to mainland Greece. My mother was Ariadne, Minos' daughter, so yes, my grandfather was King Minos! I was sent to Limnos, where it was strategically important to Crete to regulate trade into and out of the Hellespont. King

Cretheus of Iolchus sent his daughter to Limnos after my grand-father asked him if it was possible to arrange a marriage between the children. I must say, the first time I saw your grandmother Myrina, I fell in love."

"We were married not long after and produced a beautiful daughter, Hypsipyle. But sadness befell us when Queen Myrina died some years later. It was one of the saddest days of my life. The other sad day was the death of your own mother, Sikinos. I wish you could have met these two courageous and beautiful women. But, their blood lives on in you and in Hypsipyle, and now in your nephews Thoas and Euneos. One day, I hope you fall in love and marry the girl who takes your heart. Then you will truly know the meaning and purpose of life."

His voice trailing off into a breath, Thoas became sad at the thought of his two wives dying and sat down with his head buried in both hands. For the rest of the day, each person took turns to speak. There was much to tell. Many stories were shared. Many tears flowed and much laughter erupted.

Night fell soon enough, and wine suddenly appeared from a wonderful krater, kept for special occasions by Thoas. Sikinos went into the garden and returned with fresh fruit and some goats cheese. A feast was shared, and Orpheus sang. Sikinos was not sad to hear stories for the first time from his father. He must have always known there was something he wasn't telling him, as his appearance on the island was never satisfactorily believed. No one on Oinoe questioned Thoas' story of being washed up one day, as he brought so much to their island through his insistence on growing vines and producing grapes for wine. The island had pros-pered through increasing trade because of this surge in agricultural pursuits. Young people were not leaving Oinoe for neighbouring islands to find work. On the contrary, people were now coming to Oinoe to work, live and raise families!

Over the next ten days, Thoas spent much time with his

daughter Hypsipyle and Orpheus spent considerable time with Sikinos. Thoas was so happy to know that his family had grown, and often told Hypsipyle that he could now die a happy man. Hypsipyle said that he could not die yet, or not until he had met young Thoas and Euneos. Plans were made to meet up in Athens at the palace of King Theseus. It was still unsure if a meeting could take place safely on Limnos.

Sikinos took Orpheus all over his island, which isn't very big! Sikinos was proud of his father too, for surviving the boat trip, for having a daughter, and for eventually meeting his mother. After all, if Thoas had not been cast out of Limnos in a larnax, Sikinos would not be alive. Orpheus now had so much material to sing with and tell stories about, his head was bursting with ideas.

Before Orpheus and Hypsipyle left Oinoe, they all agreed to meet up at the next wine festival in Piraeus. Thoas and Sikinos agreed to be there together, and Orpheus said he would make sure young Thoas and Euneos would be there too.

This time, the father farewelled his daughter in a trading boat, filled with wine and food bound for Athens. Just as they were leaving port, Orpheus said to Hypsipyle "Now I know how Sikinos knew the words to that song!"

CHAPTER 26

Samos to Myrina

After leaving their mother behind in Athens, Thoas and Euneos set sail for Limnos. They found a boat and captain who would eventually help them reach their final destination, but the trip would take many days due to the number of ports and islands visited. Perhaps the other reason this boat was preferred was that it had intended to visit Samos. Thoas did not inform Euneos about the possibility of going to visit the girls in Samos, but he didn't think his brother would mind.

The trip to Samos was difficult. Bad weather, rough seas and a clutch of broken oars almost rendered the trip a complete disaster. The whole trip eventually took 30 days until finally they reached the town of Samos, where the island took its name from. It was not difficult to find the port as there was only one port on the whole island.

Euneos became violently ill on the trip, and the moment they reached Samos, Thoas took his brother ashore to find somewhere for him recover. The boys' winemaking reputation was known in Samos as many traders had bought and sold wine from and to Limnos. Once the local tavern owners knew who was in town, they banded together to look after and care for the sick brother.

At one of the taverns, Thoas asked how he could find his friends, the girls Helen and Ambrosia. A slave was sent to their vineyard to pass on the message. Being late in the day, and not knowing how far the vineyard was from the port, Thoas expected to see the girls the next day. To his surprise, they arrived almost immediately with their father Anastasios who they had previously met at the festival.

Anastasios had heard only good things about these two young men from many people at the festival and could sense some marriages in the air for his daughters. The fact that they were in the same business was a further blessing.

Without haste, they carefully carried Euneos to their home, which was only a short distance past the village of Samos, high on a hill overlooking the port. Euneos could not keep any food down and could only manage to sip water. Helen sat by his side and wiped his fevered forehead with a wet cloth.

After a night where the fever came and went, Euneos woke the next morning with little or no memory of how he came to be in his friends' house. The last thing he could remember was being very sick over the bow spit. The first vision he could make out was Helen's face, and that instantly made him feel much better.

With Helen's assistance, Euneos regained his strength by taking long walks around the port, village and neighbouring orchards. Thoas and Ambrosia were equally busy talking and walking. Anastasios and his wife Melissa simply went about their daily chores in their vineyard smiling at the thought of their daughters marrying such fine young men.

After seven days of this, Thoas asked Ambrosia to be his wife. She said yes. At about the same time, Euneos asked Helen to be his wife, and she said yes. Thoas and Euneos, together with their newly accepting fiancés approached Anastasios and Melissa to inform them of their intentions.

Both girls thought these two young men from Limnos were successful wine producers, but what Thoas said next stunned them and their parents.

"We are from Limnos, and we do grow grapes for wine production. Our home is the palace in Myrina because we are both princes. But don't let that change your minds."

This was bewildering news to the girls, who were both laughing in a mixture of disbelief and astonishment. Deliriously happy with their daughters' choice in husbands, Anastasios and Melissa were ecstatic as well and gave their immediate permission for the girls to get married. As per usual, there were hugs and air kisses all around.

A decision was made to conduct the marriages at the end of the wine festival in one year's time, but a venue was not agreed to at that moment. One key point was not in dispute. Both couples would eventually live at the palace in Myrina.

After a hurried feast of Samos' finest food and wine at the home of Anastasios and Melissa, the newly engaged boys departed Samos much happier and healthier than when they arrived. By this time, Euneos had returned to full health, and Thoas was already making plans to upgrade the palace for the new residents.

No one knew at the time, but the conflict brewing in Troy was becoming more serious by the day. Greek trading vessels were being asked to pay higher taxes to move through the Hellespont, and many Kings of Greece were not happy. Trade was being seriously disrupted and something had to happen. Plans were under way for a concerted attempt to encourage the Trojans to drop their tax plans and reopen free trade into and from the Black Sea.

Landing in Myrina, the boys were welcomed back with a typically huge gastronomic feast. Thoas and Euneos decided not to inform anyone of what had happened on their trip, and any news they might possess for a few days. They wanted to return to a normal routine of work before any announcements were made, or too many stories told.

Katerina knew something must have happened, because she could sense a new purpose in their work habits. All of a sudden, Euneos was cleaning the palace and making some minor plans for an extension. Thoas had many new ideas for grape production, and more parts of the island were being prepared for additional planting of some different varieties of grapes.

Thoas was also preparing for a conflict in Troy, and knew that if an army was involved, Limnos was in the perfect location to provide food and wine if needed. Tensions were high, and trade with Troy, which had been a steady flow over hundreds of hears with Limnos, had all but ceased.

Let me give you a brief history lesson here before I return to the story. You may not know it, but there was a very prosperous city on the east coast of Limnos called Poliochni that was the capital of Limnos long before Myrina, and before Hephaestia was built. Poliochni had a wonderful port and had been trading with Troy for a long time. Unfortunately, there was an earthquake in Limnos many, many years ago, and Poliochni was destroyed. Residents who survived tried to rebuild, but a further earthquake destroyed it a second time, so they either left the island, or moved to other parts to try to build a new city. That is how Myrina came into being. Myrina was always a village, but the destruction of Poliochni helped in its growth. Who knows, one day Poliochni may once again be a city, but at the moment, as some of you may know, it is but a small collection of houses now constructed out of the rubble of the long-abandoned city.

I mentioned another village, Hephaestia. Its life began well after Poliochni had been destroyed. Many rumours exist, but the main story is that Philoktetes, the returning Argonaut to Limnos, established that village, and now it is the second capital of Limnos. He travelled all over Limnos many years ago when he was an Argonaut and found an area to the north east where he believed a community could thrive. It has the benefit of a port on the western side, open to the weather, but still safe, and a port on the east side protected by a small bay. Philoktetes brought many people with him to help clear the land and build houses, and now it is a fast-growing village with hundreds of people living and working there. I did hear that he once tried to set up a village on Chryse, but he soon abandoned the thought due to the lack of a suitable port.

Now we can return to the story.

Before Thoas and Euneos retired for the night, Katerina politely asked both boys to meet her at Ambrosia's café the next morning. She was convinced they were withholding something important, and sought to discover what it might be before anyone else.

Eager to share their stories, Thoas and Euneos had a fine sleep in their own beds and woke early to stroll along the beach. Everyone who they saw during the mornings amble stopped for a chat. What would normally take only a few minutes took much longer. Well-wishers wanted to welcome back the two princes.

Having risen well before the boys, Katerina was already waiting at the café when they arrived. Ambrosia prepared the usual morning spread of grapes, nuts, goat cheese, bread and thyme honey, and of course, fine watered-down wine. After all, it was still early! It was Katerina who started the conversation. She did not hold back.

She talked about the meeting at Ambrosia's as the boys left for the wine festival, and how she informed Polyxo of the duel nature of the visit to Piraeus. She told them that her mother Polyxo died that night, knowing they knew the full story. She told them that Polyxo was not sad or upset by this and said that the inevitability of past events had finally caught up, and then she died in peace.

Many years later, Thoas voiced his thoughts to people that he always knew there was something Polyxo was not telling them all throughout their lives. He believed that she did not always tell them the truth. When he learned that she had died, he was not upset, and realised that it must have been very difficult for her to hold that information close for so long, and not tell the boys. In a way, he felt sorry for Polyxo. At least she died with that burden lifted from her chest.

For the remainder of the morning, Katerina freely shared stories of the boys with their mother before she was ostracised. They had not heard these stories before, because Polyxo did not allow Katerina to reveal any information regarding the awful deed with them. They were fascinated with her recollections, and in some way, these stories plugged any gaps in their knowledge of Hypsipyle and their infant days with her. Even though they had wonderful news for Katerina, they preferred to sit, eat, drink, listen and wait for the right moment.

Then it was their turn to talk, and talk they did. By the time Thoas and Euneos started, Ambrosia had invited Stella to come by, who invited many others to join her, and before too long, Ambrosia's café was as full as Michali's bar when Orpheus played.

The timing of this particular morning's cafe conversation was crucial to the female population of Limnos' acceptance of the tragic past events, and in the healing necessary to move ahead. Up until then, it was normal to have people share stories around Ambrosia's café with the royal princes in attendance. Weighing heavily on the women was the crushing fear of sharing too much information relating to what had become known as the '*Limnian deed*'. That topic was off limits, especially in the presence of the royal princes.

Finally, that weight was about to be lifted, and the new beginning Polyxo had talked about so long ago was moments away from reality.

In a style similar to Orpheus, Euneos was developing into quite the storyteller, and he took the lead. For all their lives, Thoas had assumed the role of being the older brother (albeit by a few minutes), but still, the older one, talking for them both in public situations. Not anymore. Euneos had grown considerably. It was now Thoas' turn to sit back and admire his brother's gift.

One time in Michali's bar, Orpheus took Euneos aside and told him the trick of telling a good story. He said that there were three things he needed to learn about how people speak. Firstly, you need to generalise. Attribute common traits to a great number of people, like saying things such as 'all sailors like drinking'. Secondly, you need to delete certain events. Not lying, not making stories up, but to delete some key points. Finally, the third thing to learn is to distort. Make some events larger or smaller than they were truly were. If you learned these three tricks, you could develop into a great storyteller.

Euneos remembered this sage advice and began to reveal the story of their trip to Piraeus. He left some minor events out, and tried using Orpheus' story telling tricks to embellish other events.

Many of the older women who were there on that particular day, remembered a younger Orpheus telling stories and setting them to music many years prior. Ambrosia told Euneos that Orpheus won many hearts back then but did not give it to anybody. He preferred to keep his heart for someone later on in his life.

Euneos told them about Michali, Nicko and his special abilities, Captain Korelli, Sikinos, Vaiyos, Theseus, Phaedra and a host of other people they met. He told them about new varieties of grape vines, of emerging methods of wine production and storage, and of soil varieties and planting techniques that were dependant on the direction of the sun.

Thoas spoke of the unfolding events in Troy, and how he had begun storing large amounts of wine in preparation. Either the armies will need wine, and if they do, we will make a lot of money, and if they don't, we will be able to sell our wine because people now know how good Limnian wine is.

Euneos returned to the speakers' chair and lovingly explained to the captive audience of two very special young girls they met in Piraeus. After a brief discussion on their positive attributes, such as a love of wine growing, stunningly beautiful and wonderful parents, he stood with Thoas and declared to the gathered guests to plan for a wedding sometime soon.

Well into midday by this stage, Ambrosia and Katerina elusively produced more wine, and Stella cleverly supplied yet more food. The gathered guests seemed to grow in number as word leaked of the princes' wedding plans.

Finally, after all the congratulatory embraces ceased, Euneos started to reveal news of their trip to Nemea and finding their mother. At news of this, the crowd were hushed. They did not know what to say or what to think. For the older women, they did not know what to think about Hypsipyle, and for the younger ones who were the children born of the Argonauts visit, they were hearing stories of the former Queen for the first time.

Gradually, Euneos outlined what happened to Hypsipyle since the moment she had been ostracised, her employment in the Nemean Palace, and to the unfortunate incident involving the baby prince Opheltes. He mentioned Amphiarus and how he spoke in favour of Hypsipyle, and if it wasn't for him, she would surely have been put to death by the King and Queen.

Sitting quietly in a corner of the café was Evanthia, a lady who had been listening intently to Euneos and Thoas' stories. Evanthia was one of the archers taught by Atalanta and Philoktetes, and who now was in charge of training young archers. She had always been a quiet lady, and one who you would never suspect was an excellent archer. She asked Euneos to describe Amphiarus to her. What did he look like now? How did he sound? Euneos didn't think anything of it and he told her what he looked ands sounded like, but more importantly, that he remembered his time on Limnos with fondness.

Evanthia smiled to herself, because she had known Amphiarus intimately one night all those years ago. One night after lessons from Atalanta, Evanthia found herself alone on the beach, firing arrows at the knot in the tree Atalanta had no trouble hitting. She could not even get close to the tree, let alone finding the knot. A young, quiet Argonaut approached her and asked if he could sit and watch. Evanthia was nervous at this strange request, but she reluctantly agreed, and Amphiarus just sat on the beach and watched Evanthia fire arrow after arrow, missing every time.

Frustrated with her lack of accuracy, Evanthia asked Amphiarus if he could help her collect the arrows.

There is something you will never hear a story teller say, but I am going to say it. I am going to cut this long story to a short story.

Amphiarus agreed and jogged down to the tree to collect all the arrows. Bringing them back to Evanthia, he whispered one thing to her. It was something like 'just visualise yourself releasing the arrow and striking the target' or something clever like that. In other words, he wanted her to imagine that she could do it.

After giving her that advice, Amphiarus left Evanthia to her practice. It was days before the two met up again, and this time, Evanthia was at least striking the tree, and even managed to score a direct hit on the knot more than once. No one noticed these two being together apart from on the beach where Amphiarus would sit and watch Evanthia practice and gradually improve every day. No one noticed them spending any nights together in her home. No one knew who the father of Evanthia's child was because as far as she was concerned, it was none of their business.

Here she was, listening to stories about the father of Amalia, her daughter, and what became of him. Evanthia was so proud of Amalia, and now was very happy to hear what became of Amphiarus. Even with this current news, Evanthia remained tight-lipped as to the identity of her daughter's father. Amalia was with her mother that morning, and silently beamed with the knowledge that her father was a good man.

Euneos spoke of leaving for Athens, staying at King Theseus' palace with Queen Phaedra, and how his mother and Orpheus met again. Stella was most interested in Theseus and what became of him. Even though she didn't have any children with him, she seemed to hold his friendship close to her heart.

Euneos shared the story of staying in the Athenian palace with Theseus. Stella always knew that his one true task in life was to make the village of Athens into a mighty city. She was so happy that her old friend, the man who helped her many years ago, had finally found his queen and started achieving his destiny.

Finally, it was Thoas' turn to speak. He conveyed his version of meeting the girls at Kratiras. He skipped over most pieces of the tale because the ending was now known, but he outlined to the guests his plans for the girls to live in the palace. No date was set, and no venue was planned for the wedding. Secretly, Thoas and Euneos wanted the wedding to be held in Piraeus.

By this stage, and well into the afternoon, Thoas and Euneos had finished storytelling, and left for their vineyard. Katerina and Stefanos walked with them and asked how Hypsipyle was. They told her that she will be at the wedding but had no intention of coming to Limnos at this stage. Katerina was very happy that Hypsipyle had survived her slavery ordeal and was finally free. Euneos mentioned that Hypsipyle and Orpheus were guests of the King and Queen of Athens for as long as they wanted.

For the next six months, Thoas and Euneos devoted their time to the vineyard and sent messages to Samos whenever they could. In Samos, the girls were doing the same — tending to their vines, thinking about a wedding and working towards a return to the wine festival once again. Life seemed all very normal.

The Trojan blockade

Apart from this story of Hypsipyle, the other main tale I have often been asked to tell in my wandering minstrel life is very much related. I won't go into any detail, but in a few words, here it is.

The King of Troy and his sons wanted to raise taxes of any vessels entering the Hellespont. Greek shipping captains and therefore, Kings of Greece were not happy and objected. They wanted unrestricted access to trade routes. Delegations were sent by both sides in the dispute, but no simple resolution could be found. There is a rumour that on one Trojan delegation to Sparta, Prince Paris of Troy, absconded with King Menelaus' wife, a lady known as Helen.

When a return delegation to Troy arrived to attempt to entice Menelaus' wife back, Helen claimed that she did not want to return to Sparta and would remain in Troy. What is funny in this story is that the lady Paris ran off with was not Queen Helen, but a slave girl who looked remarkably like Helen. The real Helen stayed behind, and her husband Menelaus, his brother Agamemnon of Argos, and many other Greek kings, used the abduction as a ruse to attack Troy and save Helen.

The various attacks on Troy failed for many years because the city of Troy had defensive walls so thick, they were deemed to be impenetrable. Finally, after what was thought to be about 10 years, Troy fell, the walls finally breached and the city razed. The end result of this long and drawn out conflict was that many people died, many men were kept away from their families for long periods of time, and Limnos kept the Greek army fully nourished with wine. Thoas and Euneos made a lot of money supplying the army, and when the conflict ultimately concluded, the wine twins were the wealthiest men in the Aegean.

I have heard many stories of how Troy ultimately fell, but the most laughable one is that the Greek army tricked the Trojans to accept a gift of a giant wooden horse, in honour of the army finally admitting defeat and a return to their families all over Greece. Stories then suggest how the Trojans were so stupid, they accepted this overly large gift, not even once considering to see what may have been hidden in its great wooden belly! They brought it inside their impenetrable walls so that they could make an offering to their gods. At night when all Trojans were sleeping, the internally hidden Greek soldiers climbed out of the wooden horse, opened the large gates, and let in the army, who then sacked the city, thus ending the blockade.

The true story is far less fantastic. The gates were opened because the Greek army had captured a number of Trojan horsemen and their mounts, swapped uniforms, and feigned a cunning plan of having Greek horseman chase the fake Trojan horseman back towards the city. On seeing their own people, or who they thought were their own people being chased by Greeks on horses, the gates were opened and the false Trojans were let in. Later in the evening, the false Trojans opened the gates and allowed the Greek army to silently enter.

Even though we now have a clearer picture of what really happened, I would guess that in the years to come, the fantastic and unbelievable story of a giant wooden horse will most likely become the preferred scenario. As we story tellers continually say — why let the truth get in the way of a good story?

With the blockade over and Troy destroyed, the true winners in this particular sorry saga were no doubt the wine twins of Limnos, who made a lot of money supplying wine to a thirsty army and to a lesser extent, food throughout the years of the conflict.

We don't have enough time for me to go into every aspect of the fall of Troy, as it too takes many days to tell properly, but I thought I would like to share that little bit with you anyway. In a way, the two stories are infamously related.

Where was I? Oh yes, life was very normal.

CHAPTER 28

Dionysus Wine festival revisited

One month after the first Dionysus festival concluded, King Theseus declared it a success, and royaly decreed the next festival in just under one year, would be held once again in both Piraeus and Athens. No one seemed to offer any alternative views, so the date was set.

Also setting a future date were two sets of twins. One set from Limnos and the other from Samos. Somehow, regardless of the tyranny of distance and time, they managed to stay in constant contact through trading boats with messages delivered by sea captains.

It is normal that a wedding would be held in the village of the bride, but this was to be no normal wedding day. To keep both families happy, the two couples decided to conduct the wedding in Athens.

Let me make another of my slight detours and tell you a little bit about Athens. I know that most of you have never been there, so I will see if I can describe the village to you.

The land immediately around the village of Athens is very expansive and relatively flat. There have been a number of small villages in the area over time, but today, these villages have merged into one larger village. Perhaps one day, many people will live there, but it will take a long time to fill up the land in-between with houses. Athens is also surrounded by hills on three sides and the fourth side leads down to the port. In the middle of this land sits a large, flat-topped mound of compacted rock, where over the years, some temples and shrines have been built on the summit and in various caves on its slopes. This rocky area is quite steep in most places and has never had any houses built on it. However, King Theseus could see that the hill needed fortification, so he set about building defensive stone walls, a palace and a temple to Athena. It was to be at this palace that the wedding would be held.

Let me return once again to the story. The wedding was still many months away.

Hypsipyle and Orpheus settled into their new life as guests of King Theseus and Queen Phaedra. As far as anyone was concerned in Athens at that time, Hypsipyle was introduced to them as the first wife of Jason, who had died some years before. The story of the Limnian deed had not reached Athens, and her life as a slave to the Nemean palace was not yet known. The story of Jason and his Argonauts was known, and to be associated with that tale was far more palatable to people than being known as a Queen who presided over a mass murder!

It wasn't that Theseus lied in regard to Hypsipyle's life, it was that he never brought it up in conversation. If any palace guest asked Hypsipyle who she was, she would simply say that she married Jason, and he never came back to see his sons. When asked why she wasn't with her sons now, she would say that they are preparing to be married here in the palace soon, and if you like, you can meet them. That normally ended any persistent and unnecessary questioning.

Nicko continued his life as an artist, gradually moving away from painting pictures on wine kraters at Kratiras to creating marble sculptures for clients. All over Athens, his sculptures were now proudly displayed inside houses, temples and some even were in public places, paid for and commissioned by Theseus himself.

Nicko even started to teach students the skills of art and sculpting. Most of his students were females, and they invariably ended up being models for his female statues, but soon enough he grew tired of his philandering life and dedicated his new life to legitimate sculpting. Gradually, he began taking male students, who also became models for male statues.

His workshop was situated at the base of the rocky outcrop high above Athens, which allowed his benefactor and friend Theseus to visit regularly. The venue of his workshop also allowed easy transportation of his raw materials to be delivered. Nicko was using marble from a new quarry northeast of Athens at a place called Mount Brillitos. Nicko claimed that the marble from this particular quarry was of exceptional quality and its faint yellow tint gave the marble a golden hue in the sunlight.

During her time in Athens, Hypsipyle came to visit Nicko often and apart from her interest in his work, she became far more concerned with his business affairs, sorting them out and helping him to see that he could be a successful sculptor and teacher, if only he organised his finances better. Orpheus visited regularly too, but not for any other reason than to drink wine with his old friend and talk.

The wine festival preparations were progressing slowly, but not gathering the same level of enthusiasm as the year before. Interest from abroad was still evident, but the festival seemed to be too close to the previous one. One by one, islands were sending delegations to Theseus saying they could not send any wine as there had been an outbreak of a grapevine disease which affected production.

It became clear that the second Dionysus wine festival would not be a success, and Theseus wanted desperately to save face. He made the reluctant announcement to cancel the festival for three years, therefore setting a precedent of having a festival once every 4 years. He borrowed the idea from King Lycurgus of Nemea who had started the Nemean games soon after Prince Opheltes died.

Lycurgus declared the first games a success and said that the next one would be held in four years' time. Theseus did not want to have a wine festival at the same time as these games, so he decided to have the festival one year before the Nemean games.

The decision by Theseus to delay the second wine festival to occur a year before the Nemean games proved to be a success. Both events have been operating now for 80 years and are still very successful.

With the wine festival on hold, Hypsipyle sent a message to her sons to see if they still wanted to have the weddings in Athens, or some other place. She desperately wanted the weddings to be held in Myrina, but that was unlikely. Even though the wine festival had been cancelled, Thoas, Euneos, Helen and Ambrosia all decided to keep the original date and hold the wedding in Athens, as long as Theseus still wanted them too.

On Oinoe, Sikinos received word that the festival was to be cancelled, but the weddings were to go ahead, so he asked his father if they could both attend the wedding. Thoas said nothing would keep him away.

The weddings were planned and invitees began to arrive in Athens. Thoas and Sikinos came from Oinoe and brought with them some fine wine and locally dried fish, which was becoming a delicacy in Athens. Helen and Ambrosia arrived with their parents and multiple members of their extended family. They too brought some Samian wine with a mixture of local delicacies. Katerina, Alexander, Ambrosia, Stella and Suneva made the trip without any fuss. Everyone in Myrina knew that Hypsipyle and King Thoas were alive and didn't seem to mind now. It appears that time had healed that deep wound. The twins and their wedding party were farewelled with some fanfare at the port. Stefanos agreed to remain behind and keep the café running. He wished the boys well before they left.

Katerina was the first person Hypsipyle saw. They embraced, cried, held each other and cried some more. Stella, Ambrosia and

Suneva stood back and watched. They too were emotional. After Katerina and Hypsipyle released each other from their long and emotional embrace, each woman took turns to do the same. There were many tears and kisses on cheeks. Hypsipyle forgave them for her ostracism and said that it was now time to move on with life.

Standing nearby were King Theseus and Orpheus. They too remembered these three women. Theseus introduced them one by one to his wife. A number of stories were told of the days all those years ago when Jason and the Argonauts rowed into their lives. Who could have predicted the multiple outcomes of that event, and the impact it had and was still having on many lives?

King Thoas was perhaps the most emotional of all. He had not cried this much since Queen Myrina died. He introduced the elderly women of Limnos to Sikinos, and he too remembered many happy stories from each one of them when times were less complicated.

In the meantime, Thoas and Euneos were introducing their best friend Alexander to their 'soon to be' new family. It was the first time either Alexander or his mother Katerina had been away from Limnos, and everything they saw or did was exciting. The city of Athens was slightly larger than Myrina, but it was still different enough for them to be as excited as a child with a new toy.

Katerina informed Hypsipyle that Polyxo had died, and just before she did, she told her to forgive Hypsipyle if they were ever to meet again. Suneva, Ambrosia and Stella also forgave Hypsipyle, and King Thoas, who everyone was still calling a king.

Many people at that wedding did not know the full story, or all the pieces of it that fitted together. Even Hypsipyle did not claim to know everything. There were enough of the main characters there at that palace who added their own pieces of the puzzle which eventually became this story.

But there was one further twist in the tale, that was not to be known until the last day of the wedding feast.

CHAPTER 29

Hypsipyle's last days

Before we move on to her last days, let me return once more to the wedding feast. Theseus and Phaedra never again had a wedding at their old palace. This was to be the first and last event like this. Their new palace high on the hill was nearly completed, and on the last day of the wedding, five days after it all began, Orpheus and Hypsipyle took a walk to the new palace together.

"You know I am technically still a Queen, don't you?"

"Yes, but do you still want to be a Queen?"

"No, not really. I think that part of my life is over now. When I was in Nemea, I wanted to tell everyone that I was a Queen, and I did at first, but after a while, I realised that nobody was listening. King Lycurgus and Queen Eurydice most certainly did not believe me. They had no way of knowing the truth about my old life, so I began my new life. All other slaves had a story of their lives prior to becoming a slave, so I soon realised that I was no different."

"And now? What is it that you want? What is your new life now?"

"My sons have new lives and new wives. They don't need me. They have a home in Myrina, and I would like to visit it one more time, but I don't see myself living there with them."

"Where do you see yourself?"

"This might sound strange Orpheus, but I want to spend my life with you."

Orpheus was stunned into silence. He had secretly loved Hypsipyle ever since he first saw her on the beach in Myrina, but Jason was first to win her heart. He had loved her from that day on but could never let anyone know it. He tried to show his love by sending money to the boys, but he was never really sure if that was the right thing to do. Now that he had seen the boys marry, and now that he was talking to Hypsipyle, he knew it was the right thing to do.

"This might sound strange to you Hypsipyle, but I have loved you for such a long time. I didn't know if it was real, but it sure felt like it to me."

Standing in the construction site that was to become Athens new palace, Hypsipyle and Orpheus kissed each other like a pair of 17-year-old first time lovers. Smiling and grinning, laughing and crying, they walked around the marble blocks kicking stones and admiring the new palace.

"I don't want to live in a palace Orpheus. I have done that, and I am happy to leave that life to my sons. I want to live where you live. I want to see what you see. I want to go where you want to go. I know that the life of a musician is a nomadic one, but I want to wander the world with you."

Orpheus said "Well, that's settled. We get married and live a life on the road."

"You said before that you always loved me. Why didn't you say anything?"

"Jason was my best friend. If it wasn't for him, I would never have been an Argonaut, never have had all those adventures, never have met such wonderful people, and never would have met you. I respected him too much to let him know of my feelings towards you. Even when he was dying, I couldn't say anything. Why do you think I held on to the sword and your blanket for so long?

They were all I had of you for myself, yet I knew I couldn't keep them. I'm now so happy that they are in the rightful hands of your brother. Doesn't that sound strange?"

Hypsipyle and Orpheus carefully chose a path from the construction site along the slightly worn cobbled stones to the old palace, where Hypsipyle announced to her father, her sons, her brother, her new daughters and their parents, and to the King and Queen of Athens that she wanted to tell them something.

So it was that Orpheus and Hypsipyle were married. With so many of the people who would normally be invited to their wedding already there, and a few days until boats were to return to Limnos, Samos and Oinoe, another wedding took place. This one was a considerably smaller and more intimate affair. The normal five days of feasting could not have occurred as all guests were bloated from the weddings of the previous week. There was enough food left over, and along with some additional fresh local supplies, Hypsipyle and Orpheus married each other.

I know what you are all thinking. Didn't you just say that the old palace did not have another wedding? If so, where did this next wedding take place?

Enough white cloth and coloured tapestries can mask any construction site, and so it was that the wedding of Hypsipyle and Orpheus was held in the almost completed new palace of King Theseus and Queen Phaedra.

Sikinos and Thoas left for Oinoe, with 'Old Man' Thoas now the happiest man alive, or so he was telling everyone he met. The young newlyweds departed for a tour of Oinoe first before sailing for Samos. Although they were married, the family business of wine production and grape growing was much bigger than they could have possibly imagined. They now had business and family connections all over the Aegean and in Athens.

Suneva, Ambrosia, Katerina and Alexander travelled back to Limnos and resumed their lives. For the next few days, they each became story tellers to anyone who was willing to listen. The number of eager listeners grew each day, and many stories were told and re-told. It was only in this time that you could rightfully say the 'Limnian deed' was now well and truly in the public domain, and given the amount of time since, explained and accepted as a past event never to be repeated.

Many older women of Limnos who were active participants in the massacre had finally forgiven Hypsipyle for not killing her father. It was a long time ago, and life in Myrina and the wider Limnos had blossomed. More people now lived on Limnos, and the island was becoming an important trade destination and serious place of commerce. A number of other villages had begun to materialise around the island, and some had risen once again out of villages ruined because of past catastrophic events.

Hypsipyle and Orpheus travelled widely. They never did settle anywhere permanent, but for many years to come, they had extended visits to Oinoe and to Limnos, but not Myrina. Orpheus' old friend Philoktetes had returned to Limnos and settled in the village of Hephaestia, where he lived for the remainder of his life. He loved the quiet life, and had a thriving business making weapons. Some even say that it was one of his arrows that commenced a set of events culminating in the demise of Troy.

One seemingly unimportant day in Hephaestia, many years later, Timotheus walked into the village to purchase some supplies and by a sheer coincidence, he met Hypsipyle doing the same thing.

"I think I know you. But you do look different," said Hypsipyle as she saw Timotheus for the first time in over 40 years.

"I remember you and your family from Myrina. But if my memory is good, didn't you and your father die at sea after taking the slave girls to Samothraki?"

It was Timotheus' turn now to be the story teller, and over a wine, bread and cheese at a tavern seaside in the protected port of Hephaestia, he explained to Hypsipyle his version of events of his life after his father Damianus overheard the troubling conversation in Ambrosia's bar regarding tainted wine.

For long into the day, Timotheus and Hypsipyle talked about their lives and reminisced on many things regarding their lives in Myrina.

Hypsipyle had no idea any male survived the murder, but Timotheus told her that he and his father not only survived, but thrived. He explained their story of overhearing the men talking and then the plot to kill all males, so they decided to concoct a story to save face, and not travel back to Limnos from Samothraki with the other men and stayed for many years in the far north of Limnos, alone.

Hypsipyle was so pleased to hear that not all men died. She introduced him to Orpheus, to Philoktetes, to her sons, their wives, and to her grandchildren. At that time, many people in Hephaestia had migrated to Limnos in the previous 20 years, and therefore did not really know or care too much that Hypsipyle was the former Queen. Euneos and Thoas shared the royal roles together, and did not refer to themselves as kings, but Princes.

Now you know how Timotheus knew so much of Hypsipyle's life.

For the next month or so, Timotheus met with Hypsipyle and Orpheus on many occasions to share stories and to listen to each other. They became quite good friends. Orpheus even wrote some songs about Timotheus, which pleased him greatly.

Gradually, the story of Hypsipyle and the Limnian deed became ancient history, best forgotten. Limnos was becoming an island where new people were choosing to settle and farm the fertile land. Not only being known as a fine producer of wine, Limnos was fast becoming a fine producer of food. New industries were emerging.

One such industry was the production of medicinal earth for use in cooking as well as in the perceived curing of any ailment. I particularly like this story because it tells us how gullible people can be. Here is my abridged version.

One day, a sailor from the mainland liked the taste of a meal he had at a tavern in Hephaestia. He asked the owner what the unusual taste was and he was told it was a special flavour derived from some soil found in the area around Kotsinas, a village not far away. He was told that local people had been using this soil in cooking for many years.

He was so impressed with the taste, he travelled to Kotsinas to learn about this soil for himself. When he arrived, he found a group of women who had on occasions used this soil in cooking, but predominantly in the production of small clay tablets, to be taken as a medicinal cure for multiple ailments.

The sailor purchased some of the tablets and took them back to the mainland. He sold them to many of his friends, and they all claimed to be cured of the problems that they faced. From then on, news spread that these tablets were a miracle cure, and to this day, people still buy the special Limnian earth tablets, believing that they do some good. If you believe hard enough, then you will be convinced of their value and worth.

In my humble opinion, these clay tablets are not medicinal at all. They are simply clay tablets.

Hypsipyle and Orpheus lived many more years together. Orpheus travelled widely and his fame continued to grow. He sang songs, told stories and recalled events that people wanted to hear. He began to embellish stories of Jason and the Argonauts, but always sung the song that Hypsipyle taught him. It was his signature tune.

Hypsipyle's final days were spent with her sons and grandchildren in Limnos. Hypsipyle and Orpheus lived together for many years and died almost at the same time. They were buried on Limnos somewhere near Hephaestia on a hill nearby where it is said that the god Hephaestus once lived. I don't believe in the gods because I have never met one, but people to this day say they exist and rule our lives. I say that people rule their own lives and use gods as an excuse to do anything they want. Hypsipyle was not a believer in the gods but was a deep believer in the comfort given to those people who did believe.

Hypsipyle had a remarkable life. She witnessed first-hand many amazing events that will be the subject of debate for years to come. Her name will quite possibly fade from memory, and people like Jason, Orpheus, Theseus and Hercules will take on a far more mythological stature because they are men and men like me will continue to tell stories. Don't underestimate Hypsipyle's role in history. After I am gone, please pass on her story of struggle, determination and love, for it is truly a story worthy of an epic tale.

Now, I am going home to Chryse to watch as many sunsets as I can. So much can happen to a person in the space of their life. To me, lives are just like sunsets. They come and go, but some are just that much brighter than others.

CAST OF CHARACTERS

Aeson   Jason's father

Alcestis   Pelias' daughter

Alexander   Son of Katerina, best friend to Thoas and Euneos

Amalia   Daughter of Evanthia and Amphiarus, the argonaut.

Ambrosia   Limnian woman and bar owner in Myrina

Ambrosia   Twin sister of Helen and later, wife of Thoas

Amphiarus   Argonaut and one of the 7 against Thebes

Anna   Limnian woman

Antigone   Daughter of Oedipus and Jocasta

Argos   Argonaut and builder of the Argo

Aspasia   Limnian woman who trained under Atalanta

Atalanta   Only female on the Argo, Argonaut and champion archer

Atsiki   Daughter of Komi and Hercules

Butes   Argonaut

Cindina   Limnian mother of twins

Cretheus   King of Iolchus

Damianus   Limnian man and father of Timotheus

Daphne   King Thoas' second wife from Oinoe, and mother to Sikinos

Davidus   Boat captain out of Piraeus

Deanus   Royal engineer to King Theseus

Eribotes   Argonaut and surgeon on the Argo

Eteocles	Son of Oedipus
Euneos	Son of Hypsipyle and Jason, twin brother to Thoas and later, husband of Helen
Eurydice	Wife of Orpheus who died young
Eurydice	Queen and wife of King Lycurgus from Nemea
Evangelos	Husband to Polyxo, and first to be murdered in the Limnian deed
Evanthia	Limnian woman and mother of Amalia
Helen	Slave to Lycurgus and Eurydice
Helen	Twin sister of Ambrosia and later, wife of Euneos
Hercules	Argonaut and strongest man in Greece
Hippomedon	One of the 7 against Thebes, and killer of the snake which killed Opheltes
Hypsipyle	Queen of Limnos and later nurse to Prince Opheltes
Jason	Leader of the Argonauts and husband of Hypsipyle and Medea
Jocasta	Wife of Oedipus
Kalliopi	Limnian woman and midwife
Kassandra	Limnian woman and first to give birth to an Argonaut baby
Katerina	Best friend to Hypsipyle, daughter of Polyxo
Komi	Limnian woman and mother of Atsiki, fathered by Hercules
Korelli	Boat captain and ex-slave trader who sold Hypsipyle to Vaiyos
Laertes	Father of Odysseus and an Argonaut, father of Sophocles, a half-brother to Odysseus
Laius	King and Father of Oedipus and first husband of Jocasta
Lycurgus	King of Nemea and husband to Eurydice
Magda	Limnian woman
Medea	Second wife of Jason

Michali	Bar owner of 'Kratiras' in Piraeus
Minos	King of Crete, grandfather to King Thoas of Limnos
Myrina	Wife of King Thoas and mother to Hypsipyle
Nicko	Friend of Orpheus, an artist and sculptor
Odysseus	Son of Laertes
Oedipus	Son of King Laius and Jocasta, later wife of Jocasta
Orestes	Orpheus' name when he did not want to be known by his true identity
Opheltes	Prince of Nemea and son of Lycurgus and Eurydice
Orpheus	Argonaut and musician
Pelias	Aeson's brother and Jason's uncle. Pelias killed Aeson and took the throne
Pelopia	Pelias' daughter
Peter	Story teller and narrator of this book
Petros	Fisherman from Oinoe who sold fish to Limnos
Phaedra	Queen of Athens and wife of Theseus
Philoktetes	Argonaut and champion archer. A cave has been named in his honour on Limnos
Polynices	Son of Oedipus and one of the heirs of the Theban throne
Polyxo	Hypsipyle's nurse and mother of Katerina
Sikinos	Son of King Thoas and brother to Hypsipyle
Sophia	Limnian woman
Sophocles	Half-brother to Odysseus and son of Laertes and Stella
Sophronia	Limnian woman and midwife
Stelios	Limnian man
Stella	Limnian woman and cafe owner, father of Sophocles

Stefanos	Sailor from Lesvos, married Katerina, stepfather to Alexander
Suneva	Limnian woman
Thanasis	Boat captain out of Piraeus
Theseus	Argonaut and later, King of Athens
Thoas (King)	Father of Hypsipyle and Sikinos, grandson of King Minos of Crete
Thoas (Son)	Son of Hypsipyle and Jason. Twin brother of Euneos
Thomas	King Thoas' name when he lived on Oinoe
Timotheus	Son of Damianus and friend of Peter
Typhys	Helmsman of the Argo.
Tinker	For a period of time, a nurse to Thoas and Euneos
Vaiyos	Slave trader and later, business man

AUTHORS NOTE:

Hypsipyle was a mythological figure in ancient Greek literature. Whether or not she actually existed is a question that is largely irrelevant. What is not in question is her place in that literature. She appears in some well-known writings from around the 5th Century BCE and ever since. In the list of Greek mythological figures, some would say she sits comfortably in the B-Grade section, along with Jason, Oedipus and Theseus. Heading the list of the A-Graders, you find such well find such well-known characters as Achilles, Hercules, Odysseus, Agamemnon, Helen and Hector.

We have Homer and Hollywood to thank for the list of A-graders, but a closer inspection of Hypsipyle's life leads me to conclude that between 2500 and 2000 years ago, she was an important mythological and literary character, worthy of the attention of major playwrights and authors. In book 7 of the *Iliad*, Homer mentions Hypsipyle once, as the wife of Jason, and father to Euneos who supplies 'a thousand measures' of special wine for the sons of Atreus, Agamemnon and Menelaus. It is curious here to note that Euneos' brother Thoas does not rate a mention. Apollonius of Rhodes in his *Argonautica*, mentions Hypsipyle quite a lot because the first stopover on Jason's voyage was to Limnos. Statius gives Hypsipyle a far greater voice in *The Thebaid* covering two chapters. The great Athenian playwright Euripides thought highly enough of her to create an entire play titled *Hypsipyle*. Sadly, only part of this play has been recovered, but in recent years, the play has had additional lines of dialogue included so that it may be produced on stage for a modern audience. Just on 2000 years ago, the Latin poet Publius Ovidius Naso (Ovid) published a collection of letters penned by mythological figures to their partners, and in *Heroides* 6 he gives us a letter written by Hypsipyle to Jason. My chapter 'A witless man' is an unashamed rip off of Ovid's work. Aeschylus wrote *Hypsipyle* in around 460 BC, but only two words have ever been found! Fragments of the play *Lemnai, The Lemnian Women* by Sophocles circa 410 BCE are also in existence.

Much more was written about Hypsipyle, but has tragically been lost to time. Her mythical life began a generation before the Trojan war, and parts of her life were inextricably entwined with characters from Homers tomes.

For my part, the Queen of Limnos started out as a collection of thoughts, ideas and research from many sources over quite a number of years. These sources range from published translations of ancient books to modern academic papers written for doctoral theses and papers for journal publications. As a part-time resident of the island of Limnos, I have spent many hours wandering and musing all over the island trying to imagine how life was 3200 years ago. Time spent wandering around the archaeological sites of Poliochni, Hephaestia, Kokkinisi, Myrina, Kaveiria, Komi and a host of other lesser known sites has given me hours of enjoyment and plenty of food for thought.

A popular place to sit, drink a coffee and talk to friends is the small square outside some of Myrina's banks. The square is named after Hypsipyle, and today, this square occupies land above the ruins of the ancient town.

Limnos has a number of physical sites named after characters in this story. Apart from Hypsipyle square in Myrina, the name of Myrina itself and Cape Petasos, there are others. Philoktetes cave sits under the archaeological site of the temple of Kaveiria, and is a popular destination for many tourists. Komi is an abandoned village close to Repanithi, and its modern church sits on top of a long-lost temple to Hercules. Limnian earth is still gathered once a year near the village of Kotsinas.

The island of Chryse is no longer visible above water, but it does exist under the sea. Its location so close to the popular east coast beach of Keros suggests that it once was accessible quite easily from Limnos until an earthquake about 2000 years ago sunk the island. Diggings in Myrina for roads, houses and for archaeological purposes, have unearthed many artefacts over the years. Around 1300 BCE, Myrina was a village of considerable size and did trade with other islands. Myrina's museum has a collection of some of those artefacts and a short distance walk, is an archaeological site visibly showing houses, roads, wells and a planned village. Clearly, more exists underground in modern Myrina, but unless the entire city is dug up, we can only speculate as to what is hidden beneath. No building like a palace has yet been uncovered, but that does not suggest one did not exist.

The place where the mythical mass murder took place is called Cape Petasos. The word petasos in Greek comes from the verb 'I throw' "Πετώ".

The legend and history of the Nemean Games is an interesting side note to this story. Some believe the games were initiated in honour of Prince Opheltes' death, and therefore, Hypsipyle is directly related to that version. The other mythical scenario includes the naming rights were associated with the death of the Nemean Lion at the hands of Hercules. Both are clearly myths, but what is not a myth is that the Nemean Games were a real athletic event held in the year after and before each Olympic Games, with the first games conducted in 573 BCE. June 2020 marks the Seventh Nemead, a modern, less formal revival of the ancient games, where the athletes run clothed!

Many of the characters in this book come from mythological

literature, and many are derived from people I know. I sincerely apologise to any of my friends and family if you have been included as a character of dubious qualities. Your names were the only inspiration for their characters, not you personally!

In the true sense of writing about ancient myths, I have chosen to add in some of my own to help with the narrative. They are hidden in plain site, and include some modern takes on ancient traditions.

Obviously, the land we now know as Greece was not called that in 1300 BCE. For the purposes of storytelling, I refer to Greece by its relatively modern name.

Finally, I hope the story of Hypsipyle can be given its due place in modern mythological literature.

Tony Whitefield
February, 2020.

Suggested Reading:

Apollonius of Rhodes (1971) The Voyage of Argo. The Argonautica. Translated with an introduction by E. V. Rieu, Penguin Books.

Bloch, D, J (2000) Ovid's Heroides 6: Preliminary Scenes from the Life of an Intertextual Heroine, *The Classical Quarterly*, Vol 50, No 1, pp 197 — 209.

Burkett, Walter (1970) Jason, Hypsipyle, and new fire at Lemnos. A study in myth and ritual, *The Classic Quarterly*, Vol 20, No. 1

Fugard, Athol (2007) Jason — The End, *Arion 15.1, Spring Summer*

Ganiban, Randall Toth (2007) Statius and Virgil. The Thebaid and the reinterpretation of the Aeneid, Cambridge University Press.

Gerolemou, Maria (2018) Euripides *Hypsipyle*, Paper uploaded to Literary Encyclopedia, http://www.academia.edu/31390806/Euripides_Hypsipyle_in_Literary_Encyclopedia

Gervais, Kyle (2008) Dealing with a massacre. Spectacle, Eroticism, and unreliable narration in the Lemnian Episode of Statius' *Thebaid*. Masters Thesis, Queens University, Ontario, Canada.

Graves, Robert (2011) The Greek Myths. The complete and definitive edition, Penguin Books.

Homer (1987) The Iliad. Translated with an introduction by Martin Hammond, Penguin Books.

Lovatt, Helen (2005) Statius and Epic Games. Sport, Politics and Poetics in the Thebaid. Cambridge Classical Studies, Cambridge University Press.

Marlow, A. N (1954) Orpheus in Ancient Literature, Music & Letters, Vol 35, No 4, pp 361 — 369

Pindar (466 BCE) Fourth Pythian Ode

Shapiro, H. A (1980) Jason's Cloak, *Transactions of the American Philological Association*, Vol 110, pp 263 — 286.

Statius, Publius Papinius (2007) The THEBAID. Seven against Thebes. Translated with an introduction by Charles Stanley Ross, The John Hopkins University Press.

Stevens, Anthony (2011) Playing with fragments https://lostgreek-plays.files.wordpress.com/2012/06/playing-with-fragments.pdf

www.ingramcontent.com/pod-product-compliance
Lightning Source LLC
Chambersburg PA
CBHW050148120726
47903CB00002B/538